A SLIGHT TOUCH OF DEATH

AND DARKER TALES

Gloria J. Brown

Contents

To
Simon, Sue and Bryony

MON REPOS

Ethel's eyes focused on the yellowing ceiling of her bedroom. She could see a spider's thread linked to the light flex and trailing a loose end out into the air. She mentally pursed her lips. How long had she been lying there for that to happen? She'd soon teach that spider a thing or two. She might not be up to painting the ceiling these days, but there was nothing her vacuum nozzle couldn't get at.

She went to get out of bed, but it was as if she was pinned down to it. Why did she feel so weak? She attempted a frown to concentrate her mind on what she was doing here.

She remembered getting up in the morning and folding back the covers for the bed to air while she went along to the bathroom. Good honest white handbasin and toilet, solid enamel bath, not like this modern plastic rubbish. That wouldn't stand the course. Aggie Skinner could boast all she liked about her new low-level suite, but there was nothing like a firm yank on a chain and the rattle of a decent flush. As if that flamingo pink would conceal the ring that dirty cow left round her bath. And we'd wait and see what Alf Skinner's filthy habits would do for the wall-to-wall carpet. Nothing like a decent bit of lino for coming up sweet every time. Nothing like a spot of elbow grease for shining up the solid chrome on her taps. No, Aggie Skinner could keep her airs and graces – just because she'd still got a husband to pay for her silly fads.

Who needed a husband anyway? Nasty untidy nuisances on the whole. As she dried her hands and neatly folded the towel over the rail, she congratulated herself that nowadays the bathroom always looked a treat. She picked her teeth out of the spotless glass on the shelf and slipped them between her gums with a practised movement. Then she gave a toothy, plastic smile to the mirror and smirked her way grimly back to the bedroom.

Here she quickly straightened the bedclothes, tucking them under in a manner that forbade a solitary wrinkle, and shook the pillows vigorously. No hair grease on them these days, thank God! And the sheets were never kicked out at the bottom. Bedmaking was twice as quick as it used to be. Who wanted a man anyway? Pity they didn't grow old in a dignified way. Hanging onto their virility as if it was something to boast about. Well, she'd set Harold straight about that. She wasn't going to put up with that for the rest of her life. She had gone armed to bed in flannelette, with a forest of curlers and a fearsome

5

hotwater bottle, and congratulated herself that on the whole she had successfully kept her husband in check.

For the last year she had enjoyed the pleasure of her own company, and was going to keep it that way. Not for her the demanding lodger, like the one Elsie Pole had acquired. Silly woman. "Can't stand it on me own. Feel safer with someone else in the house. It's nice to have someone to look after again. You don't know what it's like to be alone." Stupid fool. Doesn't know when she's well off. Lonely? Huh! A cat would be less trouble than a man, for all its hairs.

Ethel sat in front of the dressing table and extracted the curlers, putting them into their special bag and disposing of them into the drawer. More space in the dressing table now. And no clutter on top. Her cut-glass sparkled beside her brushes and combs. Amazing how there was so little dust since Harold had passed over.

She'd done him proud too. The insurance policy had run to a nice bit of polished oak with real brass handles. No-one in the road could say she didn't know what was needed, or match that send-off. No black armband on a Sunday outfit for her. She'd had full mourning, and kept her hanky firmly in her hand for all to see. Oh, she'd seen them looking round the sitting room for anything out of place, but they wouldn't find anything to criticise in her house-keeping. Thinly sliced ham sandwiches and a glass of sherry for each mourner, and then out they went! She wasn't going to have any drunken weeping and wailing at her husband's funeral. If they wanted to swap dirty jokes or tell unseemly tales of the dear departed, they could go and do it in their own homes. She wasn't having it.

She looked into the sitting room on her way down to breakfast and nodded at the snowy nets and impeccable curtains. Why some people let their nets get in such a state she couldn't think. Those Parkers at number ten, for example. No sense of decency. Curtains all cockeyed, and nets as grey as their underwear no doubt. You could see what type of people they were. All those children too! Never knew when to stop some people.

She'd stuck at Nora. One was enough after all. All that cleaning up. Messy fingers planting prints all over her polished sideboard. Plasticine trampled into the rug. She'd soon put a stop to that. One good smack beat a whole lot of argy bargy. That's the trouble with parents these days. Don't know the meaning of discipline. It never did her Nora any harm. Got her married good and early and off her hands too. True she lived rather a long way off, but then they'd never liked to be in each other's pockets. And who wanted to be doing with grandchildren at her time of life? Let the young ones look after their own, that's what she always thought. After all, it's their responsibility. If they don't want 'em they shouldn't have 'em. Stands to reason.

She noticed with pleasure how the light caught the brasses on the mantelpiece. She'd have another go at those after breakfast. No sense in letting things get out of hand. A stitch in time, that's what they need to remember. Nobody bothers about the important things any more. Look after the pennies!

And certainly she'd been able to build up a tidy reserve from her housekeeping. Other men smoked and drank half their money away, but her Harold had handed his wage packet to her every Friday. And she'd made sure he had his spending money, though she did draw the line at him going down the pub. No good ever came of those places. Much better to spend his weekends sitting quietly with his rod and line by some river. She'd packed him up with his sandwich box first thing of a Saturday and hardly saw him at all for the rest of the weekend. Yes, he loved his fishing. And he didn't get under her feet all the time. Gave her a chance to give the house a good going over in case any of his relatives dropped by for Sunday tea. Not that they did that too often, thank goodness. It was true that no-one could better her rich fruit cake, but all those mouths could get through a lot of food if you didn't watch it. And now she was reaping the benefit of her good management.

She went into the kitchen and laid a fresh cloth on the table. No hurried meals on trays for her. She knew how to look after herself. The way some of these women let themselves go when their husbands die! No respect for themselves. Anyone would think they weren't worth cooking for.

While the water came to the boil in the kettle for her morning tea and in the saucepan for her morning egg, she polished and put out the cutlery, whisked a cloth over a gleaming plate, took out her rolled napkin in the silver ring and carried the eggcup and spoon to the stove. Inverting the pink timer, she gave her egg the statutory three minutes, cooled it briefly under the tap, then placed it on the table, slicing off the top with surgical precision. She allowed herself more butter on her bread now that she was only catering for one, and turned on the wireless to the music on the Light Programme.

She did occasionally listen to the Home Service for the morning story and the morning service. She might not go to church, but she was as good a Christian as any of them. Why did she need some pansy of a man in a black frock to tell her what to think? She knew what to think without any prompting. Most of what they said didn't apply to her anyway. But she did like a good hymn.

Nowadays the morning story could prove a bit unreliable as entertainment. There'd been that one recently about the boy with a permanent candle under his nose. Who they thought wanted to listen to that sort of rubbish she didn't know. Anyway, she'd turned it off. And "Woman's Hour" seemed either all lefties and lesbians or breastfeeding and single mothers. No, on the whole it was safer to stick to music, so long as you steered clear of this new stuff. She was nearly seventy, and she'd still got her hearing – these youngsters would be deaf before they were twenty. No, she'd got her hearing all right. In fact she'd got all her faculties – the reward of a strict and regular life.

Of course, just at the moment her faculties seemed to be playing tricks. She could see straight ahead of her all right, but she didn't seem able to swivel her eyes to look round the room. She could feel the mattress under her, that awkward spring pressing in her back, but she didn't seem able to roll over and get rid of it. She could hear the clock ticking on the bedside table, but she couldn't turn her head to check the time.

What was the time? How long had she lain here? Was she ill? Was she perhaps in a stage between sleeping and waking? She couldn't recall how she'd got here.

After breakfast she'd washed up, mopped the kitchen floor and hoovered the downstairs. She couldn't have hoovered the upstairs or that spider wouldn't still be taking liberties with her ceiling. Yes, she'd hoovered downstairs and dusted, then gone out the back to beat the rugs. That's something people didn't do these days. Always half measures. As if a vacuum cleaner really gets out all the dirt.

She remembered watching Milly Sharp pegging out her washing – not that you could see much difference for it really. Her children always had grubby cuffs and collars, and you could see she didn't know how to wash her woollens. Either stretched and shapeless or so shrunk they hardly fitted her youngest. No point relying on hand-me-downs in that family. The things were ruined the moment they hit the washtub. Probably got most of her stuff from jumbles and seconds shops anyway. Never seemed to have two brass farthings to rub together. Shocking manager.

She turned back to the house just as the other woman noticed her and sent a weary smile in her direction. Ethel barged on into the kitchen pretending not to see. No point wasting pleasantries on that sort. This area was really going downhill. Never knew who you'd be rubbing shoulders with. Be having coloureds next.

Then she had moved through to the front to whiten her step and polish the knocker. Let some of them see what these houses used to look like. Once she'd finished there she'd take the brass cleaner and have a go in the front room.

While she was still on her knees, two women with bags of shopping came up the road together. They halted on the far side, and Ethel had the feeling they were talking about her. They stood with their backs half towards her, but their heads were very close together, and every now and then their eyes jerked her way. Let them gossip. They wouldn't find any skeletons in her cupboard. Jealous old biddies. They both looked too busy voicing their own opinions to listen to each other anyway.

Just then the milkman's float drew up. He called out to the two women opposite with some of his usual banter, and from a crate took the single bottle destined for Ethel Roberts. She didn't encourage any nonsense from tradesmen, and was pleased to note that he soon cut the twaddle when he noticed her.

"Hello, Mrs. Roberts. Nice morning."

"Don't you tread on my white step. I don't clean it so that any Tom, Dick and Harry can come and mess it up."

His expression didn't change. "The usual pint today, Mrs. Roberts?"

"If it's the usual pint, I suppose it must be. It's certainly getting a very unusual price these days. I suppose you want paying."

"Well, you could leave it till tomorrow if you'd rather, seeing as you're busy." He stretched past her to put the bottle on the sill.

"Busier than some I could mention." Ethel glowered across the road and struggled to her feet. "I don't believe in running up debts. Don't be in such a hurry, young man. You'll stand there while I fetch my purse."

She snatched up the milk from the sill and noted in disgust the ring it had left behind. Swinging round to give the culprit a mouthful, somehow she caught the can of brasso with her arm. It toppled off the ledge, spilling its contents over her apron and splashing across the whitened doorstep. Eyes ablaze, she turned on the guilty milkman, missed her footing on the slippery edge of the step and fell heavily onto the path. The last thing she recalled was seeing the slate edging tiles rushing towards her.

So that's what had happened. She supposed she'd been knocked out. She'd obviously been brought inside and taken up to her bed. It had to be the milkman and those two women. They wouldn't have waited two seconds for the chance to nose about her house. She'd tell 'em!"

She tried to sit up, but still she failed. Perhaps she'd broken something. Perhaps she wasn't properly conscious yet.

But she could hear all right. Oh yes, she could hear clearly enough. She could hear things being picked up and put down, drawers sliding open and shut, suppressed oohs and aahs and the occasional giggle and snort. So there they were, Maisie Jones and Rose Higgins, going through her possessions as though she wasn't there. Just wait till I get my hands on them. I'll show them.

And then she heard footsteps on the stairs. They were walking right into the lion's den. The door was pushed slightly open, and a face peered round. It vanished again, and there was whispering on the landing. Then a second face peered round and the door opened further. The two women edged into the room, holding onto each other and staring towards the bed. Well might they stare. They'd soon get a piece of her mind. She went to open her mouth to speak, but it was as if her jaw was bound tightly up. Was she paralysed? Oh damn this nonsense!

Maisie and Rose turned their attention to the rest of the room. They took lids off glass pots and inspected their insides. Powder trickled unnoticed by them onto the wooden surface. It wasn't unnoticed by Ethel. Although her eyes were still fixed on the ceiling, she could make out their movement on the fringes of her vision. Now they were pulling open her drawers and fishing out her underwear. Thermal vests and formidable bras were followed by long, sensible knickers.

Both women spluttered.

"Poor old sod. No wonder he always looked so miserable. Not much chance of getting inside them."

"Doubt if he wanted to. Would you?"

"Not me, Rose, but then I'm not a man."

"Well you wouldn't get me touching them with a bargepole."

But she was touching them. What did she mean by it? Rage boiled up inside Ethel and threatened to explode through her skin, but outwardly she gave no sign.

The women moved across to the wardrobe, and soon her hangers were squeaking along the rails as they ferreted through her clothing.

"Too bloody mean to buy herself anything new. Look at all this dowdy old stuff."

"Made to last, Maisie," Rose mimicked. "They don't make stuff like that nowadays."

"Thank God."

"That child of hers wore the same thing until it nearly strangled her."

"Yes, and it started off miles too big."

"Poor little tart was embarrassed to let the other kids see. No wonder she was such a shy little mite."

"Browbeaten you mean. Wouldn't say boo to a goose. Afraid of her own shadow."

"She wasn't afraid when it came to Sam Taylor."

"No. Fast as any of them when it came to that."

What were they talking about? How dare they discuss her daughter like that!

"Lucky they married her off when they did."

"White too. That's a laugh. At least three months gone if you ask me."

Nobody did ask them. What were they insinuating?

"Didn't take her long to scarper up north, did it? Well out of it I'd say."

She longed to shout at them, to spit their slanders back in their faces, but she was powerless to stop them. Her ears ached with what she was hearing. She wished she could block it out. Just wait till she was up and about again. She'd make them sorry they took advantage of her weakness, spiteful old bitches. Weakness had never been part of her character, and she was determined to get back on her feet as soon as possible to sort those two out.

Maisie looked out into the street, moving the curtain aside to see better. When she dropped it, it snagged on the window catch and hung crooked and untidy across the pane. She didn't bother to straighten it.

"Quite a few people out there," she said.

"Friends of hers, I suppose."

"You must be joking. Why even the butcher can't be doing with her. Drooping her nose over all the cheapest cuts. 'Is this fresh? Fat looks a bit yellow! Not very lean is it? How much! Haven't you got anything cheaper?' Drives him mad, he says. At least, it did."

11

What did she mean? Had something happened to the butcher? Serves him right. He shouldn't discuss his customers behind their backs. Especially with two of the biggest busybodies in the street.

Suddenly she found them gazing directly down on her, heads almost touching, squinting down their noses, their eyes gleaming with vindictive pleasure. She felt as if her own eyes were bulging out of their sockets, but her persecutors ignored this sign of temper.

"Quiet, isn't she!"

"Makes a change."

"Oh I don't know. Most people couldn't get the time of day out of her."

"Not unless it was to carp on about something."

"Thought she was too good for us, that's what."

"And who was she when she was out! Fat arse taking up half the pavement, shoving to the front of the queue as if no-one else mattered."

"Always running round the house, sweeping and dusting, polishing and washing."

And why not indeed? Some of them wouldn't know how.

"And what good did it do anyone? 'Mon Repos!' Fat lot of peace in this place. That poor old devil couldn't even sit easy in his own home. Reading his paper on the river bank. Waiting until it was too cold to stay out any longer."

"Oh he didn't always have it so bad. If his feet were unwelcome under her table, they weren't at number three."

"No, she always did have a soft spot for a lame dog. He climbed over her stile quite a few times they tell me.

Both women sniggered. If they were suggesting her husband wasn't utterly faithful to her, they were barking up the wrong tree. He wouldn't dare even look at another woman. He knew what he'd get if he did.

"Trouble was the poor old bastard didn't get anything at home. It wasn't only her money she was tight with."

"Those knickers!" snorted Rose.

"Those knockers!" giggled Maisie.

"Which sort?"

The two women pawed at each other in silent hysteria.

"Did for her this time though, didn't they!" And their laughter screeched raucously into the room.

And these were the vulgar sorts of nobodies she'd had to live alongside all these years. Why hadn't Harold got a better job? They could have moved to a more suitable area. But he never did have any go. Oh to be able to answer them back. She swelled inwardly with frustration.

"It's only a year since he copped his lot, isn't it?"

"Yes, if he'd known about her, he'd have hung on a bit longer."

Known about who? Some other little trollop he'd had his eye on! What was she thinking? Of course he hadn't. He'd always been thoroughly respectable. If she'd done nothing else in life, she'd managed to keep her man on the straight and narrow.

"Ah well, I suppose we'd better go downstairs. He'll be here any minute, won't he?"

She heard them go and lay rigid, staring up at the ceiling. The spider had strung a few more strands from the light fitting. She couldn't believe she had remained in that bed and listened to all that filth. If stark anger could do anything she'd soon be leaping after them and tearing them limb from limb. But stark anger wasn't enough, and the tortured soul lay in her bed and burned in fury.

It wasn't long before the women re-entered the room, hovering behind a dignified figure in black. All three grouped in the doorway, regarding the recumbent Ethel. The man wore a professional expression of cultivated solemnity. The women assumed an air of fawning respect. It must be the doctor. Now we'd see. Now we'd see how long she must suffer this inactivity. Now we'd see just when she could get her own back.

The man coughed delicately into a gloved hand. He padded noiselessly to her side. He looked her up and down as if he were sizing her up. But he made no attempt to feel her pulse or test her reflexes. Instead he put out his fingers and firmly closed her eyelids. It wasn't a stethoscope that he fetched from his bag but a tape measure. She heard him scribbling measurements into a notepad and talking of oak panels, satin trims and brass handles, while the women murmured responses in suitably muted tones.

It was then that she realised the truth of her situation. It was a truth too appalling for a body to bear. She would go to a speechless grave unrevenged and unrepented. She never would get the chance to lay into those two harridans. She never would set them straight about anything ever again. They had definitely had the last word.

THE LIGHTHOUSE

The lighthouse stood at the end of a fractured promontory approached by a wavering path across the turf. The mass of granite which supported its foundations had once been joined to the headland by an arch, but centuries ago, thinned by the gnawing of the sea, the rocks had shivered apart and sliced into the sea. Only the stumps of arms remained, reaching out across the chasm. Nowadays the gap is spanned by a sturdy bridge, allowing the passage of two men abreast.

Not that there are any keepers these days, of course. It is more than twenty years since the light has been manned. The change caused a lot of resentment in the surrounding area. There had been a tradition of keepers being selected from local fishermen coming up to retirement, or whose boats had been laid up because of fishing quotas. Now the job of maintenance was in the hands of some bloke from Trinity House, who appeared every few months to service the light and see to the emergency generator. Whenever Central Control registered a problem, there he'd be.

The local community still muttered darkly into their beers whenever such a one showed up. For the last few years it had been a craggy ex-sailor, who'd brushed off their sarcasms without batting an eyelid. But he'd just retired and they were waiting to see who their next victim was.

He had already arrived and stood on the jetty looking out to his next assignment.

In summer the lighthouse looked idyllic, the white tower rising higher and higher the nearer you approached. At night the lantern shot out a bright beam which swept the seas, and passing freighters boomed a grateful response. In winter its stark lines presented a picture of solitude.

It was winter now.

The young man leaned casually on the rail, dressed in the usual ribbed sweater with collar rolled up to the chin. His uniform jacket lay across his bag, though he still wore his cap, set at the regulation angle. He peered down at the dark water surging below his boots.

At low tide it was easy to pick out the route among the tilting rocks that separated the outcrop from the shoreline. But at high tide the waves roared round behind it, raging among the crevices and angles of the boulders. The spray flung up so violently it would have been suicide to attempt to reach it. Adam knew that with the last spring tides the seas had been so high they'd broken right over the top of the tower and smashed several panes of the lantern. It had been days before a helicopter was able to winch a man down with the materials to repair it.

He himself would need to wait to start his work until first light, when the causeway would be exposed.

He picked up his bag and swung his coat over his shoulder, stepping briskly along the jetty. Opposite was the Baron's Arms. It was a sprawling stone building with dormers nestling under the thatch. All the windows were small and deeply recessed, as was usual in these parts, and the tawny light which burned inside and spilled out into the road looked snug and inviting compared with the gloom of night closing in outside.

He ducked his head to clear the lintel as he entered, and made his way to the bar.

"You've got a room for me. I'm from Trinity."

"You don't say," said the landlady. She fetched the register and set it in front of him. "It's going to be pretty rough tonight. You know how to pick your weather I see."

She squinted at the name he was writing in the book. "Adam Darke - from round here then?"

"No," he grinned. "East Coast boy, that's me."

"Well Darke's a Cornish name, whatever you say. Got some Cornish blood in you somewhere. What'll you have? Keep out the cold."

"Better stow my things in my room first."

"Time enough for that. Annie'll be in later. She can show you up. I have to keep my eye on these old reprobates." She nodded towards a table in the corner where he found himself under the scrutiny of three wrinkled oldies, hunched round in their seats like inquisitive parrots. They promptly turned back to their glasses, shrugging and humphing.

"Take no notice of them, ignorant old buggers." She drew a pint of draught from a yellowed beer pull. "Try a glass of our homebrew. It'll knock spots off anything you can get at home."

"So long as it doesn't knock spots off me."

"Don't you fret. You'll sleep as sound as a bell after this."

"A cracked one no doubt!" The rough voice spoke from the doorway. A group of four had just entered. Fishermen, to judge by the clothing.

"You keep your opinions to yourself, Daniel Badcock. "Don't want to give this gentleman the impression we're a lot of louts round here." She turned to Adam. "Do you want a sandwich, me 'andsome? Ham and mustard or cheese and pickle? Or what about some cold chicken?

"Chicken's probably about the size of it!" Badcock levered himself onto a barstool and the rest grouped round behind him, leering somewhat boozily at Adam. This obviously wasn't their first port of call.

"Cheese and pickle would be fine," Adam responded. He tried not to wince as one of them lurched round to his side and breathed straight into his face.

"Pint of bitter, Liz."

"You wait your turn!" She leaned over the bar to Adam. "Go across to the table, me lovely, and I'll bring it over to you."

Adam took his bag and his drink to a table near the fire, where he sat with his back to the bar. He was aware of some rowdy jostling going on but did his best to ignore it. The landlady was obviously well up to dealing with it.

By the time she'd brought his sandwiches, good and chunky with thick slices of cheese, he had downed his first glass and was glad to see she'd supplied another. Plenty of head. Once he had drained this, he started to feel pleasantly relaxed and sat gazing comfortably into the flames. The handles of the fire irons gleamed with long use. The coal in the scuttle still smelled of the damp pit. Nice to see a proper fire again.

Next thing he knew the gang from the bar were clattering into the benches opposite him. He felt a heavy hand on his shoulder.

"So," rasped Badcock into his ear. "Your name's Darke, is it? How appropriate!"

They all sniggered and grimaced at each other.

A stern voice came from the bar. "You lot behave yourselves, or you're out."

"Oh dear, I'm shaking in my boots," Badcock mocked.

"I mean it. I'll get Satan if necessary."

Adam gave a startled look.

"Cornish version of a pitbull," supplied the paunchy individual to his left. "All right, Liz," he called to the bar. "We'll be good."

"You'd better be, Bob Dyer."

Badcock lowered himself ominously onto the bench opposite, the left side of his face lit red by the fire, the right in shadow.

"Want to know why it's appropriate?" His eyes glinted at Adam out of darkened sockets.

"If you want to tell me."

16

"First light keeper. Ever."

"1784," said a third drinker. His sleeves were pushed up to reveal muscular forearms, elaborately tatooed.

"1748, Tom Truscott," corrected Badcock. "Before that they had a beacon on the cliffs, but the skippers couldn't tell how far the rocks ran out below the surface. After one savage shipwreck, with all hands lost, the local squire decided there had to be a light on Dragon's Head.

"Absalom Darke was chosen, and he thought himself a lucky man, didn't he boys?" They all grinned. The effect was less than amiable.

"And wasn't he?"

Laughter erupted from the group. The laughter made Adam feel uncomfortable.

"I wouldn't call it lucky, would you boys?"

"Well what happened to him?"

Another roar of laughter.

"What didn't happen to him!"

The men eyed each other slantwise, lips twisted into sneers.

Truscott bared a gappy grin. "The wreckers got him."

"Serve him right!" This was the first time Frank Heller had spoken. His eyes glittered in his sallow face as though the offence was only yesterday.

"Wreckers?"

Badcock spat into the fire. "Absalom Darke was a bit of a goody two-shoes, you see. Bit like yourself." He winked at the others. "Wouldn't dowse the light when they asked him nicely. Said he'd been a seaman himself, and it went against his conscience."

"Huh, conscience!" snorted Heller. "What about the little kiddies, eh? What about the wives? Starving to death while the toffs fed off the fat of the land!"

"But the sailors weren't rich! Adam objected. "What had they done to deserve to be drowned? Smashed on the rocks, and then drowned!"

"Oh yes, you'd know all about being smashed on the rocks, wouldn't you?" Badcock leaned violently forward, his face suddenly plunged into darkness.

"Probably runs in the family," jeered Truscott.

"What do you mean?" Adam felt the force of their hostility.

"A rich merchantman from France was expected into Falmouth." Badcock sat back in his seat again. The threat remained. "The villagers begged Darke to rake out the brazier so they could show false lights. He refused pointblank, and they knew they had to deal with him. That night they went across to the lighthouse. But he had barred the door."

Adam was aware of a movement across the floor and that the old guys had clustered round behind him.

"Some of them carried axes, and they battered at the door until it gave way."

"Then they rushed in."

"They kicked over the brazier!"

"They knocked him down on the hot coals and beat him senseless."

"They dragged him outside and threw him into the sea!" Tom Truscott was so aflame with the picture that he leapt to his feet.

"He was battered to death on the rocks." Heller's fist smashed into the table. "He was never seen again."

"Act of God!" Badcock folded his arms in grim satisfaction.

"That's enough, Dan Badcock!" The landlady was right behind them. Adam jumped. "You and your grisly crew can take yourselves off. I won't have you bothering my guests."

Surprisingly, they all hauled themselves to their feet and trooped obediently to the door. She closed it firmly behind them and bolted it.

The old men stood uncertainly about, like guilty schoolboys. One of them started to drift back to his seat.

The landlady returned to the bar. "It's getting late. Anyone who isn't ordering is very welcome to leave."

The two loiterers grinned sheepishly at Adam and fiddled with their glasses. He knew what was expected of him. "All right," he sighed. "Four more of your best, landlady."

The two nearest the table edged into the benches, and the third hobbled back to join them.

They all sat round, shifting their feet. When they got their glasses they peered impishly at Adam and showed their appreciation by drinking deeply.

He watched the foam draining down the side of their glasses and raised an inevitable finger towards the landlady. Liz appeared promptly with four more frothing mugs and left them to it. She went to the door to let Annie in and rebolted it. Annie and Liz soon had their heads together, talking under their breaths while they busied themselves with the empties.

On his third freebie, Ned Crowhurst stretched his legs in front of him, and Arthur Bates leaned forward in his seat. Sidney Porlock just sat with a pleasantly glazed expression on his vacant face.

"Ahh...." Arthur proffered. "The light's got a dark history all right. 'Darke' eh? Get it?" He nudged Ned in the ribs. Both men chuckled, and even Porlock understood that some response was called for. He shifted fractionally closer to Adam.

Adam knew what was coming. Hours of old seamen's yarns. But he was happy to let it wash over him. He smiled encouragingly.

Arthur took the lead. "They say that over a hundred souls were drowned that night. But the ringleaders of the wreckers were caught and hanged. Caught and hanged. The rest had to go into hiding until the coast was clear. Everybody said Absalom Darke had tipped off the troops. There weren't many who didn't spit on his name." He nodded amicably at Adam.

"And ever since then there have been cormorants in these parts. And some do say they are the souls of the drowned sailors. Whenever they appear, you can expect foul weather or unearthly happenings."

Adam tried to look suitably impressed.

"The next keeper was a wreckers' man. He made sure some vessels didn't escape the rocks. But on the whole there were less shipwrecks than normal, so nobody worried too much."

"And then came one stormy night," Ned joined in. "The boys had learned of another rich cargo. Jethro Charlock had raked out the fire and everything seemed set."

Arthur took the story back. "The first lighthouse was a wooden job. Pretty flimsy, truth be told. Well, you can guess what happened, can't you?"

He paused for effect. Ned leapt into the gap.

"The seas grew rougher and rougher. It was a high tide with the wind behind it. The ship was driven towards the rocks." Ned was enjoying himself. "But the seas that shattered the ship's boards were the seas that swept the lighthouse to its destruction. Jethro Charlock was never seen again."

That seemed to be a refrain in these parts.

Sidney Porlock stirred unexpectedly to life. "But they do say that before that, before it went, lights were seen dancing round the rock.

"Phosphorescence?"

"Phosphorescence my eye! Lights like the devil's lanterns converging on the door. There were sounds of screams and cries."

"Not surprising if there was a shipwreck."

"No, no, before that! There was a splintering sound, like the cracking of bones."

"Or the splintering of wood?"

Sidney started to get agitated. He didn't want a good tale spoiled. "No, the splintering of bones! Then a great wailing cry. And it was not till then the lighthouse shifted and was carried into the water. But as it went there was a sound that made the wreckers blood run cold. It was the sound of Absalom Darke laughing."

There was a silence.

Adam broke it. "You wouldn't think you could have heard that with all the rest of the racket."

"You may mock, young man. But there's more to these tales than anyone knows." And more tales than anyone expects, thought Adam. And he was right. The old boys had clearly settled down for the duration. Another line of drinks had appeared by magic on the table, and Liz and Annie had now wandered off. Obviously no-one round here bothered about closing time. Adam was resigned to hearing more, and more came.

Arthur took the lead again. "The next lighthouse was a more sturdy affair. The lamp was fuelled by oil. It had at least ten wicks and mirrors to reflect a beam out to sea. It needed constant trimming and cleaning, and a new keeper moved in permanently, with another chap to help him. Bit of a weird type from what you can make out. A loony."

"Village idiot," suggested Ned.

"Loony," insisted Arthur. "Anyway, supplies were brought across a slatted bridge, held together by ropes, with a rope grab rail, and lashed to posts at each end.

"Everything seemed to go all right until one February there was a month of storms, and no-one could get across that bridge, not one way nor the other."

He paused to wet his whistle. Ned took up the tale.

"Those two could never have been called the best of friends. Well, they wouldn't be would they, what with one of them being off his head an' all. Things got gradually worse and worse.

"One terrible night, when the gales were blowing a force nine - "

"At least!"

"When the gales were blowing a force nine..... the loony snapped. He grabbed an axe from the wall and started to smash everything in sight. He smashed the light, he smashed the windows and he chased the keeper down the ladders to the ground floor. Then he started smashing the furniture. When the keeper tried to stop him, he bashed him on the head, knocked him to the ground and tried to hack away at his legs.

"The keeper dragged himself up and managed to reach the door. He staggered to the bridge and tried to crawl across it, hauling himself along by the planking and the cables.

"He was halfway over, when the madman started slashing at the stay ropes. As they tore apart he overbalanced and fell headfirst into the sea."

Sid could wait no longer. "The keeper hung onto the loose ropes as long as he could, but he was bleeding like a stuck pig, and the planking was jigging about in the gale like something possessed."

Arthur recovered the story. "His grip loosened, and he fell into the waves with a bloodcurdling shriek."

"And he was never seen again?"

"Oh yes he was," cried Ned indignantly. "He was washed up on the beach with terrible gashes to his legs and head. The madman was also washed up. By the time they found him, the gulls had pecked his eyes out. He was bloated and badly decomposed. But they knew who he was by his red hair."

Arthur fixed Adam with a gimlet eye. "And they knew what had happened when they managed to reach the lighthouse and saw the damage. The place was awash with the water flooded down from the lantern.

Ned carried on. "So once the new bridge was built, they decided the light would be better manned by families. And that was what happened. After the staircases were put in, the place was a sight more homely."

Arthur wiped the beer froth on his sleeve. "All went well until, in 1911, a keeper moved in with a young family. At first everything was OK until the storm birds arrived with the first signs of snow. The family were due to stock up, and the missus was expecting again.

"All the other babbies had arrived bang on time, but this 'un was early. The night the babbie came, there was such a blizzard you couldn't see Dragon's Head from the shore. The missus got into trouble, and the keeper decided to risk going for help. He didn't get as far as the bridge. His feet slipped on the icy rock and in he went.

"The missus died in the night, and the two kiddies clung to her poor cold corpse for days.

"No-one suspected anything was wrong till the light burned out. By the time they got to them, the little boy had starved to death. The girl was crouched by the head of her dead mother, almost as frozen as the poor woman herself. All about her were the remains of tallow candles. She'd been eating them to keep herself alive."

"But she might as well not have bothered," said Ned. The tears

21

were coursing down his cheeks.

"No," added Arthur, soberly. "She spent the rest of her days in the madhouse.

Sid straightened himself up in his seat. "And do you know what they found in the lantern?"

Adam was too dazed to reply.

"The place was full of dead birds. Cold had cracked the panes, and some had fallen in, you see. The birds had taken shelter. Couldn't get out again. Dead, all dead."

"I think that's enough for one night, you old ghouls. Haven't you got homes to go to?" It was Liz. But she wasn't angry.

The old men shuffled out of their seats and tottered to the door. For the last time Liz slid the bolts to.

"You don't want to take them too seriously," she said to Adam. "You look as if you've had enough. Annie's already taken your things up. I'll show you to your room."

The room was very old-fashioned, as you'd expect. But it was clean. The smell of polish amply covered any musty taint, and combined subtly with the scent of malt. The wood panelling had mellowed to a rich gleam, and there were pictures of seascapes round the walls, with a few whiskery old Victorians staring wistfully out of frames. The bed was metal framed and on high legs, but the bedding looked plump and soft, and Adam couldn't wait to get into it. He was pretty exhausted, and he had an early start.

Annie had hung his jacket neatly over the chair by the window. He went across to it and started to undress. As he removed his tie, his eyes lingered on the lighthouse opposite. It was silhouetted against the sea in a bright track of glittering moon. The broad shaft of its light arced round the horizon and swept around to the coast. Just as he was about to attend to his buttons, the beam knifed into his eyes. Three million candlepower - enough to temporarily blind him. His brain shrivelled with pain and he clutched his head, doubling over and feeling sick. For a minute he couldn't move. Then he groped his way to the light switch and turned it off. With no light in the room, his eyes could begin to relax. Eventually he could make out bits of furniture, though everything was scattered with dancing haloes of incandescence.

What in God's name could have happened? Surely the light shouldn't shine into the windows like that? He'd have to check the masking plates tomorrow and make sure they hadn't come adrift. When he noticed the beam tracing the horizon again, he pulled the curtains tight shut. Fortunately they were very heavy and let no light through.

He finished undressing in the welcome relief of darkness, felt his way to the bed and mercifully fell fast asleep.

At about four in the morning he woke up again. The moonlight was falling onto his bed. The curtains were now open. On the little table inside the window burned a candle in a frosty ring of splintered light. Its flame stretched tall and white, casting shadows about the room.

What the.....? Whoever would be fool enough to leave a candle burning? Even more unnerving, someone had been in his room to do it. He felt almost drugged with tiredness and strong beer. His legs shook as he staggered over and nipped out the flame.

Next thing he knew, Annie was coming into the room and scraping back the curtains. A winter sun flooded in and he squinted at her figure, dark against the square pane. Then she carried a tray across and put it on the chest of drawers next to his bed. She poured the tea and handed it to him without saying a word.

He stacked up his pillows and settled back with the tea in his hand.

Annie was about to move away, when suddenly she gave a scream. It was so unexpected and so loud that Adam spilled half his drink into the saucer.

"Who has done this?" she cried.

"I don't know. It wasn't me." Adam felt foolishly befuddled. He didn't even know what she was talking about.

"Look!" She pointed an alarmed finger at the floor.

He rolled over and looked where she directed. There was a trail of wax from the head of the bed to the foot and curving round at the bottom. Annie followed it round until she reached the other side of him.

He was completely encircled in candle grease.

Annie stared at him for a few moments, then turned and fled downstairs.

Adam could hardly register a problem. He heard agitated whispering from below, and then Liz entered the room.

"I'm so sorry, Mr. Darke .... Adam. She smiled wanly. "I can only apologise."

"But what's happened?" Adam couldn't take it in.

"Only Dan Badcock up to his tricks again, I expect. Just you put it out of your mind. Breakfast'll be ready in half an hour. The bathroom's along the passage."

And put it out of his mind he did. It was barely in it in the first place.

After a very adequate country breakfast, Adam left the inn. It was a fine day, and he felt good as he stepped down onto the beach. Watching his feet along the uneven causeway, he found himself at the foot of the first part of the promontory.

He had crunched along the track till he was nearly at the bridge before he noticed the birds. Cormorants! Humped on the rocks below like a bunch of depressed old men in shiny funeral gear. Their outlines were strangely primitive. They could have been welded to the rocks since the dawn of time.

But as he took hold of the handrail, they all stirred. Some of them plunged soundlessly into the sea; some of them circled round as if in search of something lost.

It wasn't till the last second that Adam saw the great black shape before him. He thought it was going to slice into him with its beak. Instead it beat at his face with its wings and thrashed at his head with paddled feet. Adam fought it off with his arms. It couldn't have seen him. A cormorant that needed specs! Still, he felt shaken as he crossed the bridge to the lighthouse.

It towered above him, gleaming in the sunshine, and its elegant lines soothed his soul. He took out the key and inserted it into the lock. The heavy clunk of its turning stirred up an echo inside.

The doors were metal, heavily riveted round the edges and opening outwards. Even the worst of seas couldn't batter their way through these doors. As he hauled one of them open, he broke the silence inside. The disturbed air shuddered up the height of the tower like a low, mournful groan.

He decided to start with the generator first, and spent the morning stripping down the moveable parts, checking and greasing them, before he was satisfied they were OK. Once they were reassembled, he gave the generator a manual test run. It powered up with a heavy rattle, settling into the usual noisy throb. To make doubly sure of it, he went up the stairs from floor to floor turning on everything electrical in sight.

When he came to the lantern, he pressed the override switch to activate the light. Immediately the lamps turned incandescent, and the prisms rotated in their mercury bed. Nothing needed here then. He put the switches back to automatic, and the slow movement stopped. None of the lamps seemed to need attention, so it was only the lenses and prisms to clean. He'd start those after lunch.

Then he remembered his ordeal from the previous night and trekked round to the shoreward side. No, the shields were firmly in place. There was no obvious explanation.

He was just about to do the regulation check of the lantern glass, when he noticed the bird on the floor. It was black; a storm crow by the looks of it. Its ragged feathers fluttered in the draught from the door, and its neck was clearly broken. But how had it got here? He checked carefully round the panes for any damage, but they were all sound. The only explanation was that it had flown in the last time the door was open to the balcony. But why hadn't the previous guy noticed it? In any case, by now it should be not much more than a few bones held together by skin and feathers. It looked as if it was only recently dead.

He took the corpse up by the legs, opened the balcony door and flung the creature over the parapet. Then he went down to wash his hands and get some lunch. Liz had packed him up with chicken drumsticks and some ham and lettuce sandwiches. She'd also put in a bottle of homebrew. He sensibly filled the kettle and made himself a cup of coffee. He'd do an inventory of the shelves and equipment later. There were always plenty of tins and dried stuff just in case. But they might need some restocking.

He pulled out a newspaper and did the crossword while he ate. Satisfied, he left the washing up in the bowl and went back to the ground floor to put the generator back into emergency mode.

He was about to turn the mains back on, when he realised he was standing in a pool of water. He gasped, and checked round for the source. He'd just been in the kitchen, so he knew there wasn't anything there.

And then he saw water cascading down the steps. By the time he'd battled his way to the next floor, he was drenched. He continued up floor by floor, hanging on to the handrail, but still the water met him. He knew there was nothing wrong with the lantern, but he had to check all the other windows. This was crazy. It wasn't even raining, let alone blowing a gale. Where in hell's name was all this water coming from?

When he reached the lantern, it was just as he'd left it. On the way down, he noticed the stairs were only slightly damp, and when he got back to the generator room the place was completely dry. He returned to the kitchen and made himself another coffee, strong and black. Perhaps the first drink had stirred up the dregs of all that beer last night. Perhaps he was still tired and hallucinating. His clothes were certainly dry, if that was anything to go by.

A second coffee perked him up again, and he carried the cleaning fluid and materials up to the lantern. He spent the whole afternoon painstakingly wiping over the prisms and lenses with a special cloth. It was important not to scratch the surfaces. Then he fetched a bucket and water and did a traditional tour of the lantern with a long-handled squeegee.

He was just doing the outside, when he felt a tug on his jacket, like a sudden gust of wind. He grabbed onto the rail and looked out to sea. Nothing. Even the flag wasn't stirring. But the light level was beginning to fall. The sun had nearly reached the earth's rim, and was going down in a misty ball of red. Perhaps the weather was changing.

The lamps in the prism were beginning to glow, and the whole unit to turn gently in its track. Adam decided to call it a day. He was tired, and his nerves were clearly on edge. He'd listen to a bit of radio, heat up some soup and have an early night.

In bed on the fourth level, he read a few pages of a P.D. James, but his eyes were weary. So he plugged in his earphones and listened to some tapes. He was just beginning to drift off, when there was an ear-piercing squeal from his transistor, and he ripped the headphones away from his ears.

He lay in the darkness listening to the rain beginning to hit the window in gusts. He'd been right about the weather. Still, one more day and he'd be out of here.

The door creaked open and he got up to close it. When he turned back to the bed, he could see it wasn't empty. A long still shape lay stretched out in his place, and by its head something was rocking and moaning with low, broken sobs. His neck and shoulders prickled into a cold sweat and his arms felt weak. It was small, like a child, but the sound that came from it was unearthly.

He stood stock still, his heart pounding and his blood throbbing in his ears. He felt he was about to faint. He took a pace backwards towards the door. And as he did so the child's head lifted. Black, hollow eyes stared straight into his out of a white, pinched face. Its mouth grew round and it started to scream. And as it did, his own screams rose in his throat and the air was ringing with fear.

Abruptly it stopped, and he found himself gaping at a pile of rumpled bedclothes. He edged backwards out of the room. As he emerged, there was a flutter of sound in the stairwell, and he clattered down to the kitchen and turned on every light he could find. He could almost hear the shouts of male laughter mocking his cowardice, but there was no way he was going to sleep anywhere else that night.

Eventually he dozed off in a chair, and wakened to the sound of the wind rattling at the windows. No-one had forecast heavy weather for that week. But he could hear the waves sucking and crashing round Dragon's Head, and the bumping and scraping of what sounded like spars of wood.

A volley of pebbles thrown up against the glass made him leap out of his chair. He got out the radio and tuned into the shipping channel. No mention of gales in any quadrant. He retuned to Central Control, but only got an annoying whine and the sound of static. The emergency channels were just the same. He seemed to be totally cut off.

The wind was beginning to shake the windows, and water was hitting the lighthouse wall. He could see the spume rushing down the panes in torrents. And then came the sound he was dreading: the sound of shattering glass. He forced himself out of the kitchen and listened hard. The stairs were in total darkness, and throwing the bar made no difference. Did he have to go up?

Another crash, clearly from the lantern, and then footsteps pounding down the stairs towards him followed by crazed shouts of garbled rage. More feet racing down the steps, thumping onto the landings as if whoever it was had leapt down several at a time. Something was clanging and ringing against the sides of the tower. The angry cries were suddenly on top of him, snarling and slavering back the spittle like a mad dog. Adam cringed into the doorway as the footfalls thudded past him, down to the generator room. Then terrified screams and pleading, a sound like breaking sticks and something heavy dragging towards the door, sobbing and snivelling.

As suddenly as it had started it stopped. Adam stayed where he was for a good ten minutes, not daring to move, hardly daring to breathe. He was shaking all over with horror.

Eventually he felt compelled to go down to the bottom level. He had to see. He crept down to the ground floor expecting to come across a terrible sight. The room was empty, apart from the silent generator. He hoped it was over, but he wasn't going to stay here a moment longer. Storm or no storm, he would have to get back to shore. If he stayed here, he'd be as mad as the rest of them.

He reached down some oilskins from the pegs and scrambled into them as fast as his trembling hands would let him. Then he tied a rope round his waist with clips at each end. He'd attach himself to the ring on the tower to reach the bridge, then work along it until he was at the top of the slope to the beach. The tide had already turned, and it wouldn't be above an hour or so before the causeway shook off the demented waves.

It was when he was reaching for the keys from the hook that he heard the boots outside. For a moment he thought it might mean help, till he heard the shouts.

"Come on Darke. Open up." The threat in the voices was unmistakable.

"Put that fire out or we'll put you out. And don't think this door will save you."

A short pause. Adam held his breath and strained his ears. He could hear the men listening outside. A thud on the door and then another pause. "Come on!" Sounds of feet scraping and shuffling and hoarse whispering.

What should he do? Should he break out the flares and send up a distress call? What kind of fool would that make him look? Wasn't it only that bastard Badcock and his damned crew? As Liz had said? He hung onto the hope. But he went to the chest anyway and loaded a flare into the gun. If they broke in here they'd get it anyway. Whatever they did to him.

It flashed on his mind that they'd never break through that door, a door to keep out the Atlantic. But the thought didn't hold.

Axes began to rain down upon it, and the wood splintered and split. A ragged hole appeared, and an arm was thrust through. He hit it with the butt of the pistol. The arm disappeared and a fierce eye glared through the space.

"Give it up, Darke! Your time has come."

"Get back from the door or you'll get this!" Adam brandished the barrel in front of the hole, and a roar of laughter went up from outside. Oh yes, that pleased them. Give them something else to blather about when the next poor sap arrived. Well it wasn't going to be him.

The smashing of axes began again and battering at the door. Then it came crashing down, and the shouts and jeers rushed towards him. He couldn't see for the panic that engulfed him, but he fired his flare.

It hit the wall at the side of the opening and showered the room with burning light. He felt hands seize him, and he was flung to the floor. Phosphorous burned into the skin of his hands and face. Heavy blows and kicks pummelled into him. He was seized by the hair and dragged out onto the rock.

For a moment he saw them, ranged around him, wielding staves and axes. They advanced upon him in a ring, forcing him towards the bridge. The air was thick with blood-lust.

He edged out onto the bridge, clutching onto the handrail and backing away as they came on. The rail shook in the wind, which tore at his oilskins and tried to lift him over the side.

As he clung on, he felt rough cable under his hands and planking under his feet. The slats were wet and slimy. He almost lost his footing. The bridge swung from side to side, and the rope gave him no real purchase. A black mass of water raged underneath. The wind howled and screamed, and the men howled and roared.

He was nearing the end of the bridge. But what was the point? They were going to murder him anyway. Even if he could scramble to the foot of the outcrop ahead of them, what awaited him there except for certain death in the turmoil among the rocks?

He was feet away from firm ground when something snapped, and he found himself plummeting down into a blaze of shifting luminescence. He was aware that the howls and roars preceded him down. As the sea reached out for the falling bodies, great showers of light were thrown into the air before the water closed over them.

Adam tried to struggle to the surface, but the current caught him and pulled him under. The surge crashed him into the teeth of hidden rocks. Pain erupted inside his skull in a dance of lights. The cold gripped him and clenched his chest, and he felt himself dying.

The last thing he remembered was a face in front of his own. The face of a mariner, lined and weathered by long years at sea, his black hair and beard streaming out and combed by the tide. It was a face with dark eyes and full of compassion. He felt a strong hand grip his wrist, and then he lost consciousness.

They found him on the shore the next morning. He was lying half on his face, and his oilskins were torn almost to shreds. They carried him into the inn on a door, and laid him out on the bed. Gently they removed his clothing, washed his body and cleaned his wounds. They covered him tenderly with a light blanket and waited for the ambulance.

A doctor examined him all over and covered him up again. Nobody could think how he had come to be on the beach, and Adam could not tell them. They had all seen him cross to the lighthouse. There'd been no sign of any problem and, so far as they knew, there was no reason why he should have left it. It had been a calm, clear night. Though there were, of course, some terrible currents around the Head.

All agreed there were remarkably few injuries considering the state of his clothing. All agreed that the sea had brought him home.

And all agreed that it was a miracle. For he was alive. Just. Whether he would ever be the same again they weren't so certain. Neither was the doctor.

As the ambulance drew away, the lighthouse stood in sunlight. The rough path wavered across the turf until it reached the bridge. The bridge spanned the last few yards to Dragon's Head. The sleek lines of the tower rose neat and white into a blue sky, and its metal door stood firmly shut.

TIME PIECE

As long as she could remember, she had always found her husband irritating.

Even on her wedding day, she'd felt a gush of annoyance when he'd stepped on her bridal train, dislodging the careful arrangement of her headdress. He had managed to slice her hand with the knife held atop the bottom tier of the cake for the photos. And she could never see the fixed smiles caught by the camera without recalling that the male hand covering hers concealed a seeping gash. Lucky the roses which decorated the cake were already crimson!

While they were courting, she had found his clumsiness part of his appeal, like the ungainly flourishes of an oversized but enthusiastic puppy. When he'd knocked the contents of his glass over the hotel tablecloth the night he proposed, she'd put his uncontrolled movements down to a natural anxiety. The egg stains that frequently graced his ties suggested he needed a good woman to look after him. She'd imagined that, buoyed up by her wifely attentions, and neatly turned out by her skills with washer and iron, he would soon go out into the world a confident and elegant figure, the kind of husband a woman could take credit for.

What she hadn't bargained for was that confidence would become assurance, that he would continue to spill food of infinite variety down his ties, that her own tablecloths would be frequently in the wash and the elbows of his newly pressed jacket constantly in the butter or jam on the side of his plate. Worse, he didn't seem to notice how this inconvenienced her.

As the hair receded from his forehead and the stomach jutted ever closer towards the table, the stains were allowed to descend onto cardigans and trousers as well as ties. The puppyish charms of the young man disappeared. No longer was there any compensation for the blows to her sensitivity.

His scramblings in bed became no more deft regardless of years of practice, and she grimly realised that she would probably make old age without ever once abandoning her senses to a flood of passion. In terms of children, his efforts were equally unproductive.

Even so, she could probably have forgiven him. It wasn't his fault that nature had endowed him with so little connection between brain, hand and eye. But the man became so appallingly complacent.

He took it as his right to collide with inoffensive pieces of furniture, to break innocent china that hadn't looked where he was going. Glasses could shatter in as many splinters as may be, and he would trample over them and tread them across the carpet to advise her that they needed clearing up.

He obviously supposed that, since he did, after all, pay for every cup, glass and plate in the house, he had a perfect right to break them. He seemed also to think that, as wives were meant to keep their husband's clothing clean, it would give her more satisfaction to wash what emphatically needed it than something only vaguely grubby.

Over the years, he developed an uncritical air of self-approval not at all like the champion's confidence she had envisaged. Who could feel proud on the arm of a man who tripped on the only bit of litter in the street, who let go of doors just as one was about to walk through them, and who increasingly puffed and wheezed as he peered into his wallet at the checkout, while the queues behind built up to rebellious proportions?

He could never be persuaded to do anything in a hurry. How often had she stood and looked at her watch and imagined trains pulling out of stations while he took forever to tie his laces? She'd build up a head of screaming impatience, while she forced her face into an acceptable mask. He constantly buttoned his cardigan wrongly, and never noticed until he'd reached the bottom. And then she would have to stand on feet that itched to do desperate violence while he undid it, with infuriating slowness, and started again.

Oh those cardigans! What had happened to the reasonably fashion-conscious man of his youth? Now he seemed to take a pride in looking as middle-aged as a fifty-year-old could. If she bought anything with a bit of colour or a bit of style, it would always miraculously be uncomfortable or scratchy, or too big or too small. It would have to go back to the shop, and he would emerge, smugly, with yet another cardigan as nearly identical to the one before as he could manage it.

It was almost as if he was trying to frustrate her. Perhaps he had read her mind when she thought she could mould him into a shape she could live with. Perhaps he had decided to wreak the revenge of all intransigent males on their opposite numbers. Marriage to Bernard had been an uphill struggle, working harder and harder, yet lacking any kind of reward.

One of the things that infuriated her the most was that he had developed all kinds of niggling little routines. These should have suggested an orderly and organised personality. Yet somehow his outward appearance, and the trail of destruction he left behind, did not coincide with this.

Among the compulsive patterns of his behaviour was an insistence on winding the ancient clock at precisely ten every evening. He would always follow the same procedure.

As the hour approached, she would feel herself tensing up. He would sit behind the evening paper, managing to mangle and crumple it even though it was only a tabloid. Occasionally he would clear his throat and loudly rattle the pages as he fought for mastery. The sight of the battered object in his stubby fingers and the assault on the silence screwed her intestines into angry knots.

At one minute to ten precisely, he would take out his watch and hold it up to his nose. He would peer at it while the sheets of the "Evening Recorder" slid to the floor. Then he would rise and kick his way, oblivious to the further damage inflicted on the hapless paper, until he stood in front of the mantelpiece. Without looking up from his watch, he would stretch his right hand to the clock and lift it from the shelf. For thirty years she had expected it to crash through his fingers onto the tiles below, but unaccountably the clock had outwitted his especial talent.

He would then set his watch on the shelf and open the front of the clock. His thick fingers fiddled pointlessly with the minute hand, which he insisted on adjusting even though the clock had kept perfect time since the day they'd acquired it. It was as if he justified his existence by controlling time if he could control nothing else. Why he could not leave the poor thing safely where it was for this operation, like any normal human being, defeated her.

But the next stage was to turn the clock over and wind it, with a deliberate thoroughness that threatened disembowelment. For thirty years also she'd expected the mainspring to give up the struggle, but it had gallantly stood the course. A more modern version would surely not survive such depredations.

At last he would replace the clock where it belonged, inflicting remarkably little violence and looking at it with evident self-satisfaction. He would then tap the glass as if it were a barometer, nod his head approvingly, pick up his watch and restore it to his pocket. Afterwards he would make his way to the kitchen and sit at the table until she made his cocoa.

Even though she longed to ignore him and finish her chapter or carry on with her knitting, she felt obliged to interrupt her own affairs and fit in with his ways. The only allowance she made to her feelings was to finish the job of wrecking the paper before she consigned it to the bin. She couldn't bear the idea of reading it after he had ravaged it.

All that, of course, was now officially over.

Bernard sat in his widower's seat, uniquely conscious of the good life he had given his wife, and what an ideal couple they had been. He wore the black suit he'd purchased at bargain price for the funeral - the respectfully grieving image only spoiled by the knitted cardigan bursting through the gaps in the buttons, and the stains of best sherry dissipating into his shirt.

The paper had arrived and, although he'd had to fetch it himself, he still rattled and thumped the obstinate pages with a degree of pleasure. It had been a good turnout, and he had enjoyed being the centre of attention. Everyone had congratulated him on bearing up so well.

At one minute to ten, his paper dutifully sighed towards the floor, and his slippered feet blundered across the carpet. Watch clutched religiously in curled, plump palm, he stretched his hand to the clock on the mantelpiece. But his fingers closed on nothing.

He had half a minute still to go, but, making no contact, he actually took his eyes off his watch and looked directly at the clock - or rather looked at the lighter patch on the wallpaper where the clock had been.

For a moment he stared at the patch without comprehension. He blinked stupidly. Perhaps one of the funeral guests had moved it. People were funny about clocks and mirrors and things where the dead were concerned - all sorts of odd superstitions.

When he failed to locate the clock, he glanced back at the mantelshelf, and there it stood, feet firmly planted, solidly in place, its figured face innocent of any misdemeanour.

For a second he frowned, but then a slow smile spread across his features. He even chuckled as he realised that his eyes had deceived him. It had, after all, been a long day, and soon it would be time for cocoa and a pleasingly roomy bed. Pity his wife wasn't there to make them for him. Still, you couldn't have everything.

He resumed his accustomed pose, consulting his watch while he reached for the clock. It wasn't yet quite ten. But as his fingertips alighted on the smooth, polished casing, he felt it slip to one side.

He looked up in alarm. Don't say he was getting clumsy in his old age! He squinted at the clock face, now registering a fraction off ten. It returned an impassive stare, the glass reflecting the myopic pupils of his own eyes.

He attempted a firmer grip, but to his amazement the clock slid sideways along the shelf, almost toppling a vase from the end. It was the remaining one of a pair.

In his effort to field the trembling vase, he fell over the companion set and considerably bruised his shins. As his legs threshed about with the effort to regain his feet, the poker caught between his ankles, and he found himself hurled across the rug and slithering through the fleeing pages of his newspaper.

Colliding decisively with the sofa, he sat up, rubbing his head. He glared at his unexpected enemy, prim and stationary on the mantelpiece, and noticed that it had now gone ten. Though not as a rule given to swearing, he allowed himself a few choice words and pulled himself up on the arm of the settee, only slightly tearing the stitching of the loose covers as he did so.

Then he turned his attentions once more to the clock. He marched purposefully over to the wanton thing and grabbed at it. This time he would stand no nonsense, though his heart was pounding with the unaccustomed exercise.

Just as it lay within his grasp, it shot upwards and hung impossibly in front of his startled eyes. Next it zoomed over his balding hairline so fast he was forced to duck. He thus struck his cheek on a carved projection of the mantelpiece. His watch fell from his unnerved fingers and disintegrated on the tiles, cogs and springs spilling into the room. He'd had that watch ever since he was a teenager, when his grandfather had died.

Right! That did it! He swung round and glared wrathfully in the direction the clock had taken. There it hovered, the other side of the sofa, jigging about in the air as though egging him on. He stepped towards it, and the clock retreated an equal distance. He started to clamber, sweating, over the sofa, but his quarry twitched back in response.

He decided to pretend to ignore it. He picked up a page of the newspaper which was still intact and, affecting to read it, upside down as it was, he sauntered round the end of the settee as though he was heading for the door.

As he drew level with the clock, he leapt after it with a triumphant cry, forgetting in his haste the occasional table that blocked his path. It crashed to the floor and splintered underneath him. And he did his own bit of splintering on top.

35

Clutching his ribs, he seized a bowl which had survived the demise of the table, and flung it at his foe. It dodged neatly, so that the bowl shattered against a valued picture, and a cascade of glass erupted over the room.

Fury fired up the widower's breast as he realised that the bowl had belonged to no-one but himself. The wretched timepiece joggled about as if it was laughing.

Snatching up a brass ornament that even he could not break, the dispossessed owner charged at his tormentor and chased it round the room. He scattered the chairs, swept photos and holiday mementos off the sideboard, dealt a hefty blow to an unwitting cabinet, and felled the standard lamp.

Finally, he caught his foot in the rug, blundered across the carpet and wrenched down the curtains in an attempt to save himself. The curtain rail flipped off its moorings and delivered a last, smart blow to the back of his shoulders.

For a moment he stayed where he was, breath coming in hoarse, despairing gasps. Then he sat up, disentangling himself from what seemed like acres of cloth.

He sobbed. He knew when he was beaten. He simply hadn't got the pace to catch the evil-minded timekeeper. It had weaved and bobbed and spun and dived like an international rugger star. Bernard was obviously no match for it.

As he lay exhausted among the curtains, blood dripping unchecked from his nose and a large bruise appearing under an eye, he noticed that the clock once more straddled the centre of the mantelpiece. It was now a quarter past ten, the room was a wreck, and he had not yet wound the beastly thing.

Slowly, he rose to his feet and advanced reluctantly towards it.

When he was squarely in front of it, he stopped and extended his hand a few timid inches. Then he jerked his arm back as if he'd been bitten, and slid one fingertip nervously into his mouth. He gnawed at the nail reflectively. He hadn't done that since he was a child! The clock, however, gave not one flicker of movement.

After a pause, he extended his hand again, very tentatively. Again the clock did not budge. His fingers quivered further towards the face.

Suddenly the glass flew open and the hands whirred round until his eyes crossed trying to keep up with them. The workings chittered, mocked and threatened. He leapt back and landed in the settee.

Screwing up his courage, he was halfway back to the mantelpiece when he felt a slight tug at the bottom of his cardigan. Somehow he had caught a thread. He followed its length into a maze of unravelled wool strewn halfway round the room. He solemnly accepted that, without his wife, there was no chance that he could mend it.

Miserably he took hold of the clock. He didn't care any more how it reacted. But it did nothing. It seemed intent on behaving itself.

He lifted it down and upended it. Mutely he turned the key. He hadn't the strength to wind it fully. He returned the clock to the shelf, where it was the only undamaged item in the room, and trailed off into the kitchen.

The next night was to see a further development.

At one minute to ten, just when he was toying with the idea of extracting his replacement watch from his pocket, the clock began to strike. It shouted out the tens and twenties until he decided not to bother.

After that, he had to wind it at all hours of the day. The slightest indication of routine had it going again.

His wife did not need to wait that long to see the fruition of her plans. She eased herself out through the wall, and set off for a brighter destination where time had no relevance.

She had witnessed her husband skipping about with a satisfying vigour. She had seen him colliding and stumbling, smashing and shattering his way round the lounge. She knew he would never again be able to sink into his old regular habits, or sit easy in an ill-buttoned cardigan. Best, she knew that any broken glass - or broken anything - would have to be cleared up by no-one but himself.

BRANTLEY RITES

A new broom had come to the Brantley Estate. The villagers knew there were bound to be changes, but nothing that could have anticipated the events that followed.

Old Sir Brantley had let the place fall into a state surpassing genteel neglect. He'd gone through three wives with never a whisper of an heir, and spent his last years alone, slobbering his wine through an unkempt moustache and peering through shaggy eyebrows at his collection of insects. Their capture to him was as much a source of pride as the elephant's foot umbrella stand and the crossed ivory tusks over the mantelpiece, trophies of an adventurous and distant youth. Even then he'd been a gambler, if only with his life. By the time he died, he'd turned a prosperous estate into one kept going only through the dedication of loyal if ill-paid locals.

Mrs. Bradshaw, the housekeeper, latterly cook, cleaner and nursemaid, had found him two months before slumped in his favourite armchair. His stained tweeds were slightly scorched from proximity to the fire, his fist curled loosely round an Ace of Clubs and resting on a game of Patience. Death had finally taken delivery.

Her husband Jim had kept the vegetable garden going and shot the occasional rabbit and pheasant for the table. Now the pair of them were out of a job.

The estate was put up for auction by some fancy London firm, and a gang of outside builders commissioned to strip out all floorboards which sagged with wet rot, all brickwork decayed by dry rot, rafters powdered and pocked by woodworm and crossbeams gnawed hollow by beetle. The roof was re-trussed and the lintels restored to an even pitch.

Those in the village who had rooms to let found themselves with spare cash in their pockets to swap the gossip over a jar at The Royal Oak. Those who had connections with the old Hall were relieved that its external character at least was retained, but worried that it would be over-modernised inside.

"I shouldn't worry about it Jim," said the landlord. "At least your missus'll have a spanking new kitchen and a good bit of help when she gets her job back."

"If she gets her job back. I'm not so sure. Story goes it's been bought by some wealthy A-rab. Probably bring in his own people to cook all that Middle Eastern stuff. Beryl couldn't manage that.... Won't want me neither, I shouldn't wonder."

"Bound to need vegetables, Jim, no matter what."

And in a way they were both right and both wrong. The new owner was an American businessman, and he had no intention of mouldering away in the middle of nowhere. He'd bought the estate to cash in on executive stress and middleclass angst about the environment and adulterated food. The Hall was to be converted into a hotel for those who needed to get away from everything except luxury. The cuisine was to be organic and home-grown, with a specialised head gardener and a specialised head chef of international repute.

The publican was dismayed to learn there would be a first-class bar and the cellar restocked. A manager was appointed who possessed not only excellent qualifications but an accent that spoke of public school. Staff were selected for youth and beauty as well as skills. Mrs. Bradshaw found herself looking for casual cleaning, and Jim was demoted to an under-gardener and allowed to drive a motorised lawnmower around the extensive lawns. But at least the pay was regular.

It wasn't all bad news. Although there'd be no new family to grace the gated pew at the head of the aisle, the clergyman allowed himself to hope for a few more attenders at Sunday Service and the occasional generous contribution in the donations box from visitors. A couple of local farmers turned their hands to organic pork and dairy products, and hoped the owner was sufficiently removed from the locality not to look too closely at their pedigrees.

So all went reasonably smoothly until the new owner focussed his attentions beyond the house and grounds. The profits from tourism were not enough. He appointed a new estate manager and expected to turn an agricultural profit too. And that was when the trouble began.

Duncan Harcourt combined a clinical knowledge of arable farming with the soul of an accountant. He moved into the old Forester's Cottage and made the front room into his office. Dan Carter stood before him like a rebuked schoolboy, as the new man flicked impatiently through the grubby sheets that showed the extent of decline in output. A map of the estate was pinned to a board. Harcourt strode over to it and jabbed it with his finger.

"Is this the best you can do with 2,000 acres? Good God, man, you should be ashamed. Is there something wrong with the soil?"

"No, sir, it's very deep, very fertile. It's just we haven't had the labour, sir, and the old master just wasn't interested. If it wasn't for me and the others it would all have turned back to scrub."

"It might just as well have from the looks of these figures. Aren't you aware of the price wheat is fetching at the moment? And with markets expanding in China it's likely to go on. How come the yields are so low?"

"Weather, sir. The crop all got smashed down by the rain, and the machines bogged down in the mud."

Harcourt gave Carter a keen look. "This is an early wheat variety. It must have been ready before the rain set in."

"It was, sir."

"So why in God's name didn't you harvest it?"

"Everyone was after the combines at the same time."

"Do you mean we haven't got our own?"

"Too much money. Everyone was in the same boat. Besides that, not all our fields are suitable for commercial machines."

"We'll see about that." He scrutinised the map. Some of the fields were a bit tight, and it wasn't acceptable any more to grub up the hedgerows. The biggest field was interrupted by a wide swathe of hatching which almost cut it in two. "What's that?"

"It's a bit of woodland, sir."

"Well what's it doing stuck right across this field."

"It's always been there."

"Has it indeed! You can walk the land with me tomorrow, and we'll draw up a plan of improvement."

The "we" did not seem to carry any great significance. And Carter found himself dismissed.

A fine morning meant it was pleasant enough to trek the old estate. Celandine shone from the banks and the grasses were coated in dew. Pheasants lifted out of toppled stubble and trailed their tawny iridescence towards the woods which fringed the estate. Harcourt was annoyed to see the stubble still lying undisturbed. Carter mumbled apologetically about winter foraging and protection of wildlife. But in any case there'd been no wages for ploughing in.

By noon they reached the hundred acre field, and Harcourt marched ahead to the strip of woodland that scythed across it. It lay across the bottom of ground which sloped gently upwards and out of sight over the curve of the hill. It was encircled by a sagging fence of rusty barbed wire. The posts in places were completely rotten and collapsed to the ground. It was easy enough to climb over.

The wood itself was in no better state. Clearly neglected for years, it was overgrown with a tangle of saplings, brambles and fetid weeds. Trees leaned at angles, some only supported by their neighbours. Dense layers of leaf mould gave an unreliable footing on ground that either crackled with dead twigs or squelched with black mud.

Harcourt hacked a path through it, a look of rank disgust settling on already disapproving features.

"There is an easier way in, sir."

"I want to see exactly what we're dealing with."

As they drew closer to the edge of the field on the village side, the wood opened up a bit into a kind of glade. They clambered over a fallen giant that lay across their path. Fungi fluoresced out of the rotting wood. To one side of them a huge beech leaned towards them, its roots and lower trunk encased in bright green moss. The copper spears of early buds showed a vigorous strength that soon would unfurl into a spreading banner of vibrant leaves. Its bulk seemed to bulge with a twisted mass of sinews.

It was as they stepped out of its shadow into the warmth of the glade that Harcourt became aware that they were not alone.

In the centre of the clearing reared a tree which dwarfed the rest. Its girth was massive, but its trunk was cleft from the bottom and separated on the side nearest them, so that it seemed to straddle the ground. It must have been fifty to sixty feet high, buttressed by huge spreading roots. At some point it may have been polled, if only by the wind, as the trunk supported a number of limbs which towered above a small figure seated on its swelling bole.

It was a young girl. She sat sideways to the trunk, her upper body turned to face it. Her soft arms spread wide to embrace the oak's rough bark, her lips moving as if she were talking to it.

"What on earth is that child doing here?"

"It looks as if she's been dressing the tree."

Harcourt looked blank. Then he noticed strands of feathery blossom draped around the lower trunk and trailing over the roots. The girl slithered down from her perch and stooped to take something out of a basket. It was a small bunch of wood anemones, which she placed reverently at the base of the tree. She clearly did not know she was observed.

"Hey, girl. What are you doing here?"

41

The child looked round, startled, then bolted into the trees on the far side of the clearing.

"It was just one of the village children. She wasn't doing any harm."

"So why did she run?"

"You startled her. She doesn't know you."

"She obviously knew she was trespassing."

"Hardly trespassing."

"It's private property."

"Well, not exactly."

"What do you mean 'Not exactly'? It's part of the Brantley Estate."

"Yes, but villagers' rights, sir."

"Villagers' rights! What rights can the villagers possibly have?"

"The right to collect fallen wood."

"Well she wasn't collecting fallen wood." The voice was sarcastic.

"She was only playing. A lot of them do it. Come up to visit the tree and wish it luck. No harm in it."

"So a lot of them do it! Where do they get in?"

He set off the way the girl had gone, passing under more beeches. The path certainly was more defined in this direction. They came to a stout wooden fence marking the end of their bit of wood and the beginning of another. There was a stile between the two.

"I see it's been made easy for them. You can put some barbed wire across that for a start."

"I can't do that!"

"Just do it!"

Carter felt he didn't have much choice, though he knew it would make no difference. And sure enough, every time he replaced it, and never when he was around, the wire was mysteriously cut. Harcourt had signs made declaring the wood "Private Property", but they disappeared too.

Nevertheless Harcourt had plenty to occupy him. First was to organise the ploughing and sowing of the fields and to work out the rotations. Next was to form a Consortium with other local farmers to buy their own combine. The estate would put up the major part of the funding and provide the housing, so the estate would have first call on

42

its services - maximised benefit for minimised cost. He forgot all about the niggling challenge to his authority presented by the village.

He was reminded of it forcibly on his way to one of those consortium meetings. His route took him through the village. A bus was making a wide turn into the High Street from Church Lane, and he was obliged to pull over and stop. He was so busy frowning at the other vehicle that he did not notice a hefty figure step into the road in front of him. But he couldn't miss the shock to his Range Rover when two meaty fists slammed down on the bonnet in front of him.

He wrenched open his door and scrambled out to face his assailant. "What the devil do you think you're playing at! Are you drunk?"

"More to the point, what are you up to?" The man leered at Harcourt. "And no, I ain't drunk."

"No excuse then. I'm a good mind to report you to the police."

"Go ahead. A fat lot of good it'll do you. Nobody round 'ere has much time for foreigners."

"Foreigner! Are you deaf and blind as well as drunk?"

"No local would behave like you."

Harcourt decided to put an end to this. "Do you know who you're talking to?"

"Oh I know who you are all right."

"So I'll thank you to watch your step. Who are **you** anyway?"

"Never mind that. What gives you the right to come 'ere throwing your weight around?"

"I had the impression it was you throwing the weight around."

"Well at least I don't pick on little girls."

"Little girls!"

"Little girls." The other man stepped towards him. Veins stood out belligerently in his neck. To his credit, Harcourt stood his ground.

"My Lucy come home in floods of tears last week. Told me how you'd shouted at her. Now she can't get past the stile with all the barbed wire. What sort of miserable bastard are you to stop the kiddies playing in that bit of wood?"

"I would remind you that it's my bit of wood."

"No it ain't."

"Oh but it is. And if I decide to deny access, there's nothing you can do about it."

"You're only some jumped up little pen pusher. You don't own the place."

"No, but I think my say-so carries a bit more weight than yours."

Harcourt's sarcasm cut no ice with his opponent.

"Well you'd better tell your boss to keep his hands off our wood."

"And who shall I say the message is from?"

"Ned Crowland."

"And what is your position round here?"

"I'm the local mechanic."

"Really? Well you needn't look to the estate for any work in future."

"I'm the only mechanic for 30 odd miles. I think you'll find I won't go short of work. Even yours," he added.

Harcourt's face reflected his increased irritation. The thought had only half formed in his mind when it came out of his mouth. "Well you can tell that little girl of yours that she'll have to find somewhere else to play. The wood's soon for the chop. Out of bounds for ever."

He climbed back in the car as if that was an end to the matter, but the man was still gripping the top of his door. Crowland bent down so that his dark eyes blazed within inches of his.

"If you think we'll let you get away with that, mister, you'd better think again."

"I don't need to Crowland. I can do anything I like."

"We'll see about that. If you know what's good for you, Harcourt, you won't meddle with things you don't understand. Lay a finger on that wood and you'll regret the day you set your piggy little eyes on it." He pushed the door into place with exaggerated gentleness, then stepped back and watched just as calmly as the car drew away.

Harcourt was annoyed with himself. Spur of the moment decisions were never a good idea. And it never did to reveal your hand. Moreover he had an uncomfortable feeling things had not gone precisely his way. Nevertheless, he knew if it came to it he could run rings round this fellow, take some of the swagger out of him. He never could resist a challenge. He decided to go ahead with it.

Of course Carter tried to persuade him it was a bad idea. It was a really boggy bit of land, as he'd seen for himself. It was no use to man nor beast. Any machine would just sink in the mire. It could even leave the lower field wetter than ever. There was some kind of spring under there. Harcourt simply asked him if he'd never heard of drainage and sent off to the Council Planning Department for permission to fell.

However, it looked as if it wasn't just Crowland who was determined to defy him. It was some time after Easter. The hundred acre field had finally been sown and was already showing green with

44

shoots of wheat. He was casting a satisfied glance across this spectacle as he drove through the adjacent parkland when his eye fell on a far less welcome sight. He slammed on his brakes in disbelief.

A whole procession of villagers, and not just children, was wending its way in a huddled line from a point near the lower corner of the field straight across his new wheat. At its head was a figure in black robes, preceded by a cross on a long staff. It was no less than the vicar - a figure of the establishment! - flouting the laws of property and ravaging his crop.

Harcourt leapt from his car and sprinted towards the hedge, shouting at the end of the line and waving his arms. No-one took a blind scrap of notice. They were all too busy chattering away, heads wagging as furiously as their tongues. By the time he reached the gate on his side, the vicar had entered the strip of wood, and by the time he'd made his way across the rows of wheat and arrived at the glade they were all grouped round that blessed tree.

He was astonished at what he saw. Two of the men had upended one of the choir boys and were bumping his head on a root of the oak, while the rest beat its sides with white wands of stripped willow. All the other children were laughing and the inverted boy, though red in the face, was joining in. Suddenly they all stopped, stood back in a circle, heads down, hands clasped in front of them.

Harcourt seized his moment. "Really, vicar. What is the meaning of this? I would have thought a man of the cloth would set a better example."

The clergyman looked up and gave a vicarly smile.

"Ah Mr. Harcourt. We are about to say the Lord's Prayer. Would you care to join us?"

Harcourt looked at the vicar's inoffensive face and wondered if that mild manner contained a hint of mockery. He decided it didn't.

"I haven't got time for this." He considered the situation. This man could be useful to him. "I'll call on you at the Vicarage tomorrow evening. About seven thirty?"

The vicar nodded assent and turned back to his flock. As Harcourt returned to his vehicle, he heard the strains of 'We plough the fields and scatter'. "Silly old fool thinks it's Harvest Festival."

Regaining his seat, he glanced back up the hill. He could just about make out the worshippers among the leaf cover. Something glittered between the vicar's upraised arm and the oak tree. "Now he thinks he's officiating at a christening. I wonder if he's quite all there."

45

But he needn't have worried. The vicar struck him as shrewd enough when he sized him up across a cup of vicarage tea in the clergyman's sitting room.

"Ah yes, Mr. Harcourt, our little ceremony. It's Rogation Tide, you know. Beating the bounds."

Harcourt did not know and confessed as much.

"Every seven years in this area. Used to be a very useful way of marking out the Parish's territory. Saved a lot of disputes one way or another."

"Since when did Parish territory extend into Estate grounds? Your so-called flock were trampling down our newly sown wheat."

"Oh yes I noticed it. Off to a fine start. And of course we invited God's blessing on the year's crops. That's part of the tradition."

"And is it part of the tradition to trespass on your neighbour's land?"

"Oh no, no, no. You don't understand. It's very much the other way round. Over the centuries the estate has gradually encroached on what used to be common land. But we still follow the old routes to the boundary markers. One of them's the Royal Oak, you know. You probably saw us blessing it."

What was the man talking about? "Do you mean the pub?"

"That is, of course, named after the oak, but no. You saw us standing round it - the great oak tree in the glade. That's our parish boundary. Been there, as they say, since time immemorial. In every sense it defines the village. We pray for its continued health."

"I think that's a forlorn hope. It's showing signs of dieback."

"Has been for years. It makes no difference. From time to time it drops the odd branch - as a matter of fact one of them was used in the construction of Forester's Lodge - but generally speaking, for its age, it's flourishing. Even seems to recover from time to time, when its acolytes have been especially attentive. Young Lucy, for example."

The name reminded Harcourt of his grievances. "Oh yes, Lucy Crowland. **She** gets in over the stile. So why did your congregation feel the need to trek through my field?"

"Well, I don't know if you realise this, Mr. Harcourt." The vicar smiled benignly at him. "But someone has barricaded that route off with barbed wire."

Harcourt said nothing.

"But in any case it wouldn't have made any difference. The route across the field is along the old boundary."

"Do you mean it's a right of way?" Just what he needed.

"Of course it is."

"Do you mean every Tom, Dick and Harry can trek across my standing crop at any time he likes?"

"Oh it's not as bad as that, Mr. Harcourt. Give and take, you know. Give and take. It's only once in seven years. Though that does, of course, maintain the right of way well within the time limit. We're no fools, you know." The vicar offered him another piece of cake. Harcourt took it.

"Anyway, it could have been worse. There's one place - the name escapes me now - where the old boundary line runs right through a newly built house, and the owners have to put up with annual invasions of parishioners passing through from the front door to the back."

The vicar continued his ruminations. "Oh no. As an act of courtesy our villagers always use the stile for everyday purposes."

"I'll have the wire removed immediately."

Harcourt knew when it was best to cut his losses, but this was all bad news from his point of view. He'd have to revise his plans. He could legitimately fell right up to the oak and still gain a great deal of land for his harvesters. Of course, it was always possible that his outside contractors might make an unfortunate mistake. There was, after all, no fence on that side.

As if he'd read his mind, the vicar added. "Of course the tree is protected too. Almost an ancient monument."

"What is it? Two - three hundred years old?"

"More like a thousand, according to folklore." Harcourt doubted that. "Legend has it that it grew from an acorn from the very tree that was cut to make the Round Table. King Arthur and all that. You can see it in Winchester, you know."

"You don't believe all that, do you?"

The vicar chuckled. "Whether I believe it or not is immaterial. It's more than your life's worth to doubt the fixed opinion of the local congregation. They also believe, of course, that these old boundary markers are guarded by spirits and demons. 'Cursed be he who removes his neighbour's marker', etcetera, etcetera."

Harcourt left the vicarage with serious food for thought. He'd apply initially to fell right up to the fence but leaving the oak standing. It would look impressive as a solitary giant. He could see it surrounded by neat plough lines sweeping around it and on up the slope. Even Harcourt could understand how attractive it would look. And you never know someone on the Council could be persuaded to let the thing through on a nod and a wink.

But he bargained without the local rag and the fact that some villagers actually read it. He soon had a deputation in his office, with Carter shuffling uncomfortably at the back. The Royal Oak was proving a nuisance. It wasn't enough for them that he wasn't going to touch a leaf of its colossal head. Oh no. Felling the manky wilderness around it would, it seemed, expose it to the wind and spell its downfall!

Much though he relished this prospect, he adopted a tactical retreat and magnanimously agreed to fell only the trees on his side of the boundary marker. This too met with dissent: trees developed a root system to cope with the prevailing wind, but the wind didn't always blow from the west; it was especially dangerous if it came the other way. Hadn't he noticed the crack in the trunk on that side? Anyway, what about the four knights?

He looked bemused at the rebellious crowd and lifted both his hands in an appeal to sanity and to a God he didn't believe in. He began to think he'd entered some kind of surreal parallel universe. "Four knights!"

A fist he immediately recognised shuddered his desk, and a work-hardened finger waved in his face.

"Yes, the four knights. What kind of ignoramus are you? The four knights, two of which are on your side of the boundary."

He still looked nonplussed.

"The beeches, you fool. The four knights!"

A crevice of light opened in Harcourt's mind. "Well - up to the beeches."

That still didn't suit, but Harcourt refused to budge an inch further. He'd given sufficient ground, however, for most of the crowd to edge grumbling out of the door. Crowland finally backed out, keeping his malevolent eye on Harcourt until his bulky figure blocked out the light. Then he turned and crunched off down the path. Carter, muttering apologies, scuttled after him.

Harcourt rang up for a new planning application, thinking how good it would be if the oak could be persuaded to give up the ghost. He began toying with the idea of copper nails. He'd heard those were pretty effective. He'd take some up with him at the next opportunity.

For a time his hands were full, however, checking the progress of his crops, taking delivery of the new combine and organising a rota and his workforce for the harvest. Once the harvest was in, arrangements had to be made for its sale and dispersal. So it was a few months before his attentions turned once again to the question of the tree.

It was early October, and the leaves were beginning to yellow and flutter to the ground. The cover provided by the strip of woodland was beginning to thin and, as he approached across the stubble he could see movement between the trees. A whole group of children were weaving in an undulating line among the trunks. At length they formed a ring around the oak, hands raised and touching while they circled to the left, then hands down but still linked as they moved to the right. At their centre stood Lucy, arms raised, looking up into the branches. On her head was a chaplet of honeysuckle.

As he looked round the clearing he realised what they had been up to. Tendrils of honeysuckle trailed from one of the beeches to the next, so that they formed a rough circle of four. In the middle, the oak was also draped in the same flower, and all the children were adorned with it.

Lucy turned to face them. The others dropped their hands and also turned to face outwards. Now he could hear what they were saying. "We call on you Gawain and Galahad, Lancelot and Bedevere. Arm yourselves. Prepare to defend your king."

Harcourt stepped into the glade. "Still playing games, Lucy Crowland?"

The children did not shift from their places, though they all turned his way, their eyes sullen.

Lucy broke the silence. "We have called on the king to protect himself, and his knights to defend him. Our task is done."

"I'm sure he's a very lucky tree."

The children broke up into groups and began to leave the clearing. In a few minutes he could no longer make out their voices as they made towards the village.

Well Arthur." Harcourt addressed the tree. "Good luck. You'll need it."

No sooner was he back at the Lodge than he started to rummage among some boxes stacked along the wall in front of the fireplace. They'd been put there to clear space in the combine shed. Somewhere amongst them there were bound to be some copper nails.

As he uncovered the mantelpiece, for the first time he noticed what a handsome piece it was. Head foresters were obviously cosseted employees. Clearly old, and cut out in deep relief, it was heavily carved with a pattern of leaves - oak leaves, of course! - twining up the legs and clustering under the shelf. Halfway down one side he realised there was a face, peering out from behind the foliage. It had round, astonished eyes as if it could not believe what it was seeing. The mouth was set into a wide grimace, stretched out by fingers slid into the corners. The tongue protruded grotesquely, the tip divided into stems which sprouted into the mass of foliage. It was a small masterpiece, like a wizened dwarf, or perhaps a gargoyle. It reminded him of something he'd seen in a book. Perhaps it was valuable.

He turned his attention back to his search, and eventually found what he was seeking. When he went to bed that night he took them with him and perched them on the dresser. It wouldn't do to let Carter see them on his desk.

He was just dropping off when an extraordinary image came into his head. It was the Royal Oak, crown perched rakishly in its topmost branches, a two-handed sword strapped to its side. It stood like a wrestler, flexing its muscles. Its limbs strained and bulged and its chest swelled and swelled until, with a violent of exhalation, it produced an explosion of nails which, as they flew and clattered to the ground, turned into miniscule daggers.

He found himself chuckling and realised that he was awake. The box had overbalanced and fallen to the floor. Nails lay scattered the across the rug. He'd pick them up in the morning.

While he slept, moonlight played softly over his face, filtered through fronds of ivy rocking gently outside his window.

He found himself looking down at a clearing through a mass of branches and crenellated leaves. The sun shone round the base of the tree and played across his feet. He felt himself caressed by soft hands. From a long way up, he saw blond hair ringed with a circlet of flowers. Then he saw dancers weaving a pattern among the gold and bronze of the forest's floor, and he smiled in contentment.

Later he seemed to be flying above a huge forest, catching glimpses of silver threading through the trees, a pattern of streams like the veins of some gigantic organism. As he flew closer, through gaps in the canopy, he saw a herd of wild pigs running free. He could see the rough bristles coating their bodies, hear them snouting among the leaf litter, champing on acorns, rooting up truffles. One particularly large boar carried a golden chain around its neck.

When he woke in the morning he felt curiously rested.

A phone ringing downstairs broke his mood. Running round the end of the bed towards the stair head, he forgot all about the nails from the night before. A pain drove into the ball of his foot and shot up his leg. Swearing, he hobbled back to bed and inspected the damage. The nail had almost disappeared into his flesh. Yanking it out of the tough skin caused more pain than when it had gone in, and left his sheets stained with blood.

Carter discovered him in a foul state of mind, limping about the sheds and finding fault with everything.

"My bloody office looks like a slum. You can stow that load of junk back where you found it."

"But what about the combine?"

"I'm sure it's not beyond your intelligence to find some corner where it won't be in the way."

"I'll do my best, sir."

"I'm sure you will. And while you're about it you can inventory the stuff. Otherwise we'll never find anything again."

So Carter spent the whole morning lugging crates and boxes across the yard and making a list in his best handwriting. Harcourt watched his progress from the desk, causing his normally adept employee to be a bundle of clumsy nerves.

Harcourt himself opened the morning's mail and made some phone calls. Then he sat tapping his teeth with his biro and sighing with impatience while the last few boxes were removed. His gaze fell naturally on the grimacing face which lurked among the carvings of the cleared hearth.

His thoughts turned once again towards the tree. He wondered, after all, if the nails were such a good idea. The glade seemed such a focus for so many villagers that someone might notice and put two and two together. The wooden eyes stared back in silent expectation.

He continued to mull over the question. Ringing would be even more obvious. No, what he needed was some kind of poison. Something copper based and very, very concentrated. Half a job would be worse than useless.

His dreams that night were more disturbing. In the centre of a moonlit clearing, etched in black shadows, a shattered tree rose stark against the sky. Its limbs and branches, ripped and jagged, told of unspeakable pain.

He felt its agony. His body began to shake. Even the earth beneath him started to tremble. Before his eyes, fissures in the bark began to split apart. Clusters of foetal shapes oozed from the cracks. Their nakedness uncurled into a mass of toadstools. Brown, pointed caps with slimy gills began to spread along the roots. They forced upwards through the poisoned loam and ran out from the base of the tree in a radiating circle. They flowed through the wood in a ruinous tide, obliterated the carved lines left by the plough, blackened and shrivelled ripened heads of wheat and washed towards him, unstoppable.

And then he saw the veins on his hands cracking open, the lines of fungus running up his arms. He raised them up in mute appeal. His mouth opened in a silent scream.

He awoke to his own cries ringing in his ears. He was sweating and shivering in fright. That bloody tree. He'd have to get rid of it, and soon, if he was to have any peace.

And so he spent a large part of the next day researching which systemic herbicide and how many gallons it would take to kill it.

Other than that, estate business kept him generally busy. His vanity was also satisfied by a personal call from the American owner, congratulating him on his progress. He took the estate accounts up to bed with him to consider the possibility of further economies. There should be a fat bonus for him at the year's end. He celebrated his anticipated success with the music of "The Four Seasons" and a bottle of good claret.

His head was just falling back on the pillow, when the wind started to get up, buffeting the house and setting up a hollow moan in the chimney. He was surprised by its force, and would have felt a little nervous had the building not been so sturdy. Its thick stone walls had clearly withstood a few gales in their time. Still, there was no way he could sleep with the windows rattling in their frames. The leads looked as if for two pins they'd give way under the assault. He imagined the small panes bursting out and flying into the room. Downstairs he heard a window fly back and shatter against the wall. It sounded like the office. Surely he had fastened them all securely.

He threw on his dressing gown and clattered down the stairs in his bare feet. He imagined his papers blowing round the room. The door to the office was slightly ajar. Inside, the light pooled and rippled like reflections on water. He pictured a bright moon with black clouds racing across its surface.

Sure enough a window swung open, the catch bar hanging loose. By a miracle the panes were still intact. It must have been something else he heard. He jerked the window shut and pushed the handle firmly into place.

He stopped for a moment and listened to the wind that raged outside. Above the screaming he could hear a persistent tapping and screeching of branches rubbing on glass. The whole house creaked and shuddered like a ship about to founder.

Suddenly the front door burst open and slammed against a bench to the side of it. A torrent of leaves whirled into the room and swirled up the papers from his desk. He dived at the door and forced it shut, dropping the latches into place and ramming a wooden bar into the brackets on the wall. He stood panting with the effort in the sudden calm that overtook the room. The floor lay strewn with printouts and dry, coppery leaves. And in the darkness that spread from the blackened grate gleamed two green points of light. They narrowed briefly and then they faded. When he flicked on the switch there was nothing there.

Harcourt returned to bed in an uneasy frame of mind. He managed to sleep, but a torrent of images flowed through his dreams. Tops of trees flailed under the lash of wind, streams overflowed their banks and bore down in a tidal wave on fleeing figures. The wild boar again, clattering on desperate hooves through tunnels in the undergrowth. All the time he could hear a drumming sound and the shouts of men. He had a glimpse of hands on bridles, iron-clad feet kicking foam from horses' bellies, the glint of chain-mail among the trees. Then he saw a blue and cream surcoat flapping round a rider's knees, an arm raised, a spear hurtling through the brambles.
One of the pigs was down. It was the one with the gold chain. It staggered heavily to its feet, the spear stuck in its ribs and trailing from its side. It flung back its head in a fierce snarl of rage and desperation. Blood and froth came gargling past its yellowed fangs in a hoarse scream of death. And a long, tortured scream came out of Harcourt's mouth and woke him from his sleep.

He didn't wait for morning. He juddered down the stairs and switched on the computer. His brain screamed with impatience at its intolerable slowness. Nevertheless, by the time the sun entered the eastern windows, the order was placed. Within a fortnight he had taken delivery of the canisters and hidden the yellow markings with their warning crosses under a pile of firewood outside the house. There they'd remain until the rising of the sap.

The morning after the gale, Carter was amazed at the mess, even more so when he heard the cause. Neither he nor his wife had heard anything, and she was a light sleeper. Nor could he understand where all those leaves had come from. There were no beeches that close to the house. The closest tree was a stately cedar, and there was no way that could have brushed against any windows. Harcourt didn't strike him as a man with an imagination and the leaves were certainly there, so he put it down to a spot of freak weather.

He noticed that Harcourt was in a funny mood.

"I think he's up to something," he told Crowland, when they met over a pint that evening.

"Well keep an eye on him. Whatever it is, it's bound to be no good."

But Carter was not there at night to plot the journeys to and from the wood. He did not witness the number of holes Harcourt dug round the tree, keeping them open with hollow tubes, scattering the soil and kicking the fallen leaves back over the evidence.

Finally his work was done. Everything was ready to deliver the death blow. Nobody would know anything was wrong till late spring, when the oak failed to produce its leaves. With the death of the oak, there could be little objection to felling the rest.

In the months following Christmas it turned much colder, and that afternoon snow began to trickle from a pewter sky. Harcourt knew he'd better act quickly before his task was made more difficult.

And so that night he waited in the kitchen until he could be sure there was no-one about. Even poachers would be inside on a night like this. He waited in comfort, armchair drawn up in front of a blazing fire, feet resting on a stool. In his hand was a good malt whisky from the crate his employer had sent him.

He heard an owl call across the fields and the bark of a fox. The time was right.

He raised his glass. "Well, Arthur, here's to you. The king is dead. Long live the king."

A sigh reverberated in the chimney and a downdraught sent smoke and ashes into the room. Harcourt went into a fit of coughing, his toast suspended.

When his vision cleared, he saw the liquid tremble in the glass. For a second it grew still, then trembled again, in an intermittent pulse. The bottle on the table started to rattle, and he could feel shaking through the soles of his shoes. For a moment he has puzzled. Perhaps a slight earth tremor. They weren't unknown round here.

He swigged the rest of his whisky and rose to fetch his coat and boots. He didn't get very far. Dust began to powder down from the heavy lintel of the door in front of him. The light fitting started to swing. He was aware of a faint drumming a long way off, growing louder as it bore down upon the house. Vibrations from the flagged floor shivered up his legs, and a dark crack zigzagged through the stones of the chimney breast. Harcourt stared in disbelief as the crack widened and the sound of drumming closed in around him. Even when chunks of plaster fell on his head he didn't move. The ceiling was supported by a massive beam which ran the length of the house. There was no way it would collapse.

The thought was answered by a mighty crack and the beam shattered, bringing tons of masonry crashing down about him. The drum roll poured into the void. The air was full of the wild shrieks of horses, and metal clanged on metal. He felt himself seized by rough hands, then the sound rolled on, fading away up the curve of the hill.

When Carter reported in next day, he found the office empty. He knocked gently on the kitchen door but got no answer. Calling up the stairs brought no result.

Later in the day, when Harcourt had still not shown up, he asked about for him, but nobody had seen him or knew his whereabouts. There were no messages. But the man's possessions were still where he had left them, and eventually Carter organised a search. Harcourt might have gone off and had an accident. If he was lying somewhere in all this snow, things could be very serious for him.

Eventually they found tracks leading from the side of the house and starting at the woodpile. Something heavy had been dragged across the snow. Occasionally there were traces of footmarks, but these seemed sporadic. Whatever it was must have gone clean through the hedge, yet there were no signs of damage. The trail scored across the plough lines and entered the wood. Once they reached the clearing, they disintegrated into a confusion of trampling. In front of the oak tree, they just disappeared.

The villagers searched in every direction but there were no further signs of him. The Police were advised, but discovered no more clues. Harcourt had simply vanished.

The village returned to normal and a new estate manager was appointed. In the wood, the beeches shook out their gleaming leaves, and the oak tree had added another ring to its girth. Its mighty trunk looked sturdier than ever. Every one of its branches was crowned with a mass of new shoots.

THE DRESS

"Look at this!"

Kate rose from the easy chair, and a load of brochures slithered to the floor. Richard was sitting opposite reading a book on the development of steam. He'd obligingly left the arrangements for Christmas to her. Not having children, and with no grandparents to consider, they could afford to please themselves. Each year they headed off to some hotel where the work was done by somebody else. While their friends slumped exhausted after Christmas lunch, surrounded by the racket of children busily breaking expensive toys and squabbling over computer games, they could relax after a sumptuous meal, prepared by expert hands, and decide what to do with the rest of the day.

Richard looked up, keeping his finger in the page. "What have you found?"

"It's a hotel near York. Used to be an old manor house. Fifty-two rooms and seasonal entertainment from November to January. It says here 'a truly Victorian Christmas'. It's obviously one of those themed places. Could be fun."

"Could be expensive!"

"True, but since when did we bother about that?" Kate knew what his problem really was. "You probably don't have to dress up if you don't want to."

"Less point going then."

"Though it is, of course, not far from the Railway Museum. We could probably spend a day rootling around that. Or the main museum, of course. That's a Victorian experience in itself."

Richard visibly brightened. "OK. You check it out. But don't be disappointed if it's too late to book Christmas proper. It's bound to be popular."

She had to admit that the thought had crossed her mind too. Still it was worth the try.

When she got through to Fentiman Hall, the receptionist sounded very doubtful and said she'd have to consult the manager. Kate heard a male voice in the background. "A Mrs. Draper, you say?" There was a pause. "Oh yes." It was almost as if he'd been expecting her. "Tell her we've reserved the master bedroom." Another pause. "It'll be all right. Bathroom en suite. Special terms."

The receptionist confirmed that something had become available, and the arrangements were made.

So, on the 23rd December, they arrived towards nightfall. A butler in Victorian gear ushered them through the door, and a footman took them to the first floor in an ancient lift with its own employee to operate the handle. He brought it to a halt exactly flush with the landing and slid open the gates with a practised movement. The footman showed them to their room and set their cases on an oak chest blackened with time.

Outside it was beginning to get murky, but they were pleased to see that the mock gas mantles cast an electric cheerfulness into all but the darkest corners. Before them stood a massive four-poster bed, high, plump and piled with comfortable pillows.

Kate was thrilled. She'd always fancied a four-poster. It was the fulfilment of a childhood dream. The drapes were rich and heavy and would exclude the slightest draught. She fingered one and looked up at the track.

"Best not to draw the curtains, ma'am, if you don't mind," the footman advised her. "They are the original fabric and won't stand too much wear and tear."

Kate looked disappointed.

"But you won't need them." He gestured to the fire blazing in the small hearth. What a touch of luxury!

He opened the bathroom door. "En-suite, madam, sir."

They peered at the giant white tub, the brass taps, the iron feet, and giggled at each other. "Room for two," Richard muttered to her.

"When you've freshened up, if you'd like to come down to the housekeeper's room, she'll fit you up for your stay. Dinner's at eight o'clock, sir, madam."

Without pausing for the usual tip, he touched his pageboy cap in brief salute and bowed himself out.

Although Kate assured Richard that fancy dress wasn't compulsory, by now he had got into the spirit of things. They went in to dinner, he decked out in evening jacket, wing collar and white tie, she in a full-skirted dress in pale grey grosgrain. Its slim bodice was topped with a small lace collar, and a row of tiny covered buttons ran down the front. Fortunately it benefited from the modern convenience of a back zip, but it looked pretty authentic, and she had pulled her hair up in some semblance of a bun. The housekeeper had insisted she wear a large oval brooch, with mother-of-pearl background and the side profiles of a man and a woman in black jet. Kate tried to reject this as "too funereal", but Mrs. Humphreys had refused to countenance a change. It was obvious who ruled the roost round here. The servants.

On the way to the dining room, their attention was drawn to a poster on the noticeboard, the evening's entertainment: "The Reluctant Heiress", a Victorian melodrama in two acts starring Richard Hawley as the Squire, Winifred Shotter as the maiden, Reginald Shindell and Hope Gaynor as the heroine's parents and Roland Chadwick as the hero.

When the meal was over, the room was cleared at one end, and the gentlemen and ladies, somewhat anachronistically, enjoyed after-dinner drinks together.

They found themselves amused by the whisker-twirling skulduggery of the wicked squire deceiving the Johnny-come-latelies of the manufacturing world into marrying their daughter to a title. The heroine was suitably demure and subdued, appalled by the apparent grossness of her suitor. The hero attempted in vain to persuade her parents of the unsuitability of the match. The audience soon caught on to hissing the villain and cheering the hero.

In the second half, the chance arrived for a just and lawful impediment to the marriage to be declared. The hero rose to his feet but was dragged protesting from the church by the squire's henchmen.

Then came the moment when the bride was called upon to say "I do". Kate felt a surge of panic, and she started to tremble. As the fragile girl lifted her pale face to say the fateful words, Kate leapt to her feet and sent her glass flying. "No, no! Don't do it! He only wants you for your money. You'll live in hell!"

There was a second of silence and then a roar of approval. Men thumped the table and women clapped. She found Richard grinning up at her and tugging her back into her seat. "Well, that showed 'em," he said. "Good on you."

Kate sat down again, smiling round at the other guests, but inside she felt dazed and bewildered. The play proceeded to a happy conclusion, but she was hardly able to follow it. She still felt shaky and upset as they went up to their room.

Richard gave her a hand out of her dress, and she hung it up inside the massy wardrobe that darkened one side of the room. Richard chuckled as he found a nightshirt and cap laid out on his side of the bed. "Don't laugh! Yours isn't much better."

Kate climbed into the ankle-length nightgown on her side, but baulked at donning the frilled cap.

"You might as well," prompted Richard. "I wouldn't fancy you tonight anyway. Not with that lot up there looking down at us."

She didn't see what he meant until she lay back on the pillows. Above them a mass of heads projected from the heavy carvings of the canopy. The delicately chiselled lips and drooping, lashless lids depicted the kind of saintly chastity that would freeze the loins of a professional stud. Slender hands offered prayers and entreaties to the luckless sleeper and showered down benisons into the dark watches of the night.

Kate spent a restless night, plagued by over-rich food, visions of wolves pursuing her through haunted forests and wakeful moments when she seemed to see the shadowy form of a woman bowed disconsolate over the writing desk which faced onto the garden.

Despite this, she woke the next day to winter sunlight pouring through the uncurtained windows and a gentle knocking at the door. Morning tea was all part of the service.

After a day spent exploring the area and stopping for lunch in the village, they returned to Fentiman Hall in good time for dinner. Kate left Richard propping up the bar, while she went up in the lift to get dressed. A maid in bob cap and apron curtseyed to her as she entered. She gave a broad smile. She could get used to this.

"Fetch my dress from the wardrobe, girl," she said loftily, and turned to the dressing table to remove her watch. When she turned back, the maid was holding up a black silk dress with three deep flounces down the bodice and ruffled cuffs and hem.

"That's not my dress. Where's the other one?"

"It's the only one there is, ma'am."

"Well, I'm certainly not wearing that. It's Christmas Eve. That looks as if somebody's died. I'm going to see Mrs. Humphreys."

Mrs. Humphreys accompanied her back to the bedroom, grumbling about people wasting her time tonight of all nights. She swept into the room ahead of Kate.

"Well, where's this dress you're complaining about?"

"She left it on the bed."

"Who did?"

"The ladies' maid."

"You're joking aren't you? What ladies' maid? Anyway, it isn't here now is it?"

"I can see that, but that isn't the point! I had the pretty grosgrain, but that seems to have vanished."

Mrs. Humphreys flung back the wardrobe door and gestured inside. "So what's this?"

Sure enough, there was the light grey. Kate was baffled.

"I might as well help you into it, now I'm here." Kate's skin cringed under the merciless fingers as the zip ripped up her back, but, impatient though the woman was, she clearly knew her business.

Once she had left the room, still puffing indignantly, Kate sat before the mirror to adjust her hair and retouch her make-up. She was applying a light dusting of mascara when she noticed a figure standing in the shadow beside the wardrobe. She just had time to register a black outline and the suggestion of frills when Richard came in. As she turned towards him, she realised she must have imagined it. There was no-one there.

"Night of thrills and spills this evening," said Richard. "Not to say things that go bump in the ......"

"What's on then?"

"Well, it is Christmas Eve - last opportunity for all the old spooks to have a little flutter. Traditional, isn't it? Ghost stories and that."

"What is it? 'A Christmas Carol'?"

"Better than that. A full-blown Victorian séance. Mme Rapsquillion."

"Rap what?"

"Squillion. Very suitable if you come to think of it. The old table turners - rapping and what not."

"Oh, I don't know if I'm keen on that. What if they have a ouija board?"

"All a lot of tosh anyway. But it's more likely to be a bit of the old 'knock once for yes and twice for no'. Should be a bit of a laugh."

Not many people seemed to agree with him. When they filed into the darkened sitting room, there were less than a dozen of them. Nevertheless, that made it better for them to all fit round the large table, which was draped in a baggy chenille cloth.

Mme Rapsquillion looked equally baggy when she emerged theatrically from the curtained recess, looking suspiciously like the bride's mother from the night before.

She gave a fair imitation of Mme Arcati and instructed them all to join the circle, fingertips touching. After a few gusty breaths, her head sank down on her chest. They waited. Suddenly she jerked upright, and her eyes snapped open.

"I feel the presence of a spirit," she intoned sonorously.

"Probably all that whiskey swilling about," put in Richard's neighbour. Richard smirked agreement.

"Shh!" Mme Rapsquillion glared at them. "You're breaking my concentration."

Kate kicked Richard under the table, and he squeezed her hand.

"Fingers touching!" The medium was convincingly fierce. "You need to have an open mind for the spirits to come." She resumed her other-world expression.

"Is there anybody there?" There was a pause. "Is there anybody there?"

"I should bloody well hope so," said Richard.

A woman opposite tutted, and Richard glared at his neighbour, who maintained indifference.

"Knock once for yes ...."

"And twice for no," Richard mouthed at Kate. She frowned at him. Give the poor woman a chance.

The table gave a slight jolt.

"Are you recently departed?" the medium asked.

The table obliged with two thumps.

"Are you a man?"

Two thumps.

"A woman?"

One thump.

"Did you die in this house?"

Kate began to feel uncomfortable. Obviously it was all tomfoolery, but she didn't like all this messing about. It seemed disrespectful somehow.

Mme Rapsquillion at least seemed totally submerged now in her role. A trill of notes on a ghostly flute drew no response from her. Her breathing grew slower and deeper.

"Were you young when you passed over?"

One thump.

"Did you die in childbirth?"

The table began to rattle.

"Try to stay calm, dear. Did you die in childbirth?"

Two thumps.

"Did you die from an illness?"

The surface began to shiver beneath Kate's fingers.

"Did you die from natural causes?"

The table began to drum on the floor and felt as if it would overturn. Kate pressed down on it, her eyes wide in shock. She tried to focus on Mme Rapsquillion, but what she saw brought no comfort. A mist was emanating from her mouth. It rose into the air and began to form a shape. The table bucked and jerked.

Kate could stand it no longer. She leapt to her feet, breaking the circle. "Stop it! Stop it!" she screamed. "You don't know what you're doing!"

She ran from the room and stumbled up the stairs. Richard chased after her and caught her up as she reached the landing.

"What's the matter, Kate? It was only playacting."

"How can you say that? What about that stuff coming out of her mouth? What about the way the table was leaping about? How could they rig that?"

"What stuff? What leaping about? Honestly, Kate, I think you must have had too much to drink. You know you can't take it."

Kate gaped at him as if he was insane. "Well, I'm leaving. I'm not staying here a moment longer."

"We can't leave now. It's gone eleven. Where would we go at this time of night? Anyway, it's Christmas Day tomorrow. We can't miss that. If you like, we'll leave on Boxing Day. Find a hotel in York - assuming that's possible at this time of year. Otherwise, we'll have to go home."

"Rather that than stay in this hell-hole."

Richard looked round at the thick woollen carpets, the shining banisters, the tasteful pictures on the wall. From the white plaster of the moulded cornicing to the gleaming handles on the mahogany doors, he couldn't see how anyone could call this luxury a hell-hole.

"You'll feel better in the morning," he assured her.

Someone had put hot stone water bottles in their bed. It felt warm and comfortable as they clambered into it. Perhaps it would be all right. Kate had automatically put on the nightdress. The flannelette wrapped around her body and cosied her towards sleep.

When she awoke, it was to find Richard's side of the bed empty. A fitful light guttered from the mantles as if the gas was running low. Shadows flickered around the room. The faces in the canopy shifted and rocked in the uneven light. The mouths grew distorted, and the hands seemed to reach out for her.

She tried to sit up and turn on the bedside lamp, but she couldn't move. She felt weak and ill. Her hands lay lifeless on the black silk. They looked almost waxen and transparent. It was as if she'd been drugged.

Figures moved back and forth through the room on silent feet. Occasionally, they approached the bed and bent over her. There were softly murmured words, solicitous, concerned, and then the shapes retreated, and she was aware of the door closing.

For a while she lay numb, unthinking. The sound of the gaslight soothed and lulled her. And then he was there, looking down at her. A man with a beard, severely trimmed, his black hair greying at the temples. He bent towards her.

"You've been so ill, my dear." The words were muffled and distant. "You must sleep now. Time to go home."

She felt something softly touching her face, something pressing down on her, gently at first and then firmer and firmer. Too weak to struggle, she submitted to the pressure, and all sound ceased.

She awoke in the morning to find Richard hovering over her. "My God, Kate, you gave me a fright. You've been delirious. The doctor's been and given you a sedative. How do you feel now? Do you feel like anything to eat? To drink?"

Kate stared at him as if he was a stranger. And then she struggled up on her pillows. Richard bent to help her.

"Where did you go? Why did you leave me, Richard?"

"I never left you, Kate. But I woke to find you cold and sweating, and thrashing about all over the place. I phoned for help and the doctor came.

"Did he have a beard - and glittering eyes?"

"Quite the opposite. Blue-eyed and clean shaven. Nice chap. Said to call him when you woke up."

"I just want to get out of here." She slid her legs off the bed. Clutching at one of the posts, she hauled herself up, but she could hardly stand.

"Just give me a hand to the bathroom. I'll feel better after a nice soak."

Richard accepted the inevitable. "I'll go down and settle up, shall I?"

"No you won't. You'll stay right there where I can see you."

Richard felt as if he was at school again, but he realised that wasn't the point. He scrubbed her back for her and helped her with the towels. Gradually she seemed more like her old self.

Down in the lobby, Richard paid for their stay and said how impressed they were with the arrangements. He apologised for the fact they had to leave early.

While he was busy, Kate looked at the portraits and photographs that lined the walls: the generations of Fentimans, starting in the seventeenth century. The old photographs were more fascinating than the paintings. She never trusted portrait artists to be faithful. But these early sepia photographs were different.

On one side of the fireplace there was a photograph of the Seventh Lord Fentiman on his wedding day. The bride wore a light-coloured dress with a row of tiny buttons up the bodice. She carried a prayer book in her hand. She was obviously happy. Kate was interested to notice, especially in that dress, it could almost have been a photograph of herself. Underneath there was an explanatory note:

"Lord Albert inherited an estate depleted by his brother's profligacy at the gaming tables. After the tragic death of Lord Roland in a shooting accident, Lord Albert's good management brought his inheritance back to prosperity. His personal life was not so happy. Lord Fentiman married four times. Every one of his brides, who brought great fortunes into the union, died in childbirth or from a wasting disease, probably T.B. This was a common fate of young women in that time."

On the other side of the fireplace there was a set of four photos. Lord Albert Fentiman with his first wife Hope, 1886. Lord Albert Fentiman with his second wife Mary, 1889. Lord Albert Fentiman with his third wife Emma, 1892. Lord Albert Fentiman with his fourth wife Myrna, 1896. There were no surviving children.

Kate felt herself go cold, and her knees turned weak. In the last photograph, Lord Fentiman had grown a beard, and his eyes looked darker and more brooding above it. Even in the earlier photographs, you could see what a hard mouth he had. But what especially horrified Kate was the image of Myrna Fentiman. In the usual stiff postures of those caught in the phosphorous flash, she held dutifully to her husband's arm, pale and fragile beside his unyielding bulk, a tragic light in her victim's eye. The dress she wore could have been for her own demise. It was black silk, with three flounces falling from the neck, and ruffles at the cuffs and hemline.

In the taxi, Kate sat with her eyes averted. Richard assumed she was still feeling unwell. On the way to the main gate, they passed a small, private chapel.

Had she looked, she would have seen, among the gravestones, a frail, slender woman, in a long black dress, whose sightless eyes, forlorn, gazed after them.

THE VAMPIRE OF PINDEFORD GREEN

A grey mist rose and hung in the fringes of the wood. Silently it flowed out to engulf the mossy gravestones of the quiet churchyard and wreathed about the ancient walls of St. Austen's. A darker shape emerged from the darkening trees and lingered among the mounds and hummocks. Concealed by a coiling surge of vapour, it gathered form by the crumbling masonry of the square tower, groping along the north side of the building until it found the low grille which led into the vault.

There it drained through the bars like some creeping miasma and extended a clammy breath over the carved tombs and sculpted figures housed therein. Satisfied at last that it had found what it sought, it sighed into the empty spaces of a solemn monument and rested below its graven lid.

The monument had not always been empty. It had contained the earthly remains of Sir Edmund Rampton, late of this parish, and those of his faithful hound, Fleet, no wife seeing fit to keep him company. But three centuries later, when Burke and Hare had set a not unfashionable example, local imitators had seized the revered bones and sold them to Guy's Hospital. A sudden glut in supply had reduced their worth tenfold and made them accessible to the most impecunious medical student. The trade had thus promptly ceased and left the remaining tombs of St. Austen's to gather moss under the stars or dust under the arched roof of the vault.

It was this dust which awoke its new inhabitant in a fit of sneezing on the first night of his occupancy. He thereupon decided to defer any mission to carry death to the small village until he had given his new home a thorough spring clean. Besides, he felt weak and tired after his long journey and thought he could carry death more effectively after a good rest. He was, after all, a professional and believed in doing things properly.

The first sign the villagers had of his presence, therefore, was not the stricken corpse, drained of its life blood, staring eyes still imprinted with horror, but a decided chill in the church the following Sunday. This seemed unaccountable, as it had been a mild autumn and the sun still poured hotly onto bronzed leaves out of a diamond sky. Nevertheless, it was indisputable that the church had developed an icy atmosphere, the walls were bedewed with moisture, and the parishioners began to rifle their cupboards for thermal underwear and heavy overcoats.

The vicar promptly sent for the heating engineers. They declared there was nothing wrong with the system and presented a hefty bill for services rendered which would provide the excuse for many an under-subscribed church function for years to come.

The vicar, reckless as to cost, promptly turned the boiler on to full thrust and the church was converted into an uncomfortable sauna. Had he been more financially astute, he could have reaped a handsome profit and, in the light of not-always-seemly stripping off on the part of the congregation, elaborated on Genesis in respect of Adam and Eve into the bargain. He was, however, a clergyman of strict moral tendency. He eschewed material considerations. In consequence, the local landowners and businessmen left attendance at church to the lesser members of their families - except on very special occasions. Those who did attend continued to ignore his precepts, but found it very difficult to ignore the intemperate conditions.

A few nights into his residency, the newcomer was feeling noticeably peckish and decided he could overlook his cravings no longer. The time for inactivity was past. As he filtered out of the coffin and streamed into the night from the bottom of the north wall, he promised himself some fine pickings: some delicately nubile maiden with snowy breasts and neck, a brace of children perhaps or a strapping young buck whose virile vigour could course through his starved being and revitalise him.

Then, at full power, he would rule the night hours. Obedient children would shiver to early beds with tales of what happened to those who defied their parents and stayed out late. Harassed fathers would have no trouble persuading their daughters to come home on time, and lustful lovers would wait in the dark unsatisfied except by the kiss of the vampire. Thus considered, a member of the undead was of great benefit to any community.

While mulling over these pleasant thoughts, his eyes fell upon the promising form of his first conquest. She sat in front of her dressing table at an uncurtained window, apparently oblivious that she could be observed. As she leaned forward with pouting red lips and the blackest of lashes, a low-cut bra revealed an ample bosom. Her strong young neck was surmounted by curls of wondrous springiness, and crimson nails betokened a wealth of vivid blood.

He had just materialised outside this lighted haven, and was about to cause the casement to blow inwards with portentous force, when he became aware that he was not alone. Someone was breathing raspingly into his ear, and a heavy hand fell on his shoulder.

Before he knew what was happening, he was spun round and found himself looking into a bunched and hairy fist, behind which glared an angry face distorted by hostile intent.

"What's your game, you dirty pervert? Get your filthy eyes off my girl before I close 'em for you. If you're not out of here in two seconds, you'll be staring at a hospital ceiling. Sod off, you overdressed pimp."

As his antagonist exhaled his abuse, the vampire's nostrils were assailed by a stench which sapped all his resources. Instead of immobilising his enemy with a hypnotic stare, he found himself gasping and retching, overtaken by the powerful smell of garlic.

With a wail the spirit fled from the scene, leaving his assailant to resume his position behind a nearby bush, licking his lips while he watched the continued preparations.

Eventually the delicious nymph - if that's not too short a term - wriggled into the briefest of tight dresses and wobbled off on five-inch heels into the arms of quite another swain.

The vampire's next attempted entry was more successful. It was obviously the time for village maidens to flock abroad, for his next quarry was also in the throes of getting ready. True she wasn't as well filled out as the last one, but she was well into adolescence and would certainly do.

The vampire decided on this occasion to materialise once he was safely inside the room. He thought in this apparently Godless society, he could dispense with the time-honoured convention of waiting to be invited. He would effect a dramatic entry with the window trick. For some reason the damsel chose to disregard this spectacle. Not only that, she seemed determined to present a moving target. The vampire mustered up a few bars of uncanny music, but still the girl jigged about as if she was demented. Some defensive ritual perhaps.

Eventually she sat at her mirror and, although she continued to cavort while she applied a thick coat of colour to each eye, the vampire was able to stabilise into one place behind her. He trembled with desire at the thought of plunging his beautiful fangs into the slender neck.

It was difficult to pick out the jugular since she was so young. Moreover, her hands and arms were constantly busy as she vigorously backcombed her hair. It was an odd hairstyle to be sure, all teased into points, and she had a black band round her head culminating in two round circles clamped over her ears. He knew he could take his time, as he cast no reflection in the glass, so he waited patiently for a moment of stillness.

As she reached for a shining canister off her table, the vampire could contain his ardour no longer. He leaned rapturously forward to take his reward. His mouth was almost melting onto the silky flesh, when a sharp noise split the silence, followed by an acid spray into his face. The girl continued to squirt copious quantities of the noxious stuff until, choking, the vampire retreated, with stinging eyes, to the wholesome dampness of the night air.

His next few sorties brought no better luck. There was his assault on a youth past the gawkiness of puberty but not its skin problems. That was a total disaster. The vampire failed to anticipate the latest cure for acne. Gagging on the repulsive cream, he left the neck untouched. Acne it did not deter; vampires it did.

A teenager engrossed in revision seemed easy meat. The tapping feet and nodding head showed the intensest concentration. He would never know what hit him! Unfortunately, it was the uninvited supper guest who never knew what hit him. Permeating the double glazing, his eardrums were all but fractured by a level 10 super woofer. Clutching his ravaged head, the vampire reeled off to the peace and quiet of his vault.

Then there was the fact that his journey across the time zones had played havoc with his sense of the calendar. The night he decided to prey on smaller fry was just an example.

Winging his way on outspread cloak above night-haunted alleys, he came on a huddle of boys. It was a stroke of luck that they chose so unwisely to linger in unlit places. Children always scattered when they were frightened. He decided, therefore, to sweep upon them with blood-curdling screech and then, as they thought to hide or fled in panic, to pick them off one by one.

He was considerably unnerved when they turned and ran straight at him. Devil-red faces thrust into his, hollow-eyed death masks squinted at him, hooked witches' noses bobbed unsightly warts before him, and sheeted figures emitted hideous cries.

For a moment he thought he'd been transported to the cosy world of his nursery. Then it struck him that these were the customs of Halloween. If only he'd realised, he could have summoned up a few ghoulish allies. Then they'd have shown these mortals a thing or two.

As it was, he'd missed his chance. Such affairs had to be set up well in advance. All Souls Night had endless alternatives for unquiet spirits.

Before he could think how to turn the situation to his advantage, he was grabbed and tugged at by four or five pairs of hands. The boys exclaimed over his make-up, his costume and his glowing contact lenses. They "borrowed" his cloak and raced up and down in it. Of course, it was far too long for them. It had dragged through several puddles and caught on the odd rusty nail before they returned it, complete with several muddy footprints in assorted sizes.

As he attempted to seize at least one of them and carry him off to enjoy at leisure, they caught at his hands and yanked at his fingernails. Worse, they poked fingers into his mouth and prised at the sacred tools of his trade. They also insisted on addressing him as Lanky.

"Gee, Lanky, where did you get it from? It's a great disguise. Wow, just look at those eyes! How do you keep the nails on? How have you stuck the teeth in? Let me try them. Go on, just once! What do you mean they won't come out? You won't half catch it from your mum!"

The vampire set up a guttural growl designed to rise to an unearthly scream fit to freeze the blood and bind up the joints of those who heard it. But before he had reached the slightest climax the boys drowned him out in a crescendo of noisy shrieks and shouts. "That was fantastic! Where did you learn that? Have you been practising? That's wicked. Really wicked!"

The idea of wickedness as an approved quality shocked the poor vampire's sense of decorum. Did these humans not fear the dynamics of evil? It was a science he had perfected over centuries. He had struggled through books on emanating malice. He had taken exams in combating the forces of goodness. He actually held diplomas for sowing doubt in the minds of believers. He could cause priests to abandon their Bibles, convinced they had seen their prop consumed in fire. He could mesmerise the faithful into removing the crucifixes from their necks. He could make his victims believe they desired him as much as he desired them. Nobody could fault his achievements.

He swung round in the circle of boys, projecting malevolence for all he was worth, determined they should recognise that their hour had come. The result was that they all laid hands on him and dragged him out of the alley and up a garden path.

"Let's try him out on old fire and brimstone."

Were these then imps of the Devil? Were they gestated like him out of hell? Had he been found wanting, and was he to be cast before the High Fiend for judgment? He would be punished by eternal agonies too terrible for even him to imagine.

Understandably, he held back before the fateful door, while a hundred burning hands tormented his tortured flesh, pushing and shoving and holding him before them. They banged on the horseshoe knocker, and the sound echoed to the bottom of the bottomless pit.

The door was wrenched open and a bald man with sweating neck and staring eyes stood glaring at the quaking form before him. Lanky was stretched between the eager hands of his smaller companions. Had he been faster to recognise that this was not a guise the Devil normally adopted, he could have shaken them off with ease.

"Well, what is it?" the man roared at them.

"Trick or treat, mister."

"I'll give you trick or treat you young ruffians. I'll treat your backsides to a good pasting. I wonder your parents let you go begging round the houses. Guy Fawkes is quite enough without all this American nonsense. Now be off with you, before you feel the weight of my hand."

And indeed it was a very large hand, the hand of the village blacksmith, and it had a brawny arm to wield it.

The boys did not wait for a second telling but scampered into the night. The vampire was left gaping until the door slammed in his face. The blacksmith considered the lanky twerp was too gormless to run with the rest and too stupid to profit from a beating.

The vampire continued to stand there. He was very taken with what he had seen. The blacksmith had all the makings of an excellent recruit. If he could exert such influence as a mere human being, if he could set to flight a whole gang of hooligans with the wave of an arm, think what he could do as one of the hosts of the undead.

The vampire had a generous spirit. He would not hold back the talents of another just in case he was overshadowed. Besides, there was the actual process of conversion! The vampire quivered as he anticipated all that strength flowing into his own hungry body. Those muscular arms, the powerful shoulders, the thick veins standing out on the bull neck, the flush of blood that spread to his forehead as he bellowed at the offenders! The point was, of course, how to conquer such a one.

He would start by bewildering his object with a sudden appearance. He would insinuate himself into the room as a subtle mist, then sweep up at his feet in a dazzling swirl of cloak. He would turn on

70

him the evil charm of his most accomplished smile. He would fix him with a quelling gaze to paralyse his senses. Then he would enfold him in his garments and sink down upon him. The nectar would flow, and he would be bathed in new energy. He would gain an enviable apprentice and for the moment the status of "master".

He was still wrapt in this heady prospect when the door again slammed back.

"Are you still there, you great gawping jessy? I'll give you something to shudder about. Try this for size." And he turned a jet of water onto his startled visitor.

It was one thing to move mysteriously through a weeping mist in remote places; it was quite another to receive the full force of a PVC super-efficient hose.

The poor undead howled his way back to his coffin, where he dripped and shivered in its narrow confines and felt thoroughly sorry for himself. What with the draughts in the vault and an ill-fitting lid, in other circumstances he would have caught his death of cold.

For the moment he decided to give up the bullnecked man. His long fast was obviously taking its toll. He couldn't cope with the antics of children or the vagaries of modern youth. Perhaps he should start at the other end of the scale. It was true an old person would not provide such satisfaction, but at least the sudden demise of such a one would arouse no comment. He would have time gradually to nourish and recoup his powers before the villagers suspected his presence. He could then strike while they were still unprepared. Once he had amassed a following of the newly converted, the villagers would not stand a chance.

It was thus that on the seventh night of his stay he loomed out of the fields behind the lonely cottage of Annie Barnes. He paused for a moment in the porch to collect himself and muster his depleted energies.

He was just about to seep under the door in an eerie and gaseous form, when suddenly it was flung open, and he was confronted by a wrinkled old woman in curlers and net.

"Walter!" she cried, flinging her arms about him and yanking him into the room. "I knew you'd come back. They all said you wouldn't, but I knew in my heart they were wrong."

She pressed him into the armchair by a blazing fire, seized each of his feet in turn and thrust them into a pair of faded checked slippers.

"My but your feet are cold!" She then took his hands between her own and exclaimed over those too, chafing the centuries old skin until it smarted. Then she attended to his face.

"How thin you've grown. I wouldn't have recognised you if you weren't my own son. Who's been looking after you to let you get in such a state? There's not a trace of blood in your poor cheeks."

The vampire felt the truth of her remarks and drooped pathetic shoulders, the corners of his mouth trembling with self-pity for his plight.

"Well, don't you worry, my pet. Your old mum knows just what you need. Just you sit there while I get you a little tot of something."

The talk of a little tot was interesting. His eyes brightened slightly as the delicious vision of a plump child with rounded, rosy cheeks floated into his mind. But then he heard her clinking about among cobweb-strewn bottles, and his hopes faded.

Sitting by the fire was beginning to get at him too. He just wasn't used to these temperatures, and the leaping flames were a lot too bright for comfort. How did these humans put up with it?

The word "human" drew his attention back to the old woman, and his eyes turned faintly pink. He didn't feel enough enthusiasm for a full-scale red. The woman did not look all that appetising, even to a stomach as shrunken as his. Still it was better than nothing, and he had to get a bit of practice. In his weakened state he couldn't have coped with anyone who could run fast.

He rose silently to his feet and drifted across the rug until he was right behind her. A practised eye scanned sagging veins and looked for the best point of entry. The withered old neck certainly didn't look too promising. Still, he couldn't afford to be fussy.

His eyes filled with tears when he remembered the old days, when it had been all full breasted virgins and tender-necked children.

While he was lost in recollection, he found his arm clenched in a sinewy grip. "What do you mean by it, dithering behind me? You know I can't stand being watched while I'm working." She then manhandled - or rather crone-handled - him back to his seat and bundled him into it. "Now you stay put. I've got something here you won't have had in a long time." She gave him a lurid wink accompanied by a toothless leer.

Somewhat fazed by the sexual overtones of her remark, he sat gripping his chair and wondering whether to make a run for it. But then he saw, descending before his gaze, a brimming glass of deep red and thickly viscous liquid. He almost dribbled. Perhaps he'd misjudged his

72

hostess. Perhaps he had hit upon a kindred spirit, some old girl who went in for the more unsavoury occult practices.

His hand trembled with lust as he seized the bloody goblet and drained it off in one long draught of sensual expectation. Then he was up and bolting to the door, throwing up the contents into the hydrangea bushes.

The old witch shrieked with laughter. "What's the matter? Can't take it any more, eh? That's the trouble with these 'ere weak stomached townies. You should have stayed with your dear old mum, stayed in the country and developed some gut on you.

The vampire collapsed on trembling legs at the table. "What was it?" he whimpered.

"Don't you recognise your mother's elderberry wine? Always got first prize for that at the village fete. Judges too drunk to go on to the other entries." She cackled with pleasure at her past nefarious triumphs.

"Never you mind, son. Just you sit there and I'll give you something you really will remember. One of my special pies - full of juicy steak."

"Is it raw?" asked the spectre, perking up a morsel.

"Raw! What do you take me for? Cooked to perfection. Just how you like them. I've always kept one on the go in case you came back unexpectedly.

She opened a cupboard whose shelves were packed with pies in varying stages of decay. She selected one that appeared to be still steaming and carried it over, placing it reverently before him, a look of proud anticipation on her face.

The vampire thought he'd better eat it. Cooked blood was better than none, and he could not go on like this much longer. He hoped his system would cope with something so solid.

The pie was a masterpiece, frilly edged, golden brown and light textured. To complete its attractions, the woman had used the pastry trimmings to spiral across the top and divided it into quarters.

The vampire was already wielding his knife and fork to plunder the interior, when he noticed the decoration. The pattern rose out at him in scalding phosphorescence and burned itself into his eyes. It glowed and smouldered in front of him, pulsing with power. It was the shape of a cross.

A fierce wind engulfed the room. Windows blew open and doors slammed back. The tablecloth flapped violently about his legs and the curtains stood out at right-angles, wrenched mercilessly from their moorings.

Holding onto the table's edge for all he was worth, the vampire was driven helplessly backwards until the table stuck in the doorframe and he was ripped shrieking into the darkness.

The old woman stood staring after him. "The blighter's gone again!" she fretted. "And he's taken his slippers with him."

The slippers looked somewhat incongruous against the ornate carvings of the 16th century tomb, but at least the spectre knew his feet would be more comfortable now. Those 17th century boots had always pinched a bit. That was the trouble with not being able to afford your own shoemaker. He settled his bruised bones back into the coffin and prepared to wait the day out and see what the night would bring.

He regretted the padded interior of his old home and wondered why 16th century English gentlemen set aside all thought of luxury when it came to being buried. You could read their attitude in the statuary on their tombs. Either they were stretched flat on top, with folds like knives in their garments, ruffs cutting into their chins and noses and hands pointing stiffly upwards, or they lay on one side, without the trace of a pillow, nursing a crooked head in one hand as if they had the toothache. The skeletons so often depicted on the side were all scrunched up as if there were too little room. Undertakers in those days must have been stingy with their materials.

And so the day passed in such diverting contemplations. There was no opportunity to sleep after the buffeting he had taken the night before and the inhospitality of his resting place. Besides, he had formed an idea for a way round his problems.

It seemed he must have lost some of his former awesome appearance. In the vicinity of his old home, he had only to appear before a lonely traveller unaccountably walking through haunted woods miles from anywhere in the dead of night, and the job was as good as done. He had only to hover in curling vapours outside a maiden's window for her to scream and fall lifeless on the bed. He had only to flap in though a window and materialise in a torrent of cloak and whoever occupied the bed would render their necks up to him, sometimes clad in delightfully scanty clothing to whet his appetite. The locals helped, of course, indulging in wild gossip that induced feckless strangers to rove the darkest wildernesses of unhallowed places where they could be sure to find him.

Either he was losing his touch, or the long journey had sapped his hypnotic energies. It could also be the case that a surfeit of horror videos had stunted the imaginations of the present generation of blood donors.

Well, he would change all that. He'd force them to take him seriously. No celluloid monster could raise the dread that he would arouse in these villagers. He'd have them rushing back to their bibles and churches, cornering the market in garlic, investing in a good few crucifixes, watching with fear as the sun faded from the sky and the creeping shadows of night laid hold of their isolated lives.

He was going to take on his favourite form. He couldn't think why he hadn't done so before. But he'd thought he'd better give them a sporting chance.

As the mist closed in on the sleeping graveyard, the vampire oozed his way out of his coffin, evaporated through the high grille to the vault and gradually took shape among the leaning tombstones. When the transition was complete, the night trembled at what it had spawned.

There in the faint moonlight gleamed the bristling silver form of a massive wolf. Its eyes flashed a wicked green, and hungry saliva dripped from gleaming black jaws. A low growl arose from the cavernous throat, sinister enough to lock the sinews of one who would flee in a profound paralysis.

The terrifying beast slipped noiselessly into the trees that led down to the unwary village and merged in a broken pattern of shadow and moonlight into invisibility.

Further into the wood, a young man rose to his feet and pulled his lover up after him. They laughed softly together, revelling in the pleasure they had just shared. The young woman brushed bits of bracken from her skirt, and they began slowly to make their way back to the village, arms encircling each other. The young man caressed the irresistible curves that lay under his fingers, and she pressed closer to his side.

Behind them the wolf scented the heat of their passion. Lips drew back into a silent snarl and it increased its pace, muscles taut and powerful under its hide. Tonight it was going to make its mark. Tonight it would strike terror into all hearts. Tomorrow there would be two families thrown into mourning, and the couple's guilty secret would be out.

The lovers, oblivious of the danger they were in, loitered in the last few trees for a final kiss. Leaves began to flutter round their feet and whirled up about them in a sudden flurry. The wind began to gust more strongly, and trees waved frantic arms above their heads. The couple looked round in amazement. Alarmed lest the fierceness of the

75

gale should bring down any branches, they fled hand in hand out of the wood and along the village street.

The wolf emerged from the trees just as they reached the green. It hurtled after them, its back alternately bunching and stretching, its feet covering the ground at terrifying pace, closing the gap at supernatural rate between the heated desires of young blood and the cold embrace of the grave.

Just as it gathered itself for the final launch, a dark van screeched up beside it. For a second the wolf hesitated, unsure which direction to take. The young couple swung round to look as the van doors burst open and two men charged towards the bristling hound. Its eyes rolled wildly, and it backed away, wrinkling its muzzle and exposing fierce fangs. A menacing snarl began to erupt from its throat, and its tongue slavered viciously.

The two men scrambled back into the van and slammed the doors as the creature leapt after them. And then its claws were tearing at the metal panels, while its teeth clashed, foaming and bloody against the glass.

It was so busy trying to rip the van open with its jaws that it didn't notice the men had climbed out of the back. The next thing it had been hurled to the ground, enmeshed in a net, and a sharp pain assaulted its brain. The men wrenched the hypodermic out of its flank and, as the drug spread through its body, it gradually relaxed into a soft heap.

The two men bundled it into the van and firmly locked the doors. They climbed into the cab, and the wolf blearily observed the backs of their heads through a mesh of wire, as they trundled back to the pound.

By the time they had reached their destination, the wolf was fully tranquillised and docile. They led him to a building with numerous doors like a prison and shoved him unceremoniously into the third cell down. Then they stood regarding him through the bars.

"Vicious bugger, isn't he?"

"Do you think it's the same one?"

"Must be! Some kind of alsation I should think. Odd colour though. If the farmer identifies him in the morning, he's for the chop."

"Yes. Pity in some ways. It's a fine animal. Still, once they take to worrying sheep there's nothing you can do with them."

"No." The other man shook his head. "See you in the morning chum," he said to the dog. "Let's hope it's not your last."

The van left the yard, returning the dog wardens to their well earned beds, and the wolf sank into the straw that had been provided.

Once the tranquilliser began to wear off, he forced himself to take stock of his position. They'd be back in the morning the men had said. If he was still there, it sounded as if they had something very nasty planned for him. Worse, if he was still around he'd be there when the sun rose, and that would be it as far as he was concerned. He'd heard grisly stories of perfectly respectable vampires being exposed to the sun's rays by heartless humans. They'd been erased from earth as if showered with concentrated vitriol. Their eyes swelled and burst, then shrivelled into their heads, their skins bubbled and smoked, their muscles shredded from the bones and rotted in seconds, tongues thrashed in agony, hair writhed and contorted and bones fell apart and disintegrated into dust. Not a pretty sight for the spectator, but think how much worse it was for the vampire.

The potential victim of these supposed horrors fell prey to every imaginable childhood fear and shivered violently, for all his thick coat. But, since he was no longer a child, he eventually pulled himself together and considered the situation.

He was in a small, whitewashed room made entirely of breezeblocks. Even his uncanny strength could not burst through that. The door was very solid with a small barred opening high up, and there were no windows. It would take him all night to chew through the thick wood, and his nails just wouldn't take the strain of scratching his way out.

He cocked his head and gazed up at the grille. An infuriating itch had him vigorously scratching his neck. That's the trouble with these animal forms - subject to parasites. It was a bit debasing for one bloodsucker to find himself feasted on by another.

Animal forms! Of course! As a wolf he was far too big to escape, but ….

He was aware that the square patch of grille was just a shade lighter and realised that he had to act quickly.

Within seconds he had metamorphosed into a bat and, with an excited squeak, he angled through the bars and winged fast towards the church. As he dived into the vault and vanished beneath the stone lid, he had a flash of inspiration. Sheep worrying - there's a thought. He'd worry 'em all right. He'd really give those farmers something to think about. Might as well be hanged for a sheep as for a….. Oh well. True, animal blood wasn't half as nourishing as the human variety, and he was told it didn't taste so good. Still, beggars can't be choosers.

With a much calmer mind than he had known for some time, he settled down for a good day's sleep.

But the sheep idea didn't work too well. The trouble was all that fleece. It might have been all right after shearing, but at this time of year for every ounce of blood he had to choke on a pound or two of wool. Besides that, it took so long, and the beastly creatures set up such a caterwauling and bleating that they always disturbed the farmer. Several times he had escaped serious injury only by the skin of his teeth, and spent half the day picking buckshot out of his buttocks.

So he moved on to other four-foots.

A picture of a vampire bat sucking blood from the heel of a cow had once caught his eye when he was contemplating raiding the reading room at a public library. He'd considered that the victims wouldn't dare scream for help in case they were thrown out, and barred from the reference section for life. However, he'd also reflected that the library shelves held too much ammunition for comfort and decided against it. The image of the blood-sucking bat, however, remained in his mind, and now he decided to act upon it.

The moment he tried out the idea, however, he discovered there were a few drawbacks. First, cows didn't believe in washing their feet, and it was amazing the things they trod in.

He therefore decided the local donkey might be a bit more fastidious, and duly settled on his hock and prepared for the feast. He had reckoned without the donkey, however. The brute had obviously had a hard day, with screaming children bouncing on its back, pulling at its mane and hauling on its mouth. It wasn't prepared to put up with any further liberties so, before the vampire could sink his teeth into the least hairy bit of foot, he found himself hurtling over the hedge, propelled by an almighty kick.

He had then moved on to smaller fish - or chickens to be strictly accurate. He found if he displaced their feathers by stroking them up the wrong way he could get a fair bit of jugular vein. It was, truth to tell, a very small jugular vein, and it needed a lot of chickens to satisfy his appetite. Nevertheless, he began to feel a good deal better and recovered his strength somewhat. His eyes glowed more powerfully in the dark and managed a passable red at the prospect of a liquid supper. His nails grew longer, sharper and a more luminous shade of grey. He was well contented.

He decided to leave his calling card, and made a practice of tying the drained carcases of his victims to the chicken wire with black crepe ribbon. This rather alerted the farmers to the fact it was not just a rampant fox, but he felt confident they wouldn't catch him in the act. The chickens were much more apt to be mesmerised by his presence than other creatures had been. While he dealt with one of them, therefore, the others stood limply about with glazed eyes and almost queued up for dinner as though on an assembly line. It was like shelling peas - not that he'd ever done any of that.

He could simply relax and get on with. He didn't even have to keep an eye out for the dawn. There was an old rooster at an outlying farm near the church which always sang out at the appropriate time, and he could be back to the safety of his dark home before the first rays hit the earliest cloud.

One night, however, he struck a problem. It seemed that the farmers did not care for his tastes in decoration, and they reinforced the cages their flocks were in. They even extended the wire underneath the pens, and the vampire had lost several of his prize fingernails before he discovered that digging got him nowhere. After his experience at the dog warden's, he shrank at the idea of percolating through anything like a mesh.

For several nights he had no luck and, on the fifth night, when the cock crew he hardly had the strength to struggle back to his coffin. As he passed the cock, descanting ever more vigorously from the fence post, he quite simply lost his head. Without a thought for the importance the bird had in his life, he seized it by the throat, dragged it from the gatepost and, totally disregarding its glossy plumage, sank his fangs into its neck. This gave him just enough fuel to streak back to his hiding place.

But the act was his undoing. The villagers were not quite as thick as he had supposed. Little by little they began to work out that they had a stranger with unusual habits among them. They tried to ignore this as long as possible. That was, after all, the only way to treat strangers. But when they discovered the bloodless form of the cock slumped at the foot of the gatepost, its tail feathers awry and its skinny neck dangling, they really saw red.

That cock had not only warned the vampire of the approach of day; it had been acting alarm clock for half the village. Now they would have to spend hard-won cash on some modern apparatus which would tick away their sleep, as well as shattering their dreams with its strident clatter. Only the owner of the village shop seemed to view the affair with equanimity.

So that very morning they had a council of war in the church. It seemed the obvious place for such a meeting. They were sure it was the seat of the enemy. The clue was the inclement weather inside its hallowed walls. Apart from their other grievances, the parishioners were getting fed up with the walls sweating icy droplets and the increased heating turning the liquid into steam. Not only could they hardly see the hymn board on a Sunday, but the pews were frequently dripping with moisture. Instead of dazzling the eyes of the Lord, and especially their neighbours, with their Sunday finery, the congregation had been reduced to plastic macs and fanning themselves for the duration of the service with a sheet of church notices.

It came as a rude awakening to the vampire to have his daydreams interrupted by the lid grating noisily off his coffin. He had hardly opened his eyes before a large cross was plumped firmly on his chest, and he found himself incapable of movement. His horrified gaze fell on a circle of faces all glaring down at him. Right next to him, and breathing excitedly into his face, was a small boy whose mother clearly didn't recognise the function of handkerchiefs. To make matters worse, he was an addict of bubble gum and puffed the unsightly, sickly stuff until it burst into the tomb. He was clearly recognised as the authority on vampires, as his school work had suffered dreadfully while he supped on a diet of black and white Vincent Price movies and up-to-date gory tales in glorious Technicolor.

The vault was full of the stench of garlic, candles blazed in every fist, hurting his eyes, and, for good measure, several participants sported bells. The Good Book bulked large in the hands of the clergyman, gratified at last to have found a direction for his calling.

At the boy's command, a thickset fellow pushed his way forward wielding a pointed holly stake and a massive hammer. The vampire recognised the awful signs and set up a piercing scream. The people round him gave astonished looks at each other. The clergyman tutted and told him to remember where he was.

The vampire gibbered and squeaked at them, begging them not to strike the fatal blow.

A hush fell on the crowd as the big man brandished his tools aloft. Looking from one to the other, the man's round face grew red and his eyes bulged. He was visibly shaken with anger.

"What do you take us for?" he bawled. "Do you think we're barbarians? We know our Bible - 'thou shalt not kill', isn't that so vicar?"

The vicar nodded, pleased that so much of his teaching had penetrated the community.

"It's simply that we wish you to realise that you are dealing with people who know what they are about," the clergyman addressed him.

"Yes, we know what's what!" interjected the boy. "Look!" he yelled, pointing to a lurid illustration in a comic.

The vampire saw what could have been his own hideously contorted face, blood spouting from a jagged hole in the chest, the skin already peeling off skeleton hands. He felt sick.

"That's what you'll get if you don't toe the line," shouted the boy.

A low mutter ran through the crowd.

"What do you want?" panted the vampire.

"It's more what we don't want," said the big man. "We don't want to be disturbed in our homes by mist creeping under doors and bats flying in at windows."

"We don't want to be woken in the night by dog wardens squealing tyres after ravening wolves."

"We don't want our sheep upset and our Sunday dinners jeopardised," the chorus continued.

"And we draw the line at our village clock being annihilated."

A woman spoke up. "It's basically this," she said kindly. "We're simple folk. We like life to go on as it's always gone on. We don't like change. We don't like strangers. Especially strangers who behave the way you've been behaving."

"In fact," nodded the big man, "we want you to clear off."

"Clear off?" stuttered the vampire. "But where would I go?"

"Easy!" said the big man. "Back where you came from. And don't go selling on your present place. Newcomers aren't welcome."

"But I come from Transylvania!"

"Then go back to Transylvania!"

"But I can't!"

The villagers all eyed each other in consternation.

"Why not?" they all demanded.

"Have you never heard of a nobleman called Dracula?" the vampire queried, and his eyes signalled the fear he felt at the name.

"Course we have. We're not ignorant," they all declared.

"Well then," continued the vampire, peering into the gloom to ensure there were no eavesdroppers. "You will know what a powerful being he is."

The boy nodded vigorously, and the audience stared at him in admiration.

"He is the richest vampire in the country," the woebegone creature informed them. "He has more shares in the Blood Bank than any other creature alive - or not alive, as the case may be. He has cornered the market in haemoglobin and acquired a total monopoly.

Anyone who wishes to tap into the reserves has to pay him a levy. The taxes have become so high and the interest rates on borrowing so crippling that the little enterprises, like my own, have been forced out of business. If I go back to Transylvania, I shall quite simply starve. I might even end up incarcerated in some dungeon at his castle, surviving on the dregs of discarded offal. He has a stranglehold on the nation. It is a place where tyranny reigns supreme and freedom is a thing of the past."

The villagers groaned.

"That is why I came to these shores," he went on. "I had heard that England was a sanctuary for the oppressed, and believed in free competition, and your little village was so remote I thought that Dracula's Secret Service would never trace me here."

The vampire's eyes filled with tears and his lip trembled

"That's all very well," spoke up a local farmer, "but most visitors don't make free with other people's blood and other people's chickens.

"But what can I do?" The tears were now streaming down the vampire's cheeks and threatening to overflow the coffin. "I can't help needing blood. That's just how I am. It's my nature. Without it I shall shrivel up and linger eternally in perpetual pain.

"Oh the poor thing," said a woman, dabbing her eyes. "Why don't you try the National Blood Transfusion Service?"

"But they don't give blood, only take it. Besides they would insist they hadn't got the right blood group. You can't even steal the stuff. It's all locked up in cold storage."

"That's right," said the clergyman, "It is."

"Besides that, I don't want to live off the State. I'm used to an independent existence. I want to make my own way in life."

The villagers said they would go away and think about it. In the meantime, they'd leave him the crucifix as a comfort in the darkness. He supposed they meant well.

The villagers set up a committee to explore legitimate ways of acquiring blood. They did suggest that there were plenty of rats and cockroaches in the area and perhaps he could take on the role of pest control. But when the vampire asked if they would welcome such a diet over hundreds of years they did agree it seemed a bit unreasonable.

Then a country vet came up with the solution. It was so simple they wondered no-one had thought of it earlier.

The vampire continued to spend his days in the 16th century coffin, but they lagged it with polystyrene to prevent his presence affecting the temperature. They gave him a key to the vault so that he no longer had to vapourise to effect an exit or entry. And they supplied him with a map of areas they'd prefer him not to visit. This did not include the new council estate.

They also got him a job with an abattoir specialising in halal meat. Night work, of course, and far enough from the village to ensure there were no hours of darkness left for him to get into mischief. In the summer, naturally, he could only work part-time.

And so the villagers learned to live with their resident vampire. They even turned his presence to good account, offering guided tours of the famous vampire-infested vault and selling furry vampire bats and vampire mugs and other such tasteful paraphernalia.

When the vampire observes the visitors to his home, all peering down on him decked in their plastic vampire teeth with their plastic red vampire eyes held in place with elastic, he knows that he has finally been accepted.

This is where he will spend the aeons of his existence until mountains crumble or Mankind insists on blowing up his world. This is where he will stay until motor-mania finally drives the M998 through his churchyard. This is where he can hang up his slippers when he retires. This is his home.

SNOWFALL

The child knelt on the floor in front of the winter fire. His shoulders drooped, his small hands curled in his lap. He was as still as the rest of the room.

The mother sat in the armchair, her head supported on one hand. Her eyes gazed motionless and unseeing on the flames before her. Eventually she stirred and turned to the little figure hunched in front of her. She found the dark eyes with their large pupils fixed on hers, the small mouth pinched and bloodless in the pale face.

She felt a sudden surge of bitterness. Why did he sit like that? Why didn't he go out to play with some of the neighbours' children? Mandy Taylor was always round him at the playschool, steering him into the Wendy House, showing him how to let the soft sand trickle through the plastic sieve. And yet he showed no response to her. He never joined in the rhymes and jingles, even though the teacher accompanied her singing with a guitar, even though the other children banged their tambourines and shook their rice-filled shakers, shouting the words with all the tuneless energy of the very young. No, he would rather sit and stare at her, his body rigid: none of the animation of youth that thrilled through other children. He was like an old man.

Why don't you play with some of your toys?"

The words came out with the controlled patience the mother invariably adopted. The boy rose obediently and went over to the cupboard. She saw his fingers aimlessly wandering over the crowded shelf. At last she could bear it no longer. She rose and went over to join him.

"Look, why don't you play with your bricks?"

She carried the box over to the rug and dumped the contents out of it. The child crouched beside her, taking one of the wooden blocks in his hand.

"Make a tall tower." The mother built up the first few blocks. "Go on. Put yours on too."

The child's hand reached out and set the brick clumsily on top of the others. The pile collapsed over the floor.

"Perhaps you'd be better off with Lego," said his mother. "At least that won't fall down."

She fetched the Lego from the cupboard and returned to her chair. Children were supposed to be inventive. Let's see what he could make of that. She watched him struggling to press the blocks together. He was so uncoordinated, fumbling and awkward even over the simplest tasks.

"Here, let me help you." She could do everything ten times as fast herself. The boy let her take the Lego out of his hands, and sat quietly while she snapped the blues and yellows into the growing shape. "We'll make a nice house, shall we?"

After a while she left the boy to his own devices and went into the kitchen. When she came back with a pot of tea for herself and milk and biscuits for the boy, she found that he had made what looked like a cross. For once he looked absorbed in his task.

"That's pretty," she said, and put the milk and biscuits down beside him.

The boy lifted the cross in one hand and stared at it, his lips parted, his eyes obviously seeing something she didn't.

"It's an aeroplane," he said, and a spot of colour glowed in his pallid cheeks.

The cup clattered down on the saucer. "No!" The plane was snatched from his grasp and fragmented. The boy just stared at her. He didn't cry and he didn't shout.

The mother felt embarrassed by her outburst. "We don't like nasty old planes, do we? You could make a little car like grandma's, or a red bus. That's it, a red bus like the one we go on when we go shopping."

But the boy climbed onto the settee. He picked up his teddy and hugged it to him, putting his thumb in his mouth and rocking his body backwards and forwards over the soft toy

The mother crossed to the television and turned it on. Comic laughter and shrills of rage filled the air, as Tom and Jerry chased across the screen. The boy's eyes turned towards it in automatic reaction. The mother left the room with a sigh of relief. Now she could get on with her washing up without the lurking feeling there was something more important for her to attend to.

Her hands busy with the immediate task, she could not keep the unwelcome thoughts at bay. Aeroplanes! She hated them. She had told the boy she didn't like them, and yet still he painted them at playgroup, and still surreptitiously she dropped them in the bin the moment she reached the lobby.

If only her husband had felt the same way about them. Then she wouldn't have had to be alone for the last year. Then she wouldn't have had the whole burden of bringing up a child alone. But he was enthralled by them, enthralled by their gleaming lines and the sense of power in the racing engines as they thrust away from the clinging earth and soared through the tingling air. Halfway to heaven, he nursed the responsive controls through a pattern than had become routine and yet never lost its thrill.

He was like that about everything he did. She was lifted along on his enthusiasms, chivvied, laughing, out of her cautious ways, her inclinations to the serious. It was in this spirit that they had started a family.

Dan was overjoyed when the child turned out to be a boy. He would have been just as pleased to receive a bonny daughter, but he instantly rushed off to buy all the trains and carriages, meccano and cowboy gear that he thought were necessary for his son to emerge into manhood. He saw himself playing with the growing child in the sunlit meadows and the warm rock pools of future holidays. And he and his wife had together wheeled the child out to show him off to friends and relatives, all caught up in the father's passionate affection. He was the most beautiful baby that had ever been, and they were to live happily ever after.

But then, shortly before last Christmas, the airline had phoned. They had chartered a flight to some important city types. Apparently nothing, short notice or the demands of the season, would stand in the way of a large contract - not even the weather, which was rapidly closing in. Elizabeth had pleaded with her husband not to go. Surely they could find someone else. What if he wasn't back for Christmas Day?

Dan had spent hours, once his small son was safely asleep, crafting a beautiful model of a plane, just like daddy's. She knew he would want to see the parcel ripped open and the child's face wrapt in joy at the marvellous creation. What if he wasn't there?

But he had laughed at her fears and hugged her, smiling. "Don't worry Elizabeth. It won't take that long. I'll be back in plenty of time."

"But what about the weather? What if something happens?"

He saw the lurking shadow in her face and kissed her. "You know me, Elizabeth. Indestructible. You don't get rid of me that easily. Just you make sure that there's plenty of turkey and brandy sauce."

So she had watched him go, only partly reassured.

But there had been no return of the loved husband. The Christmas fayre had stayed on the table until she had the phone call. Flight 116 had come down in the mountains. The wings had iced up and the plane had gone out of control. All passengers and crew were lost.

The little boy never received his daddy's last present. She couldn't bear to look at it. It lay in its dust-covered wrappings pushed right to the back of the wardrobe.

She dried her hands and opened the living room door. "Time for bed, Daniel." She switched off the television and moved to the settee. The boy was in the same position, his eyes still on the blank screen.

A wave of resentment passed through her, but she instantly crushed it. If only he were more like his father perhaps there would be more to look forward to. But he was such an uninspiring child. Try as she might she could never raise any enthusiasm in him. She bought him all the right things; she took him to all the right places. The company's insurance had made sure that they lacked nothing materially, and she saw to it that the boy had everything a child could wish for. She was a conscientious mother, always concerned for her son's welfare, and yet nothing he did caused any warmth in her heart. It was like a barren waste.

She stretched out her hand to him. "Come along," she said, and the boy slid off the settee and walked quietly up the stairs beside her.

Back downstairs she went to the garage and fetched in the tree that waited in the darkness. Last year there had been a grand expedition to the nursery out in the country. They had spent ages inspecting the field. Dan had fished out first one then another. Nothing less than perfection would do for his son.

That year Daniel was big enough to stamp through the muddy puddles in his little red boots, all smothered up in fluffy scarf and hat. He had helped to choose the holly wreath that had the most berries, wide-eyed at the magic ritual of counting. He didn't even mind when he pricked his fingers. Dan had made a great joke of it.

By the time they had lingered over tinsel and baubles, little hanging snowmen and frosted Christmas stars, darkness had fallen, and they carried home their prizes to a house filled with light.

This year the tree had come from the shop. She was determined there would be one, though she hardly felt like celebrating. She had even sent for some bells, which looked so festive in the catalogue. She imagined their cheerful tinkle whenever the tree was touched. But when she undid them she found they had no clappers - one more thing that had not gone as planned.

Even the lights did their best to frustrate her. She had forgotten how Dan had tested them before he decked the tree. Reproachfully, she took them all off again and checked all the tiny bulbs. As she wove them into the tree a second time, a shower of needles fell to the floor. It wasn't even fresh!

Her face hardened with vexation when again the lights refused to come on. She took the risk of checking them with the power on - who cared anyway? And suddenly they all lit up. It didn't help. The ornaments went on in angry haste and a careless scattering of tinsel. Finally the silent bells were lifted out of their box.

She stepped back to look at the finished effect. Well, she supposed it would do. Better than nothing anyway.

With a weary sigh she made herself a drink and sank into a chair. She hadn't wrapped Daniel's presents yet. It would have to wait till later. Christmas was such a tiring business. Before she was aware, she had drifted into sleep.

In his bedroom, the boy lay under the covers and stared at the shadows in the room. They didn't frighten him. His heart was too full of a tight anxiety to admit the elusive fears of childhood.

It seemed he had lain there for ever when he heard the soft tapping, so quiet he wondered if he'd imagined it. He looked towards the window, curious as to the cause. It couldn't be the leaves that had pattered and scuffed past the panes a while back. Then the trees were all bronzes and golds. Now he could see their skeletons against the faded sky. It certainly wasn't them.

But now he could see something else. Little white shapes were drifting against his window, and tiny droplets and trickles of water were forming against the cold glass. What was it?

He got out of bed and crossed the room, climbing on the ledge to have a better look. His warm breath misted the pane. He rubbed a clear circle with his sleeve and pressed his face against it. What was happening? The air was full of tiny flakes, powdery white and building up on the window sill. Gradually they became large, and some of them stayed on the glass for a few seconds before slithering down.

He wiped the window again and watched a dog run past on the pavement below. The white flakes had settled on its fur, but it didn't seem to mind. The boy smiled as he saw the pillar box gradually gaining a soft coat and the grey street beginning to glitter under the lamplight. It was magic. The world was changing, changing for Christmas!

He looked up at the sky. Out of its darkness was crowding more and more white stuff. It looked as if it was rushing towards him. He gazed, his child's lips open as it whirled and spun before him. It seemed to get brighter and brighter, the movement faster and faster, cascading towards him, sweeping along in a tide of excitement.

He threw up the window. "Come in! Come in!" he cried.

And suddenly he felt himself lifted by strong, warm hands, flung upwards in one swift movement. He found himself looking down into the laughing face of a fair-haired stranger. His eyes were the brightest blue and lit with a sense of fun. The child put out his hands to steady himself on the unknown forehead, and the man shook him and growled at him like a dog teasing a bone.

Daniel giggled and struggled against the man's powerful grip. But he didn't really want to get away. He punched at the tousled hair with his small fists and did a puppet dance in the air.

It was funny. He didn't remember seeing the man before, but still he felt he knew him. And he felt safe with him. He knew the man wouldn't drop him, and he knew he wouldn't hurt him.

Perhaps it was Father Christmas. An open window was just as good as a dirty old chimney. The pictures he'd seen had all been of an old man, but perhaps he could be like anything he wanted. Perhaps that was why he hadn't worn his red clothes. Or perhaps they'd got dirty with all that soot.

The man tossed him onto the bed and bounced him up and down as if it was a trampoline. The boy chuckled and sat up, flinging his arms around the stranger's neck. "Have you brought me my presents?"

"Oh yes, sonny Jim, I've brought you the best present that money can't buy."

The boy stopped for a moment and held his breath. Perhaps it was Jim the man wanted, not him.

But the man had got up and was lifting something down from the top of the wardrobe. The bright Christmas wrapper with its holly and berries was soon torn off, and there in the boy's hands was the gleaming plane. His eyes shone with pleasure and his fingers stroked the smooth lines of the wings. "It's beautiful!" he breathed. "Oh, it's the most beautiful thing I have ever seen!"

The man gave a chuckle of satisfaction and snatched it away again, his blue eyes teasing and challenging. He held it high and darted round the room, up on the bed, down on the rug, jumping over the chair and pursued by the laughing child.

"Let me, let me!"

"Now I'll help you fly," said the man. Deftly he planted the aeroplane on the table, and seizing the child he swung him onto his shoulders. "This is an angel carry!" he yelled, and did a repeat tour of the room. "Make way for the flying angel."

The Child's face glowed with fun. "Let me fly the plane now," he pleaded.

"You, my son, can do anything you like." The man set him down and knelt in front of him. "Just remember that always. Whatever you want to do you can do. Mummy loves you very much. We both love you very much, and we will be always with you."

The boy received the silver plane with gentle care. He ran his face along its silky sides and turned the little propeller with wondering fingers. The man stroked his hair, and he felt a warmth run through him.

"Off you go then!" and he was given a playful shove.

The boy raised his arm and guided the plane through the sparkling air. He scrambled over furniture, high over mountains, and swooped the plane low to the carpet, skimming the waters of a lake. Then up they climbed in a spiral. Looping the loop, he swung the plane round and round his head. He turned faster and faster. He saw the dancing light in the man's eyes as he spun past him. He turned and turned until the room whirled round him, until he felt himself falling in pleasurable giddiness. He knew the man wouldn't let him hurt himself. He let himself go.

The mother woke with a start. She returned to consciousness on the memory of a sound. Somewhere she had heard a man and a boy laughing. She had just caught the edge of it. She sat and listened hard. But there was nothing. Probably it was late revellers in the street. Through the open curtains she could see the snow clutch and cling at her window. She looked at her watch and found it had stopped at half past twelve. She shuddered. That was about the time......But no, she pushed the thought to the back of her mind.

She dragged herself out of the chair and plodded up the stairs. Outside the boy's door she paused and listened. She always did that. She was just turning away when something made her stop. She strained her ears again. Nothing. And yet there was something about the silence which disturbed her. With anxious heart she put her hand on the knob. Its coldness met her fingers and she slowly turned it.

The boy was huddled on the floor, hunched and still, a position that was not that of sleep. Beside him the window was wide open and the snow was drifting in and settling on the carpet round him. The woman froze in an agony of fear and then she stumbled towards him, snatching the little body from the floor and hugging it to her. She rocked backwards and forwards, stroking the boy's damp hair and kissing him frantically.

And then she noticed what lay on the floor where he had fallen. She shrank away from it, holding the boy more tightly to her. How had he managed to get it? It was much too high for him. Perhaps he had fallen as he climbed and had lain here in the cold, while she had slept downstairs. He had needed her and she wasn't there!

She clutched at the child's cold wrist but could find no pulse. She pushed back the panic and pressed her fingers into the side of his neck. Head and heart were pounding in fright, so she could hardly register what lay under her touch. Then she felt just the thread of a beat, faint and feeble, but definitely there.

"Oh, thank God!"

She staggered to the bed and tore off the quilt, wrapping it round the child. Clutching him firmly she ran to the stairs, holding the banister tightly lest they should fall. In the living room she poked up the fire, never for a moment letting go of the child. She held him while she boiled a kettle, only putting his down on the settee while she filled the bottle. Then she dragged the sofa nearer the fire and tucked the bottle, wrapped in some towelling, between his thighs.

Running to the phone, she forced her fingers to key in 999. Her voice shook so much it was a wonder she was understood. Somehow she managed to give the necessary details. A voice at the other end was talking to her. An ambulance would be with her as soon as possible, but they were all out on other calls.

"But how long will it be?"

"It's hard to say. There's been a pile-up on the motorway, and the usual drink-related incidents."

"But he could die!"

The operator's calm tones cut through her hysteria. She assured her she'd done all the right things.

"Give him a sweet drink if he regains consciousness and keep him warm. Ring back if there are any changes. Don't worry. They will come as soon as they can."

Left staring helplessly at the receiver, she tried the doctor's surgery. Nothing but a recorded message.

She flung down the phone and rushed back to her child. His forehead felt just a touch warmer. Perhaps he was going to be all right!

And now she tried to fight the hope that was rising up inside her. If she allowed herself to hope, things would definitely go wrong. Nothing worked out these days, nothing at all. And she had withdrawn herself out of life, afraid to be hurt again. She had even withdrawn herself from her little boy, and now she was going to lose him.

She swept him up in a torment of grief, and found that he was sweating. But he still had not opened his eyes. From fear that he would die of cold, she now was afraid that he would burn up with fever.

Half an hour ticked by, and still the ambulance had not come. She telephoned emergency services again. Most dreadfully sorry, but road conditions were appalling. An ambulance had set out but had reported in stuck in a drift. Assistance was being sent, but he could take some time to get through.

Towards morning the fever seemed to abate, and he began to sleep more calmly. She drew up a chair and sat beside him, gazing at the delicate roundness of his face, rubbing the soft, child's fingers against her mouth.

It struck her then that she didn't mind how clumsy he was. After all, he was little more than a baby. So dependent on her. And it hurt her to think how much she'd neglected him. Exhaustion and grief sent tears running over her pale cheeks. Her eyes dazzled and she could not see.

"What are you crying for, mummy?"

Immediately she was kneeling beside him, kissing and cuddling him, but crying all the same.

"Don't cry, mummy. Why are you crying?" His little hands patted her face, anxiously reassuring.

"It's Christmas, mummy, and Father Christmas has been."

She thought of the unwrapped presents still in her bedroom. "No, dear, he hasn't been yet. He's probably still busy with all the other boys and girls."

"No, mummy, he has been. He brought me an aeroplane. He said it was the best present money can't buy."

She rose obediently to her feet. She felt she couldn't deny him. "I'll fetch it for you, darling." She sent him a ghost of a smile from the doorway. "Don't go away."

In a minute she was back in the bedroom. She looked at the aeroplane lying on the floor and picked it up slowly. She turned it over gently in her hands. What care Dan had taken with it. What love had gone into every bit of carving, all the smoothing down. How silly she had been not to give it to Daniel. Of course he should have it. It was what Dan had wanted.

And he had wanted them all to be happy. What would he think of the haunted eyes of their little boy? What would he think of her constraint, her ceasing to live because he had. No, he had never ceased to live. He was always more alive than anyone else she knew. She could feel his presence as surely as if he'd been there.

The boy was waiting for her, bright with expectancy. She lowered the plane into the outstretched hands. She saw how surely he handled it, and the pleasure in his face. He looked up at her, his eyes dancing. And it was then that she realised how like her husband he was.

"Oh, my dear little one," she said, "you seemed so ill."

The boy smiled at her. "Don't worry, mummy. You know me, I'm in…" His face twisted with the effort of recalling the grown-up word. "…indestructible."

She stared at him for a long moment, then suddenly tousled his hair in a playful gesture.

"Don't go away again," she said. "I love you so much."

"Yes." The boy nodded wisely. "He said you did."

A slight draught moved the curtains in front of the windows. The fire flared, the flames licked cheerfully up the chimney, and the soft sound of bells rippled through the Christmas tree.

CAT AND MOUSE

If you must know, I got this scar as a trophy of war. No, it wasn't the usual sort of thing at all. I wasn't strafed by a Messerschmitt as I sprinted up the beach; I didn't crash land into enemy territory under a bomber's moon; I wasn't shot up still tangled in my parachute lines. No, it was a bloody woman. Trust me to know how to pick 'em.

The first day I saw her, I should have been warned. It was in France. I had been trained in explosives, and I'd been dropped in to assist the Resistance in blowing up enemy trains. Behind the lines stuff. You know.

I'd been led to their headquarters by a boy no older than your son. He didn't speak any English and I spoke very little French, but the language of sabotage doesn't need many words. More demonstration.

We went in the back way, a tunnel that started in the wood and ended in the cellar. As I came up through the trapdoor, I looked straight down the barrel of a sniper rifle. Behind it was a pair of the deadliest eyes I ever saw. But the rest of the picture was irresistible: long slim legs that looked sexy even in serge and army boots; nails long and polished in vermilion; lips to match. And what lips. And what sultry, drooping eyelids. No less hostile for that. I felt attracted and repelled in the same moment. I was done for.

Just as I braced my arms to lever myself up at her feet, I saw her finger move on the trigger. Instinctively I hurled myself back through the hole and landed in a heap on top of my guide. The finger completed its journey, and there was an empty click. The boy wriggled free and pounded up the ladder. A burst of violent language erupted from his mouth as he pushed past her. She didn't give ground.

The glance she gave towards me was contemptuous as I struggled to my feet. "Ma foi! You'll have to do something about those nerves."

I mustered as much dignity as I could and gave a rueful laugh. "Well, at least you know I've got quick reactions. Could be useful in a crisis."

"Tell that to Paul." She jerked her head after the boy. Then she turned on her heel and her figure disappeared from the aperture. As I emerged from the trapdoor, I found her calmly seated at the table dismantling the rifle, laying out the parts in a precise line.

"Not a polite way to welcome our guest, Adèle." A heavily built man made his way towards me, hand extended cordially.

She ignored him just as assiduously as she now ignored me, her whole attention focused on her weapon.

"Alex," I said, making sure my grip was firm and steady.

"Henri." He reached for my kit and led the way to another room. "Sleeping quarters in here, Alex." He dumped the bag on a wood-framed bed. "Latrines, such as they are, in there."

The bedroom was low-ceilinged under the slope of the roof. A basin and jug stood on a sturdy dresser. Shaving in cold water was going to be one of the more primitive pleasures of my daily existence. No wonder Henri had a beard. Thought I might try one myself.

Through the door I could see Adèle oiling the breach.

"Food in half an hour," Henri informed me. "You probably want to clean up first."

"Some hotel will snap you up after the war." Adèle did not look up as he passed her chair.

"I expect they'll have other uses for you," he replied without malice. "Your turn to make supper, non?" he added.

She didn't appear to have heard him. She snapped the gun together with practised speed. She too could be useful in a crisis - assuming she could be bothered, of course.

To my amazement, she then stood up, propped her gun in the corner and crossed to the range. There she began to rattle around among the pots, a length of ash gathering on the end of the cigarette hanging from her lips.

Surprisingly the food was more than edible. Apparently her particular brand of femininity had not totally by-passed the influence of French cuisine. It's lucky the plates were enamel, though, or mine wouldn't have survived the way she slammed it down.

I decided to ignore it. Whatever her problem was, we were here to do a job. And it wasn't long before we had orders to derail a troop train on its way south to the Med.

No-one was sure exactly when it would run, but German patrols along the line were noticeably more frequent, and spotter planes could be over your head before you realised.

We'd lain up in the wood flanking the track all day and couldn't make a move till it was nearly dark. Then we had about ten minutes to set the charges and spin out the wire.

I ran out with the plastic explosive and packed it under the points where a sideline went off to the coast. Less obvious there and more sure to succeed. I inserted the wires, and Henri played them out into the wood. I kicked the clinker over them to conceal them from sharp eyes.

Back in the wood, and I rigged up the plunger. Then there was nothing to do but wait.

Under the trees it was so dark that we could barely make each other out. Nobody moved much, and nobody spoke. Adèle had almost grown into the trunk she lay against, so still you'd think she was dead.

Then we were conscious of boots crunching along the cinders and the murmur of voices. The men stopped within yards of where we lay. Matches flared and momentarily lit the faces of the soldiers. The glowing ends of cigarettes swung in fiery arcs up and down. The smoke drifted across and tickled our nostrils. There was the occasional laugh as someone cracked a joke.

One by one the cigarettes were flung to the ground, and the troops began to move on.

Then we were aware of the dull gleam on the curve of a helmet as a figure faced into the woods, his outline dark against the sky. He had obviously stopped to relieve himself. I sensed Adèle stiffen, but otherwise she didn't react.

As he turned to move away, I found her at my ear. "Train's coming."

And now I could hear a soft vibration singing in the rails. She was right. As I turned my attention to the plunger, in the growing gloom, I was aware of a blacker shadow moving noiselessly towards the track. What the hell was she doing?

The throbbing in the rails grew louder as the train closed the distance. The noise was nearly upon us. Just before I thrust down the handle, Adèle slithered back down beside me. Her teeth gleamed white in a rare grin. She was wiping something dark from the blade of her knife.

"One less to bother about." She squeezed my shoulder conspiratorially.

Next second the rumbling clatter and thud of the train became the roar of detonation, the grinding and shrieking of wheels as the engine left the rails and ploughed into the trees. Carriages overturned, showering the night with sparks as the metal sides ripped open.

We didn't wait around for the body count but plunged back through the forest and over the ridge before the search started.

Back at the house, everyone was in jubilant mood, everyone, that is, apart from Adèle, who scowled at me as if I'd let the side down.

In bed that night, I went back over the events and shuddered. It wasn't what I'd done that bothered me, but what she'd done. Considering the carnage I'd just caused, this might sound hypocritical. But that was different. That was what we were there for. Taking out that bloke had been unnecessary, almost feral.

Next second the blankets were lifted away from me and she was climbing into my bed. I can't say I thought much about what to do next, but if, in the morning, I expected her attitude to have changed, I expected wrong. Ignored me just as much as if I'd been the bedpost. Back to the familiar treatment and the graceless table manners.

We had to lie low for a good while after that. No fires, no movement in the house. We spent most of the time in the cellar in case they ransacked the place. But they didn't, and eventually everything quietened down.

But after another few sorties to blow up bridges and water towers, the Jerries started to get tough. Rounding up villagers, trying to beat information out of them. They didn't have any to give, but a few suspected informers were found strung up in barns, and no-one knew whether the locals had done it or the Nazis.

Whenever Adèle heard about these episodes, I knew I was in for a good night. There was no secrecy about it, no finesse. Why she picked me I don't know. But the others seemed to take it as read. Even the boy Paul would fling himself across our legs and stare at us as if expecting some kind of side show. She just slapped him off and lay back naked and indifferent until she was tired of her own company, when she dressed and carried on as if nothing had happened.

After a few weeks, the unit decided to take on one last derailment and then close the operation down. Our luck couldn't hold much longer. We'd split up and join other teams, cutting communication links between us.

Word had come over the radio that an armaments train was coming our way. Last report it had stopped just east of the border, so we knew it would only be a day, day and a half, before it reached our stretch. Preparation had to be that night.

We decided to blow the bridge over the gully. That way there would be no chance the tanks and heavy guns would still be serviceable. The slopes either side were heavily wooded, so we could get right up to the target without being seen. We could also work our way out under the track. No chance of being spotted from above. Below there was only a fast moving river and no roads for troop movements. Perfect.

I had calculated the amount of explosive to shatter the support structure. Henri and I clambered around in the near-dark strapping the gelignite to the girders. From time to time a patrol passed over the bridge and we flattened ourselves below the parapet.

We knew too they'd be training binoculars on the crossing point from the upper slopes commanding the valley. They changed shifts every few hours, their every move observed by Adèle, Justin and Hervé from the opposite side of the gorge. There was a line stretched between the three of them. When we gave the signal that we were ready, Hervé tugged on the line. When Adèle saw the guard preparing to hand over to the next group, she tugged the line from the top.

Hervé gave a low whistle, and we climbed up the bank and through a culvert under the road, paying out the cable as we went. Then we crouched among the trees and rigged up the detonator. Nothing could go wrong. The night was heavily clouded, and the bridge concealed our handiwork in its shadows.

Unfortunately, before the train arrived the moon made an untimely entrance into the night sky. It was a full moon and glistened on every span and curve of the bridge and every handrail that skirted the parapet and stretched along the flanking road.

Another patrol filed along below us, eyes probing the darkness of the trees, guns cocked. They reached the bridge and began peering over the sides and examining the track. When they got to the far bank, some of them panned out along the road and the rest came back for a repeat performance. Had someone given us away? - or was it just sensible precaution? It was an important consignment after all.

The squad reached our end of the bridge then started back after their troop. I let out a long breath.

Just as we'd begun to relax, there was a shout. One of the men was gesticulating and pointing towards the culvert. Exposed across the bare rock below and clearly picked out by the moon, there was a line of cable where no cable should be. It would only take a moment for them to cut the wire and there would be nothing to stop the armaments reaching the front. The cable would lead straight to our hiding place and we would be done for. We decided to cut and run, leaving our equipment behind.

We reached the path which ran aslant the hill. Henri threw some wire cutters further along the track where it widened out and caught the full light of the moon. The cutters glinted on the stones. Then we took the steep way up to the top where Adèle was waiting for us. She gave me a poisonous look. "All that for nothing!"

"Merde! Shut up, Adèle, and keep your head down," Henri growled at her. She slumped in a sullen heap against a boulder.

Below us we could hear the snapping of twigs and the scrape and crunch of fallen leaves underfoot. There was a pause as they reached the path, then an exclamation and the rush of boots to where the wire cutters lay. Most of the searchers sprinted on up the path, but a few tracked down it, just in case. Only one man looked up, saw the steepness and decided against it.

It looked as if we'd got away with it. But along the track on the far side of the valley we could see the fiery smoke gushing from the train's chimney, sparks drifting back over the long darkness of the wagons, the heaping shapes waiting under tarpaulins to destroy our troops.

I felt Henri's hand grip my arm. "Another time," he whispered. He motioned the group towards him. "You know where you're all headed. We might as well say goodbye here. More chance some of us'll get away if we separate anyway."

None of us said a word. We all solemnly shook hands. Apart from Adèle. She just gave a general salute, which pointedly excluded me, and slipped silently down the far side of the hill. The others went off in different directions.

I flirted with the idea of going back and reconnecting the wires while the search for us widened, but the amount of activity still bristling in the wood and along the road meant this would be suicide. As Henri said, there'd be other trains.

I decided to stick to the top of the ridge just below the skyline. The valley ran north-south anyway, so it was in line with my route.

The sound of pebbles loosened by my scrambling was covered at the start by the thumping rattle of the train below on our side of the gorge. The brakes squealed on the descent and the jolting and buffeting collision of the wagons resounded from the rock walls, a backward echo from the thud of ordinance which lay ahead.

The further I went from the scene the fewer soldiers I saw, and I began to think I'd get well clear.

The moon had almost dropped behind the line of hills, and shadows filled the crevices in the rocks above with concealing darkness. I decided to scale them and lie up for the hours of daylight on the top. There'd be plenty of cover from aerial reconnaissance.

I found a place where sloping boulders leaned against each other to create a shallow cave. I stopped outside briefly and strained my ears for the slightest sound. There was none. I slid inside. It was dry and comfortable. Relieving my shoulders of the weight of my pack, I sank back gratefully against the rock-face.

Ten minutes later, having stuffed my face with chunks of bread and meat and washed it down with great gulps of wine, I began to give in to the fatigue that wracked my every muscle.

Imagine my shock when I was blasted awake by the sound of gunshot trapped and reverberating inside the shell of my hideout. Another bullet sparked against the rock of the entrance and I threw myself down on my belly. Something hot and wet was dripping onto my forearm. I pawed at my face and realised that a shard of stone must have scored my cheek right next to my eye.

I decided to lie still and feign dead. What else could I do? Nothing happened.

After a few seconds I rolled my eyes upwards to gauge the situation. No obvious sign of my antagonist. My hand slipped inch by inch towards the butt of my pistol, and inch by inch I stretched it forward into a firing position. I eased off the catch. No reaction.

Cautiously I edged forward using my elbows and toes. Still nothing. Now I had a better view of the rocks outside. There was nobody there. Perhaps it was just a stray bullet - or a fishing expedition to probe the hole. The attacker had clearly been satisfied there was no-one at home.

I lay still for another half hour and then wriggled free of my hiding place.

As my shoulders emerged from the cave, a boot stamped down on my wrist and paralysed my fingers. I lost the pistol. The cold muzzle of a gun bit into the base of my skull. I froze.

"Well, well, well. Qu'est ce que c'est? What have we here?"

I recognised the taunting voice immediately. I let my head slump forward. I didn't know whether to feel relieved or angry. I kept my voice low.

"Adèle, you stupid bitch. What the hell do you think you are playing at? And what the hell are you doing here anyway?"

"Couldn't let you leave without saying goodbye properly, now could I?" She didn't bother to moderate the volume.

Was she completely demented? Did she really mean what I thought?

"Well get off my bloody hand. I can't feel my damned fingers."

As she raised her foot, I tried to yank her other leg from under her with my good hand. But she was too quick for me.

"Ah! ah! ah!.......Naughty, naughty!"

"For God's sake, Adèle, grow up. We all had orders to make for our next base. This isn't a game, you know. Your idiotic gun-slinging could get us both killed."

I rose unsteadily to my feet and clutched at my injured wrist. I hobbled urgently to each side of the ridge, looking for enemy movement on the slopes below. By some miracle there wasn't any.

"It's a wonder every German for miles around isn't headed this way."

"They probably are."

"Well, we'd better split up and get out of here before we get caught. Or do you want to face a firing squad?"

"No chance of that - for me at least. For you, I'm not so sure." She raised the rifle and aimed it at my chest.

"Not this again. You've pulled that trick with me for the last time."

"Indeed I have."

The next second, gravel was spurting round my ankles, and I realised she was firing around my feet. She rattled the bolt in the breach for the next bullet.

I wasn't going to give her another chance to humiliate me - or indeed to murder me. She was a crack shot, and she was clearly as mad as a hatter. I flung myself over the top of the rocks and rolled and bounced down the steep incline. On my feet again, I slithered and dodged down through the trees, while another volley ripped off showers of bark at head height.

I didn't wait to see if she followed, but a glance upwards showed a clear skyline. The day was brightening around me, and there was no-one else in my part of the terrain as far as I could see.

I pushed on as fast as I could go, aware from time to time of German voices in the distance. Eventually, they faded away.

But I couldn't afford to be off my guard, for them or for her. By the time I made contact with my next group, I was filthy, starved and almost insane from lack of sleep. I was relieved to find that there were no women in the next unit, and passed the rest of the war in relative peace.

"Did you ever hear what happened to her?"

"No. And don't want to."

"What about the others? Do you ever have any contact with them?"

"Most of them didn't make it. Whether they were caught that night or later I don't know. Some of them just disappeared off the map.

They could be alive somewhere. Being condescended to in some piss-hole for the old and feeble-minded. I don't know."

"Henri?"

"Now he did survive." I laughed. "Owns a small hotel in Normandy! Wife and six kids to run him ragged."

"You never got married did you?"

"No. After what happened, I had every reason to distrust all women. Why give them another go at us?"

"You mean 'the female of the species is much deadlier than the male'?"

"You could say that."

"But you must have had some female companions."

"Companions, no. Females, yes."

"Well, they can't all have been like Adèle."

"Perhaps that's the trouble. They weren't. After the first flush, I found them all just unutterably dull. If I'd met up with her again, I wouldn't have hesitated to kill her. But, since I didn't, what's the point?

I fingered the edges of the scar that ran across my cheek. Nowadays, it has faded to a papery whiteness. It barely shows unless I've been working up a sweat or I've lost my temper. You'd think it was nothing. But when my blood is up, it still burns an angry red. In terms of an old war wound, it scarcely rates. But, even if you'd hardly notice it, that scar runs deep.

MIRROR IMAGE

In some ways, Gemma was an odd child. She had an expression of watchfulness, as if the world was a serious place and not quite reliable. This was unaccountable if you met her father. He was always cheerful and jollied people along. Her mother was less boisterous but invariably kind.

At fifteen, Gemma was still the ungainly adolescent, her clumsiness almost a mistrust of her right to be there. She didn't lack friends, though none was especially close. She stayed on the fringes of their activities, approving and applauding but taking no active part. She seemed to be waiting for something to happen, a permanent audience expecting the curtain to rise.

Although she was intelligent, she hadn't achieved as much at school as her potential suggested. Now she was halfway through her GCSE course, and the strain was beginning to tell.

One of her set books was "I'm the King of the Castle". The tensions that underlay the action struck a resonance in her own personality. Kingshaw's suicide filled her with angry horror and a lurking fear at its inevitability.

Her teacher seemed to have an obsession with death, which she justified by referring to the "thematic" requirement of the Board. Most of the children enjoyed the gruesome possibilities this presented, but it only deepened Gemma's depressive tendency. It widened the gap between what she felt she should be like and her unwilling grasp of her own nature.

Her instinctive responses did not help much when it came to the written work. The ideas that frothed up inside her refused to submit to order, and she was left in a state of permanent anxiety. Her eyes became strained and hunted, and she took frequent baths to soak away the cares that piled up chaotically in her bedroom.

Standing one evening in front of the mirror, she was about to rub off the condensation when she noticed the black points of her eyes staring vaguely out beyond the mist. She scoured two vicious circles in the greyed glass and glared at herself discontentedly. Next she drew a gloomy mouth where she thought her own must be and watched the tears from the disturbed moisture trickle down the result. Then she destroyed the apparition with an angry wipe of the towel.

To her surprise she found that the face behind the mask was smiling back at her, the eyes alight and mischievous. She hadn't realised her expression had changed, but the smile relaxed right through her and left her feeling quietly happy. She fingered the smeary mouth that remained on the glass and lifted the corners into a ludicrous grin. Her mother would yell at her for messing up the mirror, but that was all part of the game. She slept better that night than for many a long while.

But work crowded in with relentless pressure, as the deadline for folders drew near. The teachers' demands grew increasingly shrill, and they lost their customary tolerance: "Gemma this, Gemma that! Gemma you really must .....! Gemma Watson, this just won't do!"

She began to hate the sound of her own name. It was a silly name anyway. Her father said they'd chosen it because she was a little gem, a precious jewel. He only laughed when she denounced this as "pathetic".

"Cheer up, old dear. Just think, we might have called you Rhinestone - or even Carbuncle! At least that's what it 'boils' down to!"

Gemma groaned at his heavy-handed humour and stamped off to her cell.

The geography teacher had told her that if she didn't hand in her completed project tomorrow he would halve her marks. "Just think what that will do to a barely scraped C, eh?"
She wasn't sure if he'd keep his threat. She didn't think he would want her to fail, but he'd always been very strict. So here she was, scribbling frantically away in a room knee-deep in screwed-up paper, while her mother ran up and down stairs with "something to keep her going".

At one o-clock, however, she was still crouched over her work, with hunched shoulders, a head that ached and throbbed, and eyes that could hardly see. Somehow her hand kept moving and her pen left tracks of God-knows-what gibberish behind it. It was as if her arm was being steered and her fingers guided across the page by someone quite other than herself.

It couldn't last. Her mother peered in anxiously at two o'clock and found her slumped in sleep. She eased the pen from her fingers, and her father carried her to bed.

This is where she woke the next morning to find the alarm by her side switched off to let her rest as long as possible. With a wail, she threw off the covers and lurched across to the table.

Her mother was listening out for her and came straight in.

"Don't worry. Dad'll run you to school. You won't be late. You can eat in the car."

"But my project! It isn't finished. Oh mum - " She broke off in exhaustion and despair.

"Well, it looks finished to me. You've even put 'The End' and a flourish of squiggles. Hope that won't lose you marks, young lady."

Gemma snatched up the pages and scanned through the last few sides. It was all there. And it made sense. It was even good. She'd done it! "Let's see what old Carter makes of that."

She scrambled into her school clothes and was off with as much spring in her step as if she'd slept for a week.

And 'Old Carter' was impressed. He even gave her a B.

Encouraged, she went on to improve her performance in several other subjects. "Sure this is all your own work, Gemma?" Miss Maxwell had said suspiciously. Nevertheless, by the time the folders were in, Gemma was confident she'd do quite well in most areas. Credit was given for the recent display of brilliance, late though it was, and now it was only the exams.

Her lightened manner increased her circle of friends. One even collected her in the mornings and walked back home with her from school. She and Sally decided to tackle their revision together.

But Sally went down with tonsillitis. The others had already made their arrangements and did not think to include her in. Gemma's studies became more random and aimless, and her room disintegrated into the jumble that reflected her mind. As the calendar ground away the days, the threat of exams became frightening. With three subjects crammed into the first two days, panic splintered her thoughts into a sharp wilderness of worry.

Her mother decided that a tidy-up was the answer, and Gemma returned to discover her pencils freshly sharpened, her pen, ruler and rubber ready to hand, her textbooks ranged neatly on the shelves and her papers stacked in a single pile. She would never make sense of them now.

Just as the old despair overtook her, a sweet and refreshing fragrance spilled all round her. Its scented arms reached out and seemed to enfold her. Filling her consciousness, it carried away the bleakness in a pastel tide of colour. She breathed in deeply, saturated with its purity, feeling the calm re-gather in her spirit.

She spread herself luxuriously on an unusually tidy bed and eyed the surfaces of dressing table, chest of drawers and formerly cluttered ledges. All the little pots and ornaments were carefully arranged, and the wood shone through where the dust had been. She lifted a long-favoured teddy from the friendly mob around her and cuddled his balding body contentedly to her chest. When she finally visited the offending desk, she knew it would not take long to reimpose order on order.

She emerged from her room with the flippant air of youth and surprised her mother by the energy of her hug.

"Thanks, mum. It must have taken you ages." Another surprise. "I love that new polish. It made me feel really good."

"Polish? Surprising what a quick flick of the duster will do, isn't it. You should try it some time!"

Her parents were amazed by the change that came over their daughter. From shadowed diffidence emerged a new vigour. Examinations were plainly the elixir of life! The music she chose for her CD player had distinctly more attack. She even sang along in brief snatches of discordance.

Once or twice in the pauses between bouts of cacophony, she caught a lingering echo which still haunted the spaces of her room, and was surprised it was so melodious. Her estimation of her abilities rose accordingly and she redoubled her efforts.

Her mother somehow feigned deaf, and only her father actively grumbled. "How you can work with that racket I don't know. You're making enough noise for two."

In the second of silence that followed this remark, she saw an odd look pass between her parents. It was about her, yet it wasn't. For a moment she felt excluded, outside some wordless secret. But she didn't care. She could take it all.

Besides, she knew that her parents loved her. Her mother had even resumed the habit of kissing her goodnight before going to bed. Although she was nearly asleep, she was aware of soft hands caressing her cheeks and the feathery touch of lips. Challenged, her mother had naturally denied it, but Gemma knew what she knew and was happy in this affection.

The night before her exams were due, with the hot steam blooming through the bathroom, the words "GOOD LUCK" appeared in stages on the glass. She grinned. She never realised her mother was a vandal.

The exams were finished, and she was waiting for the results. Sally, who had recovered in time for the pleasure of the ordeal, had chivvied her into playing tennis. Normally too inhibited to enjoy any sport, now she waited on the pavement, bouncing the ball on the ground with her racket, while her friend popped into the off-licence with a message for her uncle.

Gemma was seeing how many bounces she could manage without missing the ball. She never got beyond four and, in a flash of temper, she slammed the wretched thing hard on the ground. It struck the edge of a paving stone and ricocheted into the road. Without a second's thought she dashed after it.

In the moment that her foot struck the tarmac, she saw herself leap gracefully after the ball, catching it deftly in full flight. She looked radiant. Her bright hair shone and her eyes sparkled, full of life and fun. As she landed she turned, her face exuberant, and waved. Gemma froze, astonished. Then the darkness rushed in upon her and the vision was replaced by blankness.

The driver clambered, shaking, from his cab and ran to the front of his lorry. He stopped short in disbelief. There was nothing there.

He had not felt the bump - he was too busy with his brakes - but he had seen her straight ahead of him. There'd been no time to swerve. She had to be underneath.

He threw himself down on his belly and peered into the oily darkness. She had to be there! Yet she wasn't. It was as if she'd been spirited away.

Then he noticed the crowd gathered at the kerbside, grouped around something on the ground. His heart sank. He pushed his way forward and looked down on Gemma. She lay on her face half across the pavement, her blond hair hanging in the dust, her hand reaching out. The racquet had fallen from her grasp and the ball still rocked in the gutter opposite.

"I couldn't help it!" the man jerked out. "She jumped right under my wheels. I didn't have a chance. There was nothing I could do."

He went to lift her, but somebody held him back. "Better leave her till the ambulance arrives. You could do more damage if you touch her."

He didn't see how more damage could be done. The girl lay without moving. There was no sign of blood, no obvious bruising even, but she was clearly dead. He thought of his own children, the hopes he had for them, and he shuddered.

By the time the ambulance arrived, a miracle had happened. The girl was sitting up, gazing bewildered about her. The driver sat weakly on the kerb beside her. The colour had returned to his cheeks. He must have a guardian angel.

The ambulance men, after expert inspection, lifted her deftly onto a stretcher and put her into the back. "Probably just shock, but best to have her checked over."

Sally returned to the scene too late for the action but climbed importantly into the ambulance to sit beside her, claiming to be a close relation.

Her parents were sent for and hurried to the hospital. There they found Sally telling everyone of the part she'd played and Gemma looking vaguely distracted, but generally behaving as if nothing had happened.

On the way home her mother hardly stopped talking. The anxiety that shuttered down at the news of the accident was swept aside in a torrent of words.

"But mum," interposed Gemma, when she could get a word in, "I don't know what all the fuss is about. I only fainted. What happened to the other girl?"

"What other girl?" asked her father.

"The girl who caught my ball. They said something about an accident. There was a lorry, I think. She wasn't hurt, was she?"

"There wasn't any other girl, Gemma. It was only you. You were knocked down by the lorry. You ran into the road after the ball."

Her mother looked as if she was going to cry again.

"But I didn't, dad...mum. Look, there isn't a mark on me. I just fainted with the shock. It was the other girl. She stopped me going on. But it was the oddest thing. She looked just like me, dad - just like me!"

Her parents exchanged a long glance over her head, and they reached an unspoken decision.

Next morning, Gemma stood with her parents in a quiet corner of the cemetery. She gazed at the headstone to a tiny plot marked out in big pebbles. Her mother knelt and removed the dead stalks from a vase and replaced them with sweet peas. The delicate colours dispelled the grey. Their fragrance surrounded Gemma, drawn out by the sunlight. It was the perfume that had filled her bedroom.

"I always bring them to her at this time of year. They were flowering when you were born, and they were still flowering when she died. I always felt she would like them."

Gemma laid her hand on her mother's shoulder. She looked at the name on the stone. "Naomi. That's a nice name, mum. Better than Gemma."

"Gemma for Gemini. Your star sign. The twins." She smiled fondly at her daughter. "We lost little Naomi, but we thought we could keep her alive in your name."

Her father took her free hand and held it close. "We never told you about her in case it upset you. Kids can get funny ideas, you know. But it seems she has never forgotten you, even if you didn't know about her."

They stared at each other in the thought of what might have happened without her. Her sister. Her guardian angel.

They stayed for a moment longer in silence by the grave. Then they retraced their steps towards the gates.

Gemma felt warm and grateful. She had often been alone. She had often felt lonely. She had often experienced an odd sensation, as if something was missing. Now she had a sister, a twin. Even if she never saw Naomi again, she knew she would never be truly alone. Naomi would always be a part of her.

At home she stood facing the bathroom mirror. Her own reflection stared thoughtfully back at her. When she moved, it moved. When she frowned, it frowned.

She misted the surface with her warm breath, and traced a smiling face on the glass.

THE BLACK TAXI

Abby watched her husband over the top of her book. The children, mercifully, were in bed, and here she was, as usual, keeping herself occupied while he gave himself completely to his papers. He might be a manager, but did he really have to bring his work home every night?

At least he was in the same room as her. Most of the time he was in his study and she was trying to keep the children quiet. How could you expect a seven year old and a five year old to be quiet? It just wasn't fair on them. She hated herself for constantly shushing them and telling them to keep the noise down. Always dragging them off to the kitchen to play in there, while she got on with her chores.

And when were they supposed to have their friends round? It was so awkward to keep farming them out to their friends' homes when they could never invite them back. It was a wonder they still had any friends, or at least that she had. The only time they got a chance to let off steam was in other people's houses or at school. Jonathan's teacher had already had her in about his behaviour and Sally was such a restrained, quiet child it made her heart bleed.

It wasn't as if Andrew was unkind. It was almost as if he wasn't there at all. Lately he'd become more and more withdrawn. It could, of course, be the pressure of work, but she didn't think it was as simple as that.

Perhaps he hadn't wanted children in the first place. They'd certainly put it off for several years. There was always some reason, some excuse. They needed to establish themselves. They needed a bigger house; they needed a bigger mortgage; they needed a place with a garden. Had it all been excuses?

Admittedly they'd both had to work long hours, she with her nursing, he scaling the ladder of advancement. Night classes, economics and management exams. Had he just got so in the habit of slogging away he just couldn't stop? Did he actually like all this work, work, work? Or was it a substitute for discontent? Did he just not like being with them?

Earlier in the evening, she'd broached the subject of the approaching birthday.

"I was wondering what we should do for Jonathan's party."

"The usual sort of thing I suppose.

"Well, a lot of his mates are going for special days out. Mark Southerby's mother hired the local pool for a swimming party. Peter

Gordon's parents took them all to a bowling alley. Jonathan told you about it if you remember."

Andrew shrugged. "Did he?"

"Jonathan was asking about taking a group of his pals to Alton Towers."

"Seems a bit extreme. What are we supposed to do, hire a coach?"

"Naturally he'd have to limit the numbers."

"I can see that happening."

"But some of the parents would be able to muck in. We could take several cars."

There was a pause. She thought Andrew was considering the logistics.

"It's too much of a responsibility. What if something happened?"

"Such as?"

"Kids wandering off. Getting lost. Falling off a ride. Anything."

"Well, what about the adventure course at Abbots Court?"

"Same difference."

"You suggest something then."

"I don't see what's wrong with having the party here. It won't cost so much. And the children always enjoy it. Besides, Sally is far too young to join in all this other stuff."

"I suppose. But Jonathan's going to be very disappointed. Can I at least tell him we'll take the two of them to Alton Towers later in the year?"

"I don't know. I shouldn't make any promises."

Then he'd gone off to fetch his briefcase, and that had been that.

She thought back to when the children were born. It had been all right then. Andrew had seemed pleased enough. He'd even taken a turn with the bottle, though he drew the line at nappies. He'd accompanied her on walks and sat with the pram while she pushed Jonathan in the baby swing, but as he'd graduated to the ordinary swings and started to hurl himself down the slides Andrew had gradually dropped out of the picture. He'd kick a ball about with them in the back garden, but nothing the least bit exciting. Outings had always been her pigeon. He'd mostly got something else to do. When it came to the school run, he'd opted out altogether.

It dawned on her that Andrew was no longer jiffling with his documents. She looked directly at him. He was rubbing his eyelids with the heels of his hands. He looked drawn and strained. She put down her book and went across to him.

"You've done enough for one night." She pressed his shoulder lightly. "Put that lot away, and we'll have a nightcap."

By the time she'd made the drinks, he was relaxing in an armchair with his feet up, watching a replay of "My Family" on the box. Another dysfunctional family; another reluctant father. But the real thing wasn't so funny.

She waited till the end, until the eternal adverts were muted on the set, and returned to the subject of the birthday.

"What are we going to do about Jonathan's present?"

"What have you got in mind?"

"Well I think he has his heart set on a bike."

Andrew started flicking around the programmes with the remote.

"Several of his friends have bikes now, and he's beginning to feel left out."

"Doesn't always have to follow the crowd does he? Anyway, it's too dangerous for a bike round here. Too much traffic."

"It'd be all right if he stayed in the cul-de-sac."

"Yes, but how do we know he would? You know what boys are like. One of his friends would decide to bunk off to the park, and the rest would follow. Besides, have you seen the way some of the idiots floor it round here?"

She somehow felt he was usurping her role. "He has goes on the others' bikes now, but he wants one of his own. It's not surprising, is it?"

"No, it's not surprising, but he's too young. If the other parents think it's okay for their kids to risk life and limb, that's their affair. I'm not prepared to take that chance."

"We can't wrap him up in cotton wool all his life. I could always take him to the park to ride it."

"It's too risky."

Andrew stood up abruptly and headed towards the stairs. When he reached the bottom he seemed to relent. He turned to face her and gave her a brief smile. "Anyway," he added, "I heard him say he wanted a Playstation 2. I'll get one from town when I'm passing through. Save you the bother. I'll find him some decent games too. You see how his mates come flocking round when he has one of those. He can have it in his room."

Abby said nothing. He tried again. "You can surprise him with one of your fabulous cakes. What's he into this year?"

"Shrek, I should think - or hobbits."

"Well, there you are then. Two nice surprises."

Abby felt slightly mollified. At least it would mean a few return play sessions, even though Sally would be left out of the loop.

She turned off the plugs and the lights and followed him up.

So far the party had gone down better than she expected. Perhaps Jonathan's friends were not too old for party games after all. Or perhaps they were getting blasé about themed parties and this was a refreshing change.

Her friend Phyllis had stayed to give a hand, and they'd already gone through treasure hunts, musical chairs - without too many spots knocked off guests or furniture - and various team games in the garden. Tea was over, and now it was time for some winding down before their parents came to collect them. They'd started off with pass the parcel - they were never too old for that one, mercenary little devils - and now they were onto the pièce de resistance, at least in Abby's book.

She'd left Phyllis organising the kids into a circle while she went to collect the tray from the dining room. The table presented a delightful chaos of half-drunk squashes and half-eaten fairy cakes. Streamers and silly string littered the cloth, with liberal portions of crumbs, gobbets of jelly and crumbled bits of cheese. Who would have thought a few kids could make quite so much mess? Phyllis had reduced Shrek to a goggle-eyed head, and the party bags were complete with the ritual pieces of cake.

Everything had gone off like clockwork. Andrew had been a bit stiff and awkward to start with, but at least he was there. And she'd got him to lead the chorus of "happy birthday".

The relighting candles had caused a lot of giggling, as everyone tried to help Jonathan blow them out. He was allowed his wish anyway. Andrew too had looked as if he was enjoying himself.

Abby gathered up the pencils and pads and put them with the tray. She looked at the collection of objects she'd put on it. All very intriguing. She was glad she'd remembered the box of knickknacks Andrew's mother had given her when the children were small. She'd dug them out from the loft and wondered why she hadn't thought of them before. The children had been too young at the time they'd been given; now they were almost too old.

She'd always loved the tray game. It had been her own favourite as a child. How thrilled she'd been whenever she'd remembered the most things. Feeling a surge of anticipation, she entered the room.

She found the children looking pleased and excited, and incredibly still in their places. Even Andrew remained in his chair, though he'd tried to sidle off after tea.

She allowed each child thirty seconds to take in the objects on the tray. She watched the children's earnest concentration, the screwed up faces, the counting on sticky fingers as they tried to remember what they'd seen.

Then she arrived at Andrew.

"Oh no, not this! You can't expect me to join in this. It wouldn't be fair."

"Don't you be so sure. You might be able to spell, Andrew, but I bet you any of these kids can remember as many as you. Probably more."

She put the tray in front of him. He bent forward as if to focus and then he froze, his face a blank.

"Come on. You're supposed to be trying really hard to memorise the lot. Or are you afraid to show yourself up?" She laughed.

Still he did not move. Abby started to feel disconcerted. It was as if he was turning to ice. His face had drained of colour and his mouth was rigid. Slowly his hands stretched out and he lifted a toy car off the tray. It was a black taxi, an old Corgi, battered from use. It must surely have been his own. Yet all he registered was shock.

And then in front of her eyes he started to crumple. His shoulders shook; his chest heaved. His face collapsed into a mass of woe before he bowed his head over his hands, still clutching the car. He began to rock backwards and forwards in his seat. For a second he choked. And then he began to howl. A low, broken howl. She stared in horror as the howl grew and grew. The sound rang in her head and paralysed her in alarm. What on earth was wrong?

Then Phyllis was marshalling the kids into the garden. Some of them looked scared, some of them simply curious. Scot Appleton was grinning like a lunatic. He always was a nasty little tyke. Jonathan looked horrified. Phyllis had hold of Sally and was propelling her gently towards the door. Abby saw her agonised face. "Mummy!"

And then they were outside and she heard Phyllis's reassuring voice. "It's all right, baby. Daddy's not feeling very well. But he'll be okay in a minute. Come on petal, I need your help to give out these

114

masks. We're all going to be wild animals. Let's see if we can scare the boys."

Thank God for Phyllis.

Abby turned back to Andrew. He'd stopped howling and had started to shiver as if in shock. He was staring mutely at the taxi, still in his hands. Abby crouched down in front of him and folded his hands in hers. She did not try to take the toy away from him. She felt desperately frightened.

"What is it, Andrew? What's happened?"

Andrew's voice choked. "It's his."

"His? Whose, Andrew? Who do you mean? I thought it must be yours."

"It was his." The tears flowed down his face. He made no attempt to wipe them away. Neither did she.

"Who, Andrew?" She stroked his hair.

"My brother's."

Abby was perplexed. What brother? Andrew didn't have a brother. Like her he was an only child. "What are you saying, Andrew?"

"It was my brother's. It was my brother's. And I killed him."

"Killed him?" Abby heard herself idiotically repeating everything he said. She felt helpless, and stupefied. What was all this? It was as though she was caught up in a nightmare. Nothing made any sense.

"It was my fault. I killed him."

Abby took hold of the taxi and eased it from his fingers. He didn't resist. "You're not well, Andrew. You need to go to bed." She put an arm round his shoulders and tried to help him up. He rose obediently to his feet and she walked him up the stairs.

Once she had got him in bed, she telephoned the doctor. Outside she could once more hear the shouts and shrieks of mock fear as the children pursued each other round the garden. Parents had begun to arrive and Phyllis was handing out the party bags. When she left with her own lad, she took Jonathan and Sally with her for a sleepover. Abby had never felt so grateful.

The doctor examined Andrew thoroughly and gave him a sedative. Downstairs he wrote down the name and number of a colleague and gave it to her.

"He's a very good man, Mrs. Mason. He'll get to the bottom of all this. I've written a sick note for Andrew for at least a month. I've put it down as nervous debility due to exhaustion. They shouldn't ask too many questions. With luck he'll be able to get back to work then, at least part-time. Probably the best thing he could do to get him back on track.

Abby checked on Andrew and found him fast asleep. He looked exhausted and haggard. Perhaps it really was nervous debility. And he had been overdoing it. Nevertheless, she decided to get at the root of it. She telephoned Andrew's parents in Ilkeston.

Andrew's mother answered in her bright, expectant voice. "Oh hello, Abby. How's the birthday boy? How did the party go?"

"Pretty well, Marcia, but something's happened. Something I don't understand."

"That sounds ominous. What is it?"

"This is going to sound crazy, Marcia. But did Andrew have a brother?"

There was a long pause. Marcia sounded odd when she spoke again. "David."

Another pause, and then there was Brian at the other end. "Hello, Abby. Can't talk at the moment. I'll ring you back."

It was gone ten before he did ring back. Marcia had been upset, so he couldn't phone before. Abby told him that Andrew had had some kind of breakdown, and it seemed to be connected with the death of his brother. Abby hadn't realised that he'd had a brother.

Yes, he did have a brother. David. But David had died when he was eight. Same age as young Jonathan. Andrew had only been four at the time. Younger than Sally. Marcia had gone completely to pieces, and Brian had been fully taken up with looking after her and dealing with the necessary arrangements. Fortunately Marcia's sister had offered to look after Andrew. When he came home, he seemed to be back to normal. It was almost as if nothing had happened, and they'd tried to keep it that way. They'd done their best to shelter him from the distress, but it had obviously gone deeper than they'd realised.

"But Andrew seems to think that he killed him."

"Of course he didn't. It was just a terrible accident. Nobody's fault."

"Then why does Andrew think it was his fault?" Abby hazarded a guess. "Was he jealous of David?"

"Jealous. No. He idolised him. And David loved Andrew too. But he was with him when it happened. Perhaps he thought he should

116

have saved him. Perhaps he thought he'd let David down in some way. We didn't think of that."

"I need to understand. Do you….do you mind telling me how it happened?"

"It was shortly after David's birthday. We'd given him a new bike and he'd been tearing about up and down the lanes on it. He was an athletic little chap, always in scrapes of one kind or another. But he always bounced back, just as confident as ever…."

Abby felt him struggling, but she had to know. Just when she thought she'd have to press him, Brian continued.

"He was a generous boy too. Spent a lot of time raking around with Andrew, even though he was quite a bit older. The day he had his bike he was swanking around the yard, and Andrew was sitting on the step watching him. Then he went off to the shed, and came back pushing his old three wheeler. He cleaned it up, while Andrew held the rags and the polish for him. And then, with a grand gesture, he presented it to his little brother.

"Andrew was overwhelmed. He stroked its frame as if it was gold. He could hardly reach the pedals, but he lifted his feet up as David shoved him round the yard. When David had flown off to show his new bike to his mates, Andrew chugged patiently up and down, determined to prove to his brother how well he could ride."

"And was that when David had the accident?"

"No, it was a week or two later. David and Andrew were out together. The first we knew of it a neighbour was running into the kitchen. Her husband had been driving home and had found them on Shooter's Hill. Both bikes were tangled together. Andrew was sitting next to the wreckage in a shocked state. He was covered in blood and grit where he'd been dragged across the road, and David ….. David was in a heap next to the wall. His neck was broken."

"Oh my God, how dreadful." Abby's eyes filled with tears. Just imagine if it had been Jonathan and Sally. And poor little Andrew. What on earth had he gone through? She wanted to gather him in her arms, to make it all better, but she didn't know how. She hoped to God the psychiatrist would be able to undo this mess.

When Andrew woke up next morning, he lay dully on his pillows as if incapable of movement. Abby sat beside him and told him she knew about David.

"Your father said it wasn't your fault, Andrew."

He turned his face away from her.

"Nobody blames you, Andrew. Your father said nobody blamed you."

"Of course they blamed me. Or why did they send me away?"

"Because your mother was too upset to cope."

"Exactly. I destroyed my mother's life. And when I came home again, it wasn't my home at all. They'd moved to Ilkeston. And they'd got rid of all David's things. There was no sign I'd ever had a brother. Nobody mentioned him. I never mentioned him. It was obviously something I'd done wrong. They sent me to boarding school. They didn't want me any more."

"That isn't true, Andrew. You mustn't think like that. How could it be your fault? You were only four. It was just a horrible accident."

She was obviously not getting through to him. "David was eight. Much older than you. If anyone was to blame, it was more likely to be him."

Andrew gave her a look of dogged hostility, and she knew she'd said the wrong thing. He rolled with his back towards her and lay rigidly on his side.

Abby hoped that anger was more healthy than guilt. But now it was her turn to feel guilty. How had she never suspected? How could she so have misjudged him?

She decided it was best to leave it to the professionals.

A few days later the visits to the psychiatrist began. Graeme Frampton specialised in hypnotherapy. Abby had filled him in on everything she knew and, after a few sessions with Andrew, it was clear to him that they were dealing with a case of repressed memory. Andrew couldn't in any way recall the accident itself. Until he could be convinced he had not caused the death of his brother, he would never be able to trust himself with his own children. Regressing him though the accident was nevertheless a risky business. Success would require him to readjust all his relationships. Failure could leave him even more overwhelmed by guilt.

Andrew would not submit to hypnosis without the safeguard of a witness, so Abby accompanied him to all his appointments. She was humbled by his faith in her. She didn't know if she could reveal her innermost thoughts to him - or anyone else if it came to that. She admired the skill of Graeme Frampton in edging him closer to the brink. Andrew's resistance intensified the nearer they came, and his levels of anxiety increased. Life at home was getting harder for everyone.

Then came the critical moment. Frampton had asked him to watch the two boys as if he was their uncle. "It is the day David was killed. It is the day David took his little brother out on his tricycle. Tell me what they are saying, Andrew."

Andrew's voice took on the tones of the two boys.

"Where are we going, David?"

"We're going down into the village. I've had my pocket money. We'll get an icecream."

"It's a long way. Mummy says I shouldn't go too far from the house."

"S'okay. She won't mind. I'll look after you. Mum! It's okay if we go out on our bikes for a bit, isn't it? There you are. Said it would be all right."

There was a pause. Andrew's breathing became laboured. Frampton prompted him. "What are they doing now?"

"David is cycling on ahead. It's a long incline. Andrew is finding it hard to keep up. David keeps coming back and trying to push him from behind, but he's almost falling off himself and wobbling about."

"Come on, Andy! The shop'll be shut at this rate. Use your legs!"

"I can't, David. I'm tired."

"Just a minute. I've had an idea. You stay there. Sit on that bank. And don't move till I get back."

Andrew starts fiddling with his fingers and gnawing his lip. He keeps looking to his left, as if he's worried about something.

"Is David coming back, Andrew?"

"Yes, here he comes .....What's that, David?"

"It's a rope."

"What's it for?"

"Wait and see."

Frampton asked, "What is he doing, Andrew?"

"He's tying it to Andrew's handlebars. Now he's tying the other end to his saddle stem."

"Now we'll see how fast you can go."

"David's almost standing on the pedals, and Andrew's pushing away as hard as he can. It's not very fast, but at least they're getting up the slope. Now the road's levelled out. David is cycling fairly slowly, but Andrew's legs are pumping up and down. Here's the hill down to the village. Andrew can see the old lady's house at the bottom and further on the shop with the icecream board outside. David draws up and Andrew stops beside him.

"We could just coast down this bit, Andy. But it must be getting late. I'll keep towing you. It'll be quicker."

"How's that for speed?"

Andrew stops speaking. His face goes white.

"What's the matter, Andrew?" Frampton watches him intently.

"He's going too fast. Andrew can't keep his feet on the pedals. He takes them off. The pedals thump into his legs. They bite into his skin. The handlebars are jolting. Jerking about. He can hardly keep his grip."

"Why doesn't David stop?"

"He doesn't realise Andrew's in trouble. He thinks it's great. He takes one hand off the handlebars and waves back at him. Andrew tries to wave back. But the bike is bucking about. Andrew is terrified."

Abby sees he husband's agonised face. His eyes are staring; his mouth is trembling. He is trying not to cry. She longs to intervene, but Frampton is urging him on.

"Why doesn't he call David to stop?"

"He can't. They'll miss the icecream shop. David will be so disappointed. He can't let him down. He's got to hang on. He's got to be brave. David is relying on him."

Andrew suddenly shrieks and throws his hands over his face. He rolls off the couch and lies kicking and screaming on the carpet. Abby wonders why Frampton doesn't stop. He waves an arm at her to make her sit down.

"What's happened to the boys, Andrew?"

Andrew sits up, looking grey and shocked. "It was the gravel. There was gravel at the side of the road. Andrew went into a skid. His back wheel came off the ground and the bike went over. It slithered across the road, dragging Andrew with it. David was half round in his saddle when the rope snapped back and his bike lurched towards Andrew's. As the bikes collided, David was thrown over the handlebars into the wall."

Frampton helped Andrew back into the couch.

"Now, Andrew. I'm going to count backwards from ten. When I say 'one', you will wake up. You will remember how the accident happened. And you will remember that Andy was only four. You will see him as a frightened little boy who did not want to let his brother down. And you will realise that his brother did not mean to hurt him. You will understand that it was an accident. A tragedy, but it was nobody's fault."

Learning to take on the role of parent, learning to trust himself with his children, was a long and painful business for everyone, with months and months of regular visits to a cognitive therapist.

The first time he drove the children to school was a disaster. Abby went with him to give him support. It was lucky she did. At the end of the cul-de-sac he came to an abrupt halt and buckled over the wheel. They had to swap drivers under the eyes of other children, including, inevitably, Scot Appleton.

Later, Abby was called into the school. This was becoming a regular occurrence. It seemed Jonathan had once again attacked Scot Appleton. He'd refused to say why, but the head teacher was beginning to talk about suspension. Whatever the reason, such conduct was inexcusable.

At home he told Abby that Scot and his cronies were always singling him out. They taunted him about his father. He was barmy. He was a cry baby. He was a snivelling little coward. Jonathan was embarrassed and ashamed of his father's behaviour. And his shame erupted into violence. Eventually this did at least mean that they left Jonathan alone, but Abby was alarmed at the change in her son.

Andrew's progress and his temper remained erratic, and Abby began to wonder if anything would ever really change. She grew more and more concerned for her children. Everything considered, they had both been very good. They understood daddy was ill. They knew he wasn't going to die. But a shadow of anxiety lurked in both of them. Jonathan took himself off for hours on end. Whatever he did when he was out, Abby began to catch her friends giving her sidelong glances. Sally spent more time in her room. She heard her upbraiding her dolls, telling them they'd been very naughty. She'd started to wet the bed again. At this rate, they would all need therapy. It had got to stop.

She was seriously thinking of leaving and taking the children with her. Children were resilient. In the relaxed atmosphere of her parents' home, they would eventually get over it and start to live their own lives. She still loved Andrew, but she had to put them first. Once Andrew was ready, if he was ever ready, they could come back. That is if he still wanted them.

Meantime she did her best to keep the children distracted.

One evening, they were sitting round the table playing "Frustration" - that was apt - "Popamatic" as she used to call it. The

121

game produced the normal rowdy competition they enjoyed when Andrew was at work. Jonathan was stomping round the board and gleefully pounding his mother's conquered piece; Sally was out of her seat, jumping up and down with excitement when the front door slammed.

Instantly everyone froze, and Sally's face grew pinched, her dark eyes huge with fear. Jonathan's hand stiffened, his piece still in his fingers. Abby removed her own piece and returned it to base. She popped the dice again, trying to recover the game.

The door opened and Andrew strode up to the table. He swept the board away. "What's all this rubbish?" he said. "We don't need this!"

Abby heard the tone of his voice and looked at him in wonder. The children looked confused. Andrew plonked himself between the two of them at the table and spread out some papers with a flourish. They weren't office papers. They were coloured brochures. "Look at this," he said. "You know what this means!"

Both children shook their heads and eyed him up, glancing uncertainly at their mother.

"It means…." Andrew drew Sally towards him and scooped her into his lap. "It means that we are all going on holiday. And guess what sort of holiday?"

Both children stared again. Neither said a word. But Sally wrapped her arms around his neck and Jonathan leaned an arm across his shoulder, craning forwards to look at the brochure.

"Skiing! Something we can all learn together. It's a beginner's centre. Mummy and I will probably spend all our time on the nursery slopes, and you can help us." He ruffled both their heads, then looked across at Abby. He smiled at her unspoken question. "I've made a breakthrough, Abby. No more living in the past. No more worrying about the future. I'm going to need you to keep me to it, but I know it's going to be all right."

Abby put her hand over her mouth. She felt like crying. But a huge weight lifted off her.

"You must be hungry." She bent to kiss the top of his head. "I'll get your tea. Oh, and by the way…" She paused at the door. "Don't forget it's your turn to read the children their bedtime story."

A PRESENT FOR HENRY

The podgy hands shook out the investment pages of the "Financial Times". Sheila looked at them with distaste, shuddering at the thought of their fleshy propensities. She had endured a million such breakfasts in the eleven years they had been married. As the greying hairs had increasingly graced his morning pillow and increasingly deserted his plump, round head, the charms of his bank balance had faded. In any case, he hated to see that balance diminish for anything other than necessities. "Necessities" included whatever in the end would make his money grow.

At one time he seemed to develop a heart problem and promised to make her a wealthy young widow, but, when she studied her reflection in the glass and observed the lines beginning to form on her forehead and round her mouth, she found herself becoming tired of waiting.

Despite his continued hold on life, her prospects recently had taken a turn for the better in the manly shape of Foster Grant, a business associate of her husband's. She smiled as she thought of Henry's instructions to "make a fuss of this young fellow". That had been supremely easy. He certainly was not typical of Henry's friends, though all had their uses or they would not be invited home. He had shown a distinct partiality for Sheila and was a frequent visitor to the house. Sheila pulled her dressing gown firmly round her body and imagined its embrace to be two strong, fair-haired arms.

"For God's sake, woman, stop smiling into thin air and get me another coffee. This one's putrid."

"Well, if you will sit over it so long, what else can you expect?"

Henry glared at her truculently. "Like everything else in this house, bloody cold!"

Sheila sighed and rose obediently to fetch the percolator.

"You'll have to pull yourself together tonight at any rate. Firm's do - I suppose you've forgotten."

"How can I have forgotten?" She poured his second cup with tight lips. "Who's been driving round for the last two weeks trying to find you a suitable costume? Why they couldn't stick to the usual collar-and-tie affair I don't know."

"That's your trouble, Sheila - no imagination."

Sheila gave a somewhat bitter smile, and shook the dregs down the sink with vicious energy.

Henry rose from the table and thrust his paper into his briefcase. Sheila dutifully collected his coat, hat and brolly and waited by the hall table. He shrugged himself into the coat, found his keys and moved towards the door. "My case, Sheila."

Sheila took the suitcase from the window seat and held it out to him.

"Everything here? I don't want to be let down at the last minute."

"Yes, everything's there. Cavalier costume, buckled shoes, sword, toiletries, handkerchief, hairbrush -"

"All right, all right, I don't want an inventory. Just make sure you're at the hotel for eight. And try to look presentable. Don't forget I've got an image to keep up."

She watched him strut to the Mercedes and squeeze his bulk behind the wheel. The car revved up and spurted along the drive, scattering stones into the flowerbeds.

Sheila closed the door and her mouth firmed into a wry smile. "Lack of imagination, eh? Oh no, my darling, I won't let you down at the last minute."

She crossed to the phone, and lifted the receiver.

The office was bustling with an unusual atmosphere of ill-concealed animation. Miss Taylor had resuscitated last year's paper chains, and under the fluorescent lights they looked tolerably festive. Someone had taped a sprig of holly on the old man's chair, but Miss Taylor had hastily removed it. Henry Carter's bonhomie was strictly a Christmas affair and would not spill over into a regular sense of humour. Dusty garlands of tinsel trailed across the tops of filing cabinets, and some coloured balloons, already wrinkled, bulged from each corner. From the centre of the ceiling near the door to the adjacent room, a young or evergreen hopeful had pinned a bunch of mistletoe.

"That mistletoe was a mistake," said Miss Taylor, but it was too late to alter it now.

By the time Henry Carter arrived, the typewriters were rattling and the phones were ringing; business was in full swing as usual. Christmas was all right in its place, but it should never be allowed to interrupt the important things of life.

"Good morning, ladies," smirked Mr. Carter, treading with proprietorial step across the plain flooring of the outer office and onto the carpeted opulence of his own domain. He sat down at the "executive mahogany" desk and surveyed the pile of opened mail before him. Then his eyes alighted on the envelope marked "Strictly Private and Confidential".

"Good old Foster." He grinned in anticipation. "Let's hope this is a nice little Christmas present for Uncle Henry."

His fat fingers trembled slightly as the ivory paper knife slit carefully along the edge. His eyes gleamed at the contents and he reached for the phone. Contacts in the City were very useful. A little insider dealing to put some flesh on the bone was always a good thing, but especially now. It was an expensive time of year. A few words into the ears of his stockbroker, and he settled down to read his morning's postbag with an air of self-congratulation.

Mr. Tonks from Accountancy looked in on the two women in the outer office.

"Merry Christmas, ladies. My, you look cosy in here."

Miss Taylor peered at him over her glasses. "So we should, Mr. Tonks. We work hard enough all the rest of the year."

"Can't risk slacking when the boss's in, I suppose." Tonks nodded towards the closed door.

"I assure you, Mr. Tonks, that we in this office don't have the opportunity to slack."

Tonks caught Janet's eye as she flicked through the files. She was well covered, that one. Nice little armful for someone all right.

Miss Taylor intercepted his glance. "Do you want something, Mr. Tonks?"

"Oh, just a word with the b - Mr. Carter," he corrected.

"I'll see if he's free," said Miss Taylor stiffly. There was something about this young man she didn't quite like. Too cocky by half.

Tonks stood in front of his impassive boss, fidgeting with the report that Carter had demanded for that morning. Christmas certainly didn't mean any let up for the junior staff, though the open bottle of whisky on the side table showed that celebrations already flowed for the upper ranks.

Carter left Tonks standing while he shuffled the papers on the desk and scowled thoughtfully at some documents before him. It didn't do any harm to keep these youngsters waiting. Taught them what to expect out of life.

Eventually he honoured Tonks by extending an autocratic palm across the desk, while keeping his chair faced firmly away. Tonks obediently deposited the report in the outstretched paw, and felt himself going redder as the balding head bent over meticulous columns of figures. At length Carter strode out of the room, glowering and tutting at the report in his hand.

Then he could be heard shouting at Miss Taylor in the outer office, fuming about inefficiency and heads rolling and all sorts of other unseasonal remarks. Tonks registered Miss Taylor, flustered and twittering, making excuses for his own department as if she personally were responsible. She wasn't a bad old girl really, for all the acid drops.

Tonks's eyes skimmed briefly over the polished desk with its neatly stacked in-tray, the work of Miss Taylor, and its toppling out-tray, the work of his indefatigable boss. It was amazing how quickly some people could operate if there was money at the end of the road.

And then he noticed the corner of something tucked under the edge of the blotter. He slid it out and perused the same information that had gladdened the heart of the older man earlier that morning. He straightened, and gnawed his lip in a calculating way. When he heard Carter commence his return, snorting and blustering across the lino, he hastily thrust the paper back into its hiding place and stood with a long-suffering expression on his thin features.

"Get out!" snapped Mr. Carter. "And take this rubbish with you. You'd better tell Baker to move his arse on this one, or there'll be two people missing from the party tonight.

"Miss Taylor!" he bawled at the timid little woman, who jerked uncontrollably at his tones. "Get some coffee."

"But Miss Stone usually does -"

"Never mind who usually does what. What's this I employ - a shop steward? Who pays your wages round here? I have other work for 'Miss' Stone."

Miss Taylor rapidly left the room, her dignity severely ruffled.

Henry Carter sidled up to Janet and put a plump hand on her firm, young shoulder. "Well, Miss Stone, perhaps you would be so good as to find the correspondence on this and then come into my office."

While she stooped over the files, he stood next to the cabinet and stared fixedly down the top of her blouse.

Janet felt herself colouring up. "I can manage, Mr. Carter." She tried to speak coolly. "I'll bring the correspondence as soon as I've sorted it out."

"No hurry, young lady." He moved closer to her, watching her fingers flutter over the folders. He sensed her agitation and bent across her. "I think you'll find this is what you're looking for." He leaned across her and allowed his hand to rest on the back of her trim waist.

126

She extracted the papers with admirable speed and pranced on into his office. Grabbing her pad and pencil as she went, she left him puffing in the rear. She stood rigidly beside his desk, and her flesh cringed as she felt his heat behind her. Ducking quickly into the secretary's chair, she rammed it dexterously back and into his midriff. "Oh, I'm so sorry, Mr. Carter, I didn't realise you were there," she expostulated, her eyelids signalling affected concern.

Carter was not unduly perturbed. He was used to the tricks of these little tarts. He lounged back in his chair and dictated his letters with a speed carefully calculated to leave Janet always one sentence behind. When he had got her thoroughly unsettled, he advanced on the door to usher her out, while she still scribbled frantically in her notebook.

It was then he saw the mistletoe and decided to get his revenge. As she passed him, relieved to get back to her machine, he caught her to him and pressed a moist, rubbery kiss on her scarlet lips. To Miss Taylor, standing in the door, cup of coffee trembling in the saucer, biscuits decidedly soggy, he pointed smugly to the mistletoe.

"Spirit of Christmas, Miss Taylor," he chortled, and swept back into his office.

Janet was in the ladies' room, frantically scrubbing her besmirched lips. "Randy old bugger," she scalded. "I'll get him for that, you see if I don't."

Her threat would probably have remained a threat but for the advent of lunchtime, and then, when she took the chance to leave the letters for signature on his desk, she noticed the case with his costume.

She didn't realise how far-reaching would be the results of her subsequent action.

Even while she was taking the scissors out of her top drawer, Tonks was making his own preparations for a prosperous New Year from a callbox down the road. He had telephoned a number that he kept in his pocket book, and this time he felt his information was worth a cool £50,000. If he played his cards right, he might even be able to screw considerably more out of them. It was the best opportunity he'd ever had to get out of this rat-hole and strike out on his own.

"You can let me have the payout at the office party tonight. It's at the Franchester at 8 o'clock. Wait till it gets in full swing, and then you can contact me without attracting attention. You'll recognise me easily enough. I'm going as the Frog Prince - green and yellow frog, crown and all!"

At 7.00 p.m., Carter decided he might as well get ready. The employees had been told they might well have to work late to get business finished for the Christmas break. It was safer, therefore, if they planned to change at the office and go straight on to the hotel. Accordingly, the offices and cupboards had been filled with a motley collection of finery.

Inside Miss Taylor's desk was a glittering sequined mask with which she hoped to convert her usual "little black number" into something exotic. Not much bigger than the mask, and draped from a hanger on the wall, hung Miss Stone's contribution to the evening's festivities. She claimed to be going as the "Snow Queen", and certainly, to judge from the minute quantity of white fabric, it was obviously intended for someone who didn't feel the cold.

The two women heard Mr. Carter shuffling around and pom-pomming to the strains of his electric razor. Then they heard the click of case latches and a few seconds of silence.

Suddenly there was a roar like Rudolph, nose lit up with the full mains voltage. The door slammed open, and out shot Carter, very nimbly for a man of his size, waving the remains of his cavalier costume. The jerkin was unimpaired, but the breeches would not even cover a Gay Rights follower's idea of modesty.

"Look at it!" he bellowed, purple with rage. "Ruined! Who's been in my office today?"

"Must have happened during the lunch hour, Mr. Carter," put in Janet, not batting a glistering, ice-covered eyelid. "Did you see anyone, Miss Taylor?"

"No I didn't. Whoever could have done such a thing?"

"Well, it's not good enough. I can't be expected to go in civvies. After all, I've got certain standards to set."

Carter careered down the corridor. He raged through the departments, bursting in on all sorts of employees in varying stages of undress, and to his credit with no discrimination on grounds of sex.

Eventually he arrived in the Accounts office. And there on the wall was just was he was looking for: a costume without anyone in it, or indeed near it.

By the time Tonks had carefully shaved and applied a liberal dowsing of aftershave to his less reliable parts, he emerged from the men's toilets ready to transform himself in green and yellow.

A horrifying spectacle met his gaze. What had been a tall, thin frog costume for a tall, thin man was stretched round the ample girth of a short, round man. The frog's flexible skin had met the challenge admirably in the wider parts and sagged into becoming wrinkles everywhere else, so that Carter looked like a reptile who had been over-ambitious with its dinner. Nevertheless, honour was satisfied. The boss was appropriately clad for the office fancy dress.

"Good of you, Tonks," he grunted. "I appreciate it. Not a bad fit really."

And Tonks watched in disbelief as his costume padded out of the door.

Foster Grant drove slowly along the approach roads to the town. Sheila leant contentedly beside him against the rich green leather. Henry would have been proud of her. Her pink dress scintillated under the passing lights, revealing curves her husband had forgotten she'd got. Her make-up was carefully blended to suggest that youth had not escaped her. In her dainty handbag was a small packet of crushed tablets that Henry had also forgotten, for the heart that he'd managed without quite ably for several years now.

"So you told him about the plans for a merger," she mused. "It should be easy enough to get him to celebrate the season tonight."

"Then it'll be a case of Happy New Year," grinned Foster. "What a shame he'll miss it."

He drew into the car park and handed Sheila out of the Porsche. She pressed not too obviously against him as they entered the hotel.

Shortly afterwards, a large frog eased his Mercedes into a reserved space. Walking was sufficiently a problem to occupy his attention, so that he did not notice a dark shape emerge from the shadows and head towards his car. After a glance round to make sure he was unobserved, the figure slid beneath the bodywork, reappearing only seconds later to make for the hotel, where he vanished into the privacy of the gentlemen's changing room.

By 9 o'clock the noise had reached almost intolerable levels, punctuated by shrill squeals as colleagues were recognised in unexpected guises, and sloshing still higher with the aid of quantities of liquor and a conscientious band.

At the balcony table reserved for the boss and his guests, Sheila tinkled seductively for the benefit of the guest, while the guest plied his host with unstinted measures of spirits.

Carter, ever mindful of the importance of his role, constantly slipped off to keep an eye on proceedings and let his employees know that once a year he could let his hair down with the best of them - metaphorically in his case, of course.

Wherever he went he was pursued by the anxious figure of Tonks, watching for the expected coming of the bearer of gifts. He had to intercept delivery before it fell into the wrong hands. The trouble was he didn't know who was to be the messenger boy. Every time he saw a masked or veiled form sidle up to Carter, he nearly had a fit. Fortunately for his nerves, there were few employees who actually made the first move. More were in the business of avoiding these jovial encounters.

Eventually Carter returned to his seat. He was getting decidedly merry by this time. Sheila and Foster looked meaningfully at each other and, when next Carter staggered to his feet to look over the balcony at his faithful minions, Sheila tipped the contents of the small packet into his drink.

"With all that alcohol, it can't fail," she said. "No-one could possibly suspect anything at such a function. Look at his face," she added. "It's red enough for a seizure now."

And indeed it was extremely red, as it sweated inside the neck of the Frog Prince.

In the crowd, Janet caught sight of Mr. Tonks, hovering to one side of Mr. Carter and a little behind him. The happiness of the occasion, the music, the rich food and the flowing drink had warmed the fair Snow Queen to her barely covered heart, and she blew an alcoholic kiss at the thin and tormented Mr. Tonks.

Carter, of course, imagined that the little minx was finally coming round to his way of thinking. As she wriggled and swung her promising hips in her white maiden's garb, he leant even further over the balustrade.

Just then a figure dressed as a highwayman moved swiftly up to Carter from the concealment of the hotel's ample greenery. Tonks could tell from the decisiveness of the movement that this was it.

Janet suddenly saw Mr. Tonks surge forward, and Sheila looked up just in time to see a large, bulging-eyed frog describe a graceful parabola off the balcony.

For a split second everyone was still, open-mouthed and incredulous as their respected boss continued his fall to the lower floor. He landed on the table below, already groaning with the weight of mince-pies and sausage rolls. It gave an indignant creak and crashed to the ground. Crisps showered down like confetti, and everything came to a shocked halt. The frog's legs lay spread-eagled among the fairy cakes and spattered with aspic jelly.

Janet couldn't believe what she had seen. Who would have thought Mr. Tonks could have it in him! What could have inspired that murderous rush? Surely it wasn't the cavalier theft of the frog costume. Though he must have felt out of place as the only one not in fancy dress. Some kind of last straw, she supposed.

Sheila had glimpsed the push to her husband and the dart through the rush of attenders on the fallen idol. She couldn't understand it at all. She looked at Foster in horror. It was one thing for her to murder her husband. She had every justification. After all, she was his wife. But a perfect stranger! What could it all mean?

Tonks had seen it too, but it didn't take his accountant's mind long to work out the reckoning. So they wanted him out of the way. As a source of information he was becoming too expensive. Besides, he knew a lot about their operations. It was he, after all, who was supposed to be dressed as a frog. Carter had muscled in on someone else's action once too often.

He felt weak, appalled by the image of himself taking that fatal plunge. He staggered across to the adjacent table and gulped down the whisky standing conveniently to hand.

After the Police had questioned everyone with anything to tell, the partygoers were allowed to leave, with the prospect for some of renewed stardom at the inquest.

Janet's account had made a particular impression, and now she looked forward to seeing her picture on the front page of every newspaper. How lucky she'd invested in some waterproof mascara, and how she'd hold centre stage at every gathering this Christmas!

The grieving widow, who had managed almost genuine hysteria for several minutes after the sudden carnage, was escorted from the scene by the faithful family friend.

"We might as well take your car," said Foster. "It'll look better, and it'll give me an excuse to stay the night. Not that I need it really - the shock of young Tonks's death was enough to upset anyone.

"Sporting of old Henry to do the job for us like that!"

"Didn't you see what happened?" whispered Sheila.

"Just fell, didn't he?" queried Foster. "Just like I told the inspector. Had too much to drink and overbalanced. Serves him right for ogling that young floozy."

"But he was pushed!" Sheila said. "I saw someone push him."

"Yes, odd thing that. That's what that young girl kept on saying. She seemed to think young Tonks had committed hara-kiri out of remorse. Another one with too much Christmas spirit."

"The police reckoned he'd had a heart attack with the shock," Sheila offered wryly. She looked at Foster, and they smiled at their own cleverness.

Foster revved up the car.

They passed the village sign that signalled the approach to home. He squeezed the accelerator and the car leapt forward, speeding towards the sharp bend at the top of the downhill run.

"New Year, here we come! Make way for the Merry Widow!"

And they were still laughing when he stamped on an unresisting brake, and the executive Mercedes left the road in a graceful parabola!

DEATH ON THE A5

Wipers flickflacked in front of his straining eyes. Baxter had well exceeded his maximum hours, but if he pushed on he'd be home and dry by two o'clock. A bit of nifty fiddling with the tachograph had given him quite a few days off, time for some jars down the pub and a game of darts.

Water cantered down the windscreen. The wipers raced, but the road ahead blurred and cleared, blurred and cleared, visibility lessening with each sweep. Headlights seared into his eyeballs and crazed the glass into a pattern of molten light. Another lorry, a blaze of splintered red from front to back, surged slowly past him, blinding him with spray.

He pressed his foot down, clawing back the yards, and forced his way forward until he was parallel with the other driver. The two lorries roared along the screaming tarmac, a tidal wave of male aggression.

At the last second he saw him. A dark figure caught for a fraction of time in his headlights. Coat flapping round his gaunt figure, face haggard in the beam. One hand was thrown up to ward off danger. The other still clutched the neck of a bottle.

Baxter hardly felt the bump, but he knew he'd hit him, and he knew that would be it. Curtains.

He should have stopped. He should have gone back to see what he could do. But he knew he could do nothing. Instead he veered away from his rival at the next junction and pulled into a layby a few miles on.

His heart was still thumping and leaping, and the blood pounded in his head.

"Stupid old fuck! What was he doing in the road anyway? Asking for it. If it hadn't been me it would have been the next guy."

He told himself that nobody could have seen what he had done. Nobody could identify him. Who could see numberplates with it pissing down like this? The best thing he could do was get back home and get his head down. Keep it down too. He'd feel better in the morning.

It wasn't on the news for several days. People swept up and down those roads in droves, focussing always ahead, at the rear of the car in front, at the white lines flashing past, at the rearview mirror, at

133

the long straight channel narrowing into the distance.

And then the police had noticed the crows, flocking at the side of the road, the odd stray snapping and snarling to keep off other scavengers. The body would be hard to identify. Nothing in missing persons. Just some old vagrant no-one would miss. Dead in a ditch, unmourned and unimportant.

Baxter breathed again. Home and dry. He had a shave, put on his check shirt and his best jeans, and went to his local to see if he could pull.

A month of so later, he'd managed another few days off. It was too wet to tempt him out, so he lounged in front of the tele, at his knee a bag of chips, at his right hand a half empty glass of bitter. Rings of sliding foam clung thickly to the sides, marking every swig. He hadn't bothered to build a fire. It was much easier to turn on the electric. His fingers played deftly over the controls on his knee, and manipulated the violence of his favourite videogame.

He was so intent on the on-screen bloodshed that at first he didn't notice the scuffling in the wall. When he did, he realised it was coming from the chimney breast. And a powdering of soot sifted into the grate. What the devil! At the thought the sound stopped, and he went back to his game. Perhaps a gust of wind had dislodged some of last year's build-up. He'd have to get it swept.

But the noise resumed as a distinct scratching of nails. He listened with half his mind to whatever it was scrabbling about, bringing down more and more dirt. Bloody bird, I should think. Well if it had managed to get in, he supposed it would manage to get out. Perhaps he'd give it an incentive by lighting a bit of paper in the grate.

A frantic fluttering suggested the bird had read his mind. Either way, it ruined his concentration. His alter ego was obliterated with less than 200 dead warriors to show for it. He'd never beat his score at this rate.

He put the machine in pause, got up and rattled a poker in the fire basket. The scrambling intensified, and with a thump a large bird suddenly flopped down in front of him. A puff of soot smutted his shirt and smarted in his eyes.

Squinting, he made a grab at the scraggy bundle that wallowed in the grate, but it stabbed at his fingers with a vicious beak and lifted off into the room. Wherever it flew, it scattered a dusting of black. Chasing it and lashing about with the poker only made matters worse. He leapt to the window and flung it wide open, but this invitation seemed quite lost on the stupid runt. It bashed into walls and cupboards, everywhere scattering filth from every feather. An attempt to round it up left him with claw marks to hands and face.

When Baxter finally had the sense to retreat to a corner, the bird at last hurled itself from the room.

He looked at the devastation in disbelief. How could one bird make all that mess? Well he was damned if he was going to clear it up. He'd get in a woman in the morning.

He was still trembling with frustration and effort. He reached for his glass. He was about to drink when he noticed the oily slicks floating on the surface. Flinging a newspaper over the chair, he slumped down in it with a fresh bottle and stared in disgruntlement at the frozen screen. No point carrying on with that tonight.

He flicked over to the TV channels in time to see a brief newsflash on the progress of the police in the case of the Body on the A5. They were linking it to the disappearance from a Nursing Home of an old boy with dementia.

"DT's more like," was Baxter's response. "Did him a favour if you ask me."

And once again he set the matter easily to the back of his mind, even when his lorry sped past the same section of road, with its straggle of birches and bushes on either side of the carriageway. It was, after all, one of his regular runs, and he had other things to think about.

Shortly before Christmas, on the same run, snow sliding relentlessly into his windscreen, he was beginning to think of putting up for the night. The monotony of the engine and the hum of the fan blasting hot air into the cab affected his concentration. He seemed to be sliding into a torpor.

One second he was staring at the white flakes swooping towards him; next there was a wild flurry of tattered rags and his vision was blotted out by a solid ball of pure darkness. There was a loud thud right in front of his eyes, then the object was whisked away in the slipstream. It took his shocked brain a second to realise what it was.

But he'd automatically stamped on the brakes, and felt the lorry slide sideways till its wheels were half over the ditch. A blaze of light and a blare of sound sped past him on the outside. The stink of burning rubber hit his nostrils as an articulator slithered to a standstill, and its back end slewed round screeching across the carriageway.

As he opened the cab door, the other driver appeared at his side, face swollen with rage.

"You bloody halfwit! What were you trying to do, get us both killed? Look at my fucking lorry.

Baxter just sat where he was.

"Did you hear what I said? What did you brake like that for? I nearly went into the fucking back of you."

Baxter went into automatic. "Then you shouldn't be right up my fucking arse should you! Specially in these conditions. You should learn to drive mate!"

"Don't tell me about driving! Stamping on the brake for no reason. Like a fucking lunatic."

"There was a bird. Hit my windscreen."

"A bird! At this time of night?"

"Probably dazzled by my headlights."

"What kind of bird flies at this time of night?"

"Could be an owl," another voice chimed in.

By this time a small knot of other vehicles had collected behind the blockage. One had a flashing light on its roof and the dark figures of two policemen were pushing aside the onlookers. They arrived in time for Baxter's response.

"Not an owl. Definitely not an owl. As black as pitch. If it wasn't for the glass it would have hit me in the face."

"Pity it didn't," snarled the other driver. "Somebody should."

"All right, all right, sir. We'll take care of this." And the man was shepherded back to his vehicle to give his own separate account, while Baxter was required to step down from his lorry and do the same. Both drivers had their names and details taken, and both were breathalysed. And it took over an hour for the haulage equipment to arrive and drag the two lorries back into position.

The Policy were inclined to disbelieve the tale of a suicidal bird and suspected the driver of dozing off at the wheel. Nevertheless, they had no proof, so they had to let him go with a stern warning. Baxter was considerably shaken up. He'd have to watch his step from now on.

Towards the end of February, after a winter of bitter rain and leaden skies, he once more sat in his warm cab eating up the miles from Oswestry to London. On Talk Radio James Whale was making his usual inflammatory remarks to some tosser who'd phoned in about delinquents on his estate. Dunno why he didn't just give 'em a quiet going over. 'Stead of a load of bollocks to bore the pants off you.

He reached across to switch to Radio One. If you wanted to be brain dead might as well do it to music. He helped himself to a twix from the dashboard.

He was ripping it open with his teeth when a sharp explosion came from under the chassis and the steering wheel wrenched through his fingers. Once again he found himself facing onto the side of the road, the powerful beams illuminating the spindly trees.

Baxter thumped the wheel in exasperation. A bloody puncture now! This stretch of bloody road seemed to be bloody jinxed.

He reversed onto the carriageway and drew forward into the edge. Clambering from the cab he walked the length of the lorry, shining a torch on every tyre. On the near side he found it. Had to be a front tyre didn't it! He might have got away with one of the doubles at the back. Driven onto the next service station and had it fixed while he grabbed himself a bite to eat. Could've been sat in a nice warm café instead of standing about round here in the sodding rain.
Still he couldn't be arsed to wait around for the breakdown service.

Trudging to the back, he hauled out the heavy bottle jack, fixing it under the front axle and blocking the rear wheels with wedges. Then he trundled the spare alongside the body of the lorry and bent to undo the wheelnuts and ease off the flat.

As he worked he became aware that someone was standing at his side. He noticed the boots first, very battered and scuffed. Then the bottoms of some greasy trousers, ripped and stained with dirt.

"It's all right mate. I can manage."

But the fellow made no attempt to move. Baxter's nose was assailed with a stale reek emanating from his clothes, sharp and sickly. Impatiently he swung round to tell the old bleeder to clear off.

But there was no-one there.

He looked up and down the road - still no-one. He swung his torch in an arc through the trees and thought he caught a flicker of movement among the dead brambles. What looked like the tail of a coat fluttered into the light before being extinguished in the dark of the wood.

Above the wood the sky still carried some light from a nearby town. Low down he saw the heavy rake of wings, black against the amber glow. They descended into the surrounding treetops and set up a bleak and raucous cry. Rooks. Fooled by the artificial dusk. He'd heard of that.

Once more he scanned the woodland with his torch and, for an instant, suspended in the beam, he saw a ravaged face, the eyes and mouth hollowed in shadow. One arm was thrown up, like an image caught in phosphorous and burned onto his brain.

It wasn't possible.

"Hey you! Come here you old bastard."

The image blinked out.

Baxter started into the wood, determined to have it out with him. But he hadn't gone a few yards when the air was full of beating wings and battering discord.

He turned on his heel and sprinted towards the lorry. As he reached it and made to snatch open the door, he found himself under attack. Beaks stabbed at his arms, his face. Claws ripped through the leather of his jacket as if it was paper.

He swung round with the torch, battering at the frenzied rooks. For a second they wavered. He wrenched at the handle and tried to scramble to safety, but they were back. The onslaught was even more ferocious; the noise was overwhelming. In the darkness their eyes burned with yellow fire.

Covering his head with his arms and shielding his face, he dropped into a crouch and dived under the lorry. He grabbed up the lever that still lay by the wheel and lashed out at any rook that tried to follow him.

He didn't hear the soft clunk as the engine was knocked out of gear. He didn't see the brake lever shift in its socket. He didn't hear the wedges slither to the side or see the rear wheels start to turn. But he did hear the grate and groan of the jack as it lurched under the pressure. And he saw the axle drop. Trapped by the crushing weight, and dragged along, he finally came to rest, as did the lorry, with his body firmly wedged beneath its back wheels.

> "Light thickens, and the crow makes wing
> To the rooky wood."   (Macbeth)

LEGEND

She stumbled past the beckoning arms of the King's Tavern. Lights glowed invitingly through the low windows, gleamed in the highlights of the bullseye panes. Clinging to its warped wood frames, the top storey bulged over the cobbled forecourt. Nothing was quite at right-angles. If you thought you weren't drunk when you staggered out, a backward glance would convince you that you were.

Gwendoline left the lights behind and set off along the gravelled path. She could feel the stones pressing up through the thin soles of her shoes. She dragged her party stole closer round her shoulders, and regretted that she'd run out in such a temper. The night was filthy. Rain beat into her face, needled with cold. She could hardly see where she was going. But still she pressed on to her refuge, her place of dreams, where she could leave behind the petty treacheries that stung her heart.

The way dropped down through the defile. Now she could hear the breaking waves above the noise of the wind, battering the rocks that lined the shore. High tide. She could imagine the water roaring through the cave that bored from one side of the promontory to the other.

Before she reached the bottom of the path, she veered off to the left, following a winding sheep track that led up to the castle ruins. Inside their ragged stone walls she could shelter from the gale. She could feel in touch with a world where honour meant something, where courage and nobility were expected qualities, where feasts took place under iron circles of blazing candles, and dogs waited hopefully for bones on strewn rushes. Wine and conviviality flowed.

Not the restrained and mealy-mouthed correctness that passed for hospitality in her home!

She wandered between high walls towards the great arch at the end. Here a set of steps carved for tourists descended to a lower path, where a bridge spanned the breach that had grown between the mainland and the headland. Even before she reached the opening she was caught by a forceful gust. The descent would be difficult. The other side would be dangerously windy once she'd tackled the precipitous route to the top. The haven to the east usually gave some shelter, but the west was exposed to the rushing tides of the Atlantic.

Yet when she stood in the archway the sight that met her struck her with amazement.

No steps descended the cliff face. Instead a graceful curve across a shallow depression carried a wide bridge to the headland.

Torches flamed in brackets along its sides. A crush of people and horses coursed across its length. The men were dressed in rough tunics, their leggings crisscrossed with strips of leather. Women chattered noisily as they joined the crowd. Woollen skirts flowed around their ankles. A couple wore jewelled belts around their hips. A jolly woman bustled along, her red face flaming from the white cloths which swathed her head. A set of keys jangled from her waist, and she picked her skirts up shamelessly high to avoid the droppings of the horses.

Gwen was drawn into the throng and found herself carried along on a wave of excitement. All round her people laughed and jostled. The royal sails had breached the skyline an hour or two earlier, and a brisk breeze now carried the vessel rapidly shorewards in the half-light.

As the crowd entered the portals on the other side, she hardly had time to notice the defence walls she had passed through. No longer the crumbling ruins she was familiar with. Low stone walls now supported a great timber stockade. Once through it, they turned down the fall of land to the harbour, where a great slab of natural rock produced a landing stage, the Iron Gate. There to greet the king.

The moment he stepped onto the quayside, he almost vanished in a tide of retainers, tugging at his clothes, slapping his shoulders and flinging arms around him. Gwen could see his flushed face above the crowd. His dark hair looked thick and tangled under the circle of grey metal that crowned his authority. His lips showed red and laughing through his beard and moustache, and his eyes gleamed with the joy of homecoming.

Behind him the warriors were greeting their own families, hugging their wives, swinging their children off the ground and planting them with rough kisses.

On the beach of the haven another craft had been drawn up and was already being unloaded. Horses were being led up the beach; men shouldered barrels and crates onto a waiting cart.

Gradually the mob around the king moved back along the path leading to the settlement. And there was the man himself, back from defeating the Saxons. The red of his cloak was pinned at the shoulder with a brooch scrolled in gold. Every inch the royal hero, followed by his fighting men.

Gwendoline stood at the side of the path. She didn't know whether she was expected to curtsey. She wasn't even sure that she was visible and, if she was, what they would make of her. But as Arthur drew level - and surely it was Arthur, despite the lack of surcoats and armour - he stopped and blew her an ironic kiss.

"Ah, the Lady Morgwynna, Dragged herself away from her scribblings to greet her ageing cousin. Well, Gwenny, since you are here, consider yourself commanded into the royal presence at the feast of welcome. It could be that, among my errant men-at-arms, you may find you have a suitor. And don't give him short shrift this time. At nineteen it's high time you were married off!"

Gwen wondered if she should tell him about Morton, but was not sure he would be able to hear her, let alone be pleased that the favoured follower had a rival.

"Cat got your tongue? Just remember - beauty does not linger for ever. Before you know it, you'll be a shrivelled old crone who's sick of her own company."

Gwendoline was disconcerted, until his hand fell on her shoulder and he roared with laughter.

She could still hear him laughing as she felt another hand, this one gently shaking her. She looked up to find it was Robert, the family gardener and general help. She was lying against the sheltered end of the lower courtyard on the mainland. Despite this she was soaked through with the soft mist that now drizzled from a dark sky.

"Come on Miss Gwen. This is no place to be at this time of night."

She rose stiffly to her feet and he wrapped a jacket round her shoulders. "You'll catch your death."

She was touched by his concern. She'd known Rob ever since he was a boy trailing after his father, who was then head gardener. In the long summer holidays, when her school friends were away with their families, she'd often appreciated his company, though he'd never presumed on their friendship - too well trained.

"Your mother and father were worried about you."

"Worried were they? Not worried enough I'd say. If they're so bothered, they shouldn't have driven me away!"

Robert put an arm round her shoulders. "You'd better come home. I'm freezing even if you aren't."

She looked at his concerned face, then noticed that the jacket she wore was his. Without another word, she let him steer her towards the exit. She trudged by his side until they reached the landrover.

"How did you know where to find me?"

"I know you well enough by now. Where else would you be?"

Reversing in a wider section of track, he ground the vehicle up the rough incline to the tarmacked road.

Just outside Tintagel, he turned into the long driveway of

Trevena Manor. Although the windows were all still brightly lit, the visitors' cars had gone. So she'd spoiled the Christmas celebrations. So what! They'd been spoiled for her the moment she'd introduced Morton Anders to her parents.

Her mother's smile had frozen in mid-sentence to Mrs. Angela Hope, who was gushing noisily over the sheer honour of being invited. Having bundled her out of the way in the direction of the buffet, she turned her full attentions to the tall figure which stood beside her daughter. And she didn't offer him her hand. Her father made a point of turning to the next arrival and shepherding him to the far side of the room, where he introduced him to another of his business acquaintances.

Her mother eyed Morton frostily up and down, as if his immaculate dress had turned to stinking rags. "I don't think we've met, Mr....er..."

"Anders, mummy. You know perfectly well who he is."

"And where do you come from, Mr. Anders?"

"London, Mrs. Robartes."

"London's a big place. Which part of London?"

"I have a mews house in Bayswater, Mrs. Robartes."

Her mother seemed less than mollified. Gwendoline did not supply the knowledge that it was actually an apartment. After all, it was only his Town address. His main residence was somewhere in the wilds of Yorkshire. Bayswater was just his pied-a-terre.

"And what do you do for a living, Mr. Anders?"

"Morton came here for a party, mummy, not an interrogation!" And taking his arm she marched him away in the direction of her friends, who gathered round him and soon negated any effects of his initial reception by admiring his good taste in girlfriends and laughing at all his jokes.

Gwendoline was able to avoid further contact with her parents until the party was winding down. Then she discovered that Morton had been put in the annexe with the other waifs and strays.

"I'm sorry, dear," her mother told her calmly, "but the main bedrooms are full of family. I'm sure Mr. Anders -"

"Morton!"

"...will be comfortable enough."

Morton gave an easy laugh. "I can make myself comfortable anywhere, Mrs. Robartes."

"I'm sure you can, Mr. Anders. I'll have Henderson show you the way."

Morton winked at Gwendoline with a quizzical smile and followed Henderson obediently from the room.

"Mummy! How could you be so rude?"

"I thought I was politeness itself."

"You know perfectly well you weren't. I've never been so humiliated. And daddy was just as bad."

"I'm not aware that your father has even spoken to him."

"That's just the point. He hasn't! You know how important this evening was for me. I'll never forgive you for this. Either of you!"

And before her mother had time to object, Gwendoline had banged out into the night and disappeared down the drive.

It wasn't surprising she'd made for the castle. As a child she'd spent hours raking around the headland, pestering the tourists with extended eulogies on every minor feature. They didn't seem to mind. They were bemused that such a small girl should have such apparent knowledge. She created dens in the outlines of iron-age houses, and danced in and out of the ancient chapel walls. She picked the heather and decorated the well at the top of the rise. Sitting among the mounds that lined the walled garden, she listened to bards singing songs in praise of Arthur. She played upon lutes and harps and threw sticks to the hounds. She heard the women swapping stories, and watched them making their husband's shirts. For hours she sat on the north cliffs, arms folded round her knees, watching for a sail.

At home, in her father's study, she'd pored over tales of chivalry and romance, of black knights and imprisoned maidens. She crept into caves hung with icicles, where Sir Gawain slept in his cold armour. The only shelter in the snowy wastes on his journey to meet The Green Knight. She followed Sir Galahad on his quest for the Grail, and wept for courageous warriors slain by ravening dragons. She shuddered at the treachery of Mordred and Agravaine, and waited for Arthur, the Once and Future King, to come galloping up the slopes of the headland brandishing Excalibur.

As she grew older, she puzzled over the crumbled walls extending round the old chapel on the south side, and thought of the original Arthur. If his own dwelling had not been on the site of the medieval castle, surely it would be here, adjacent to the chapel, close to the walled garden and the well, and surrounded by the homes and workshops of his people. And if he was buried anywhere, it had to be nearby. Did those mounds at Tintagel Church hold the secret of his resting place?

And now she had left behind her personal Avalon, her place of healing, for the aggravation of her so-called home.

Her parents came to the door the moment the landrover swung over the gravel. They both looked relieved, though clearly strained. She even thought she detected tears in her mother's eyes. She was certainly clutching a handkerchief. If they'd been so worried, why hadn't they looked for her themselves instead of sending Rob? To be fair Rob was the best choice of help, and the house had been full of visitors. But she didn't see why she should be fair to them when they'd been so unfair to her.

Next thing she found her mother's arms around her and her father leading them both back into the house. Rob went to garage the car.

They sat her in the big armchair in front of the fire, and Henderson put on a few more logs. Her mother was actually patting her hands and kneeling at her feet. Her father had pulled up another chair beside her. What was going on?

"I'm sorry dear. I didn't mean to upset you." Gwendoline didn't respond. Her father cleared his throat. "We only want what's best for you," her mother added.

Her father leaned towards her. "The thing is, Gwenny, we don't know anything about this chap."

"Anything about him? Has he got two heads or something? No, what you really mean is that you don't trust me."

"Of course we trust you," put in her mother. "It's him we're not so sure about."

"What is there to be sure about? Was he improperly dressed? Did he eat off his knife - or wipe his fingers on the table cloth? What I meant was you don't trust me to be able to choose for myself."

"Well you are rather young, dear."

"And more to the point, Gwenny, he is rather old. He must be twice your age - at least!"

"Age is a matter of opinion father. And my friends didn't find anything wrong with him. Didn't you notice how well he got on with them all?"

"Yes, but he isn't marrying any of your friends, Gwendoline. He's marrying you!"

Gwen's face flushed with triumph. "I'm pleased to hear you say that."

"What your mother meant to say was, 'What's in it for him?'"

"Me, father, me! Or do you think he'd need his head testing to find me remotely attractive!"

144

"No of course not, Gwenny. But why haven't we met him before? Where has he come from? We know nothing about him. And you can't have known him very long."

"If someone's right for you, you don't need 'long' father. I knew at our first meeting that here was someone very special. I just knew he was the one!"

"Oh you and your love at first sight, Gwendoline! Life isn't like all that romantic stuff you fill your head with. You can't assume that because someone's good looking he's also noble, loyal and true, let alone that he'd make a reliable husband."

"Didn't you just know that daddy was the man for you?"

"Not initially, no. In fact at first I thought he was too wrapped up in his veteran cars and his horses."

"But weren't you attracted to him?"

"To his estate, certainly." Her mother gave a knowing smile at her husband. "And the rest of him grew on me the longer I knew him." She actually reached up and touched his cheek.

"But in this case, my dear," her father submitted, "it isn't him who's got the estate. It's you."

Gwen saw what he was driving at. "But how do you know that? You know nothing about him."

"Exactly our point. We don't even know how you met him."

"He was at one of Terence Forster's parties. In fact it was Terence who introduced us."

"And how did Terence know him?"

"He was a guest of Angela King's."

"And yet he attached himself to another young lady."

"They're only friends, daddy. Apparently Angela pointed me out and he was keen to meet me."

"And what had she told him about you?"

"I don't know - just that we were a West Country family and I was up in London for a few weeks."

Her father glanced across at her mother. "I wonder what he concluded from that?"

"I think he thought that I might be glad of someone to show me around!"

"And did he?" Her mother's voice had something of an edge.

Gwendoline adopted the same tone. "Yes."

"Well, Angela King might know a lot of people, but she's hardly what I'd call discriminating. And Terence is better at spending his father's money than making his own. How does this Morton make a living?"

"I don't know, mummy - something in the city! But he never expected me to pay for anything, if that's what you mean."

"Could he be playing the long game?" This from her father.

"Really, daddy, I don't know why you should think he's up to anything at all? Why should he want your estate when he's a place of his own in the north?"

"What kind of place? Where in the north?" Her mother returned to the third degree.

Gwen rose suddenly from her chair. "Oh I don't know! Somewhere in Yorkshire. And then there's his London flat."

"Oh, a flat. I see. I thought it was a house. That's what he said."

"House! Flat! What does it matter! I'm going to bed. If you can't be happy for me, you'll just have to stay unhappy. I'm old enough to do as I like. If I choose to marry him I will. It's nobody's business but ours. Nobody needs your permission!"

This time when she slammed the door at least it was into the house.

Richard Robartes looked solemnly at his wife. "And on those terms do you think he'll go ahead with it?"

"I shouldn't think so for one moment. Though perhaps we've given her something to think about."

They had. But it didn't make any difference. And they were wrong about Anders too. She left with him the following morning, before the others were up, and within a month they had received notice that the wedding would take place in May. It didn't seem to be an invitation.

It is true that Morton Anders would have preferred more time to get to know his future in-laws. In fact he had tried to persuade Gwendoline of the wisdom of sticking it out and giving him a chance to bring them round. But she was adamant. Nothing can be so headstrong as a young woman determined to teach her parents a lesson. Nothing would suit her but to shake the dust of her detested home from her heels. Morton, however, took the time she was flinging her newly unpacked cases back together again to cast his eye over some of the grounds. He had, after all, arrived in the dark. It was interesting to confirm what he'd driven through.

Once in Bayswater, Gwendoline set all her energies to arranging a wedding in the area. No expense would be spared. All her friends would be invited and as many of Morton's friends and relations as he thought fit.

"Oh I don't know about that. You don't make so many real friends in the City. Colleagues, yes, but most of them best kept at a distance."

"What about your aunts, uncles, cousins and things?"

"Well you know how it is. Lost contact with most of them - scattered to the four winds. Half of them dead, and the rest either incommunicado or disappeared into the ether. You know."

Gwen did not know. Most of her relatives seemed obstinately glued to the West Country, and determined to make their presence as noticed as possible. "If only your parents were still alive."

"Yes."

She put her hand on his. "It seems so awful that you're getting married and they can't be here to see it. You must miss them dreadfully."

"Well not really – not any longer anyway. They have, after all, been dead for some years now, and I'm a bit past the age to consider myself an orphan."

"Yes, I suppose so, but - "

"But your parents, Gwendoline, are not dead. In fact they are very much alive. Don't you think they'll be rather hurt if you don't ask them?"

"If **we** don't ask them you mean."

"No. If **you** don't ask them. In fact, if you don't at least give them the chance of marrying you from home you could end up regretting it. I gather they're quite the sticklers for family tradition. They might be so humiliated that they cut off contact altogether."

"They can stew in their own juice so far as I'm concerned. They didn't care about tradition when they made you so unwelcome as a guest in their home. They turned their backs on you. Now let them see what it feels like."

"We probably took them a bit by surprise, you know. And perhaps they expected me to do the old asking-permission thing. It must have seemed very sudden. One minute they'd never even heard of me and the next their only daughter is unofficially engaged to me."

"All the more reason, then, to get to know you."

"To be fair, they really didn't get much of a chance - and having all their other guests to look after they were bound to be a bit distracted."

"Distracted! They were jolly rude."

"Probably not intentionally."

"Don't be so forgiving. You never heard the way they went on

147

about you. How much older you were."

"Well that's true, of course. But you know what they say about old wine....." He gave her a playful squeeze. "Anyway, it takes a lot of maturity to recognise a good thing when you see it."

She wasn't deflected. "And they had the cheek to imply you were only after my money."

"What money's that then? Yes, that was a bit of a cheek. Still, as you say, they don't really know me. Why don't we give them a chance?"

"No way!"

"You know, you'll regret it if you don't. You don't realise how these things build up. What happens when you have children, and they're kept out of that? What happens when they get old, and one of them dies? There's nothing worse than losing someone and knowing you've missed the chance to tell them what you really feel."

"I don't care."

"You will care, Gwendoline."

He switched mood, grabbing her and tickling her. "And what if the wicked squire cuts you off without a shilling?"

"I don't care about that either. It's not as if we need their money, is it?"

"Of course not .... but it's a pity to waste it!" He sat astride her and nibbled her neck. She shoved him off but did not seem really to mind. He followed up his advantage.

"But what about you? Don't you want to be married from that Tintagel Church you're always on about? What about taking your vows within sight and sound of the presiding spirit of the place? Wasn't there something about some mysterious mounds in the church precincts?"

Now he had touched a vein that ran deep. He saw her hesitate and knew the battle was won.

She left it to him to write, however, and he took full opportunity of the chance to cast himself in a better light.

After some preliminaries as to how concerned he was that they had left without even saying goodbye, he set out his stall. He had never quite persuaded Gwendoline to say what had so upset her, but he imagined they would have more idea. He had tried to get her to resume some contact, but she'd refused. They must know how strong-willed she was. It was one of the many things he most admired about her. When it came to getting married with none of her family around her, however, he had pressed her more firmly, and she had confessed that the situation was causing her distress. She had asked him to write on her behalf:

"You are of course invited to the Bayswater wedding (he enclosed a tastefully printed card, RSVP), but I am worried about Gwendoline. I can tell that she is missing you both deeply, though she is too proud to own to that personally.

"As you will know, she has always cherished the idea of a wedding from home, to be led up the aisle of Tintagel Church on the arm of her father and surrounded by family. I feel certain that, if you were to write directly to her and suggest it, she would be overjoyed to accept a change of venue, and this painful rift between you would be healed.

"I am sorry to have been the unwilling cause of this rift, though I can never regret the fact that we love each other. I know it must concern you that I am somewhat older than she is, but I assure you that I will devote myself to her happiness. When I met her and we were so obviously compatible, I could hardly believe my luck. I feel now that in some ways I have been waiting for her all my life. What I want is what she wants.

"For this reason, although our plans at this end are considerably advanced, I would be quite prepared to cancel everything if you preferred to put on the wedding at Tintagel. I have formed the impression that, whatever the fashionable idea is here, outside the Capital people still prefer what is traditional. Gwendoline's real feelings on this are obviously the same as yours.

"A quick reply would be helpful."

"I bet it would!"

The Robartes exchanged glances. Richard sat back in his chair and tapped a finger on the table. "Far better than having to shell out for an expensive London affair."

Neither of them believed for a moment that the sentiments expressed were genuine. Nevertheless, they conceded that it was a chance to repair the bond with their child.

What Anders said about her temperament was certainly true. In most things she was sweet-natured and loyal, but now that sense of loyalty was endangering their continued relations. She had transferred it to someone they considered unworthy of her. But she'd never allow herself even to think her parents could be right. And once she'd made up her mind, there was no shifting her.

They wrote to her as requested, apologizing for any misunderstandings. They begged her to allow them to put on the marriage from Tintagel, in the ancient church their family had attended

149

for generations. It would, of course, be easier to do this if she was on hand to say exactly what she wanted. She and Morton could bring lists of guests and wedding gifts when they came, assuming Morton could leave his business affairs for a few days.

Morton could. In fact he spent more of his time in Cornwall than they were comfortable with. However, he kept himself busy with lots of confidential calls, the odd overnight stay and long weekends in London.

Gwendoline was satisfied that her parents had made amends, and where Morton was concerned they were certainly on their best behaviour. They bought her an extravagant trousseau for her honeymoon and filled the church and house with flowers and music. The most expensive caterers were employed, and the locals were satisfied that everything had been done in a manner befitting one of the oldest families in the county.

In the event, the only guests on Morton's side were his best man, the best man's sister and a few hangers-on. The sister's taste in make-up seemed a little over the top and her neckline a little below it, but she clearly enjoyed all the wine and attention, and trotted round after the happy couple with a slightly tipsy leer. Gwen was too happy to notice anything but her handsome new husband.

They came back from three weeks in the Seychelles with a healthy tan and stayed another week before returning to London. Gwendoline seemed ecstatically happy and Morton maintained a sleek and well satisfied demeanour.

Near the end of their stay, Richard waylaid Morton on his way out of breakfast, and led him into his study. Morton was amused by this old-fashioned approach. Richard closed the door and crossed to his chair. As he sat down, he motioned the other man into the chair opposite. It was a bit late for any pre-nuptial words of wisdom, and Robartes had had the sense to leave the topic unbroached. Now, however, he opened his drawer and fetched out a bulky envelope. He reached across the desk and gave the packet to Morton.

"As you will see, it is addressed to Gwendoline, but as her husband you have a right to know the contents."

Morton's response was lighthearted. "I doubt if Gwendoline would agree with you!" He fingered the packet and anticipated a considerable leap in his fortunes.

"Inside is my daughter's marriage settlement."

Promising! Morton looked politely interested.

"I for one am old-fashioned enough to believe in doing the right thing, and I want to ensure her future welfare."

"Well of course she has me to do that," Morton smiled.

"Be that as it may. I have drawn up a Trust in favour of my daughter and to operate within my lifetime and beyond. The trustees will ensure that monies spent are for the benefit of my daughter and any children. My Will makes provision for my wife's continued occupancy and enjoyment of this property until her own death, when the bulk of my estate will pass in trust to my grandchildren. Failing grandchildren, it will pass to my brother and his heirs, of which there are many."

Morton's expression did not change. He felt a grudging admiration for the old fox. He'd been bested!

"I don't understand, sir, these seem extraordinary lengths to go to. Who could have Gwendoline's best interests more at heart than I would? I am astonished at such an apparent lack of trust, not only towards me but towards your daughter. She is no longer a child. After all, she is a married woman."

"I am only too aware of that. As for my daughter, I would trust her with my life. But as to yourself, I have no great reason to trust you with hers."

Morton shot out of his chair, registering outrage at the slur on his character. "Really Mr. Robartes – "

"Really Mr. Anders! Did you think I would hand over my daughter and what will one day be a small fortune to someone I knew nothing about? No. I too have contacts in the city – wide contacts - and in a position to know. And let me tell you, Mr. Anders, not one of them had heard of you."

"The nature of my business, Mr. Robartes, is strictly confidential. It does not pay in my business to have a high profile."

"You might, I suppose, draw the wrong sort of attention from the authorities – perhaps even the Fraud Squad?"

"I cannot see how you are justified in these preposterous suspicions. If you were anyone other than Gwendoline's father I would sue you in every court in the country."

"I doubt that. You see I hired a detective to look into your affairs. No fixed office but merely a postal address and a telephone number that were constantly changed to outstrip any creditors – after you'd relieved them of their assets, of course. And what of this mysterious property in Yorkshire? Torn up by a freak hurricane I suppose. You have, of course, got an old mother in a council home in Walthamstow – and she hasn't seen you for years, has she?"

"I don't know where you're getting all this twaddle. Both my parents are dead."

151

"Impeccable sources, Mr. Anders. And, just in case you're thinking of giving my daughter a hard time, just remember I have contacts in high places who could have your backside behind bars as soon as look at you."

Morton shrugged his shoulders indifferently.

"I think you'll find my daughter can be very generous, and she won't be kept too short. Be a good boy, Morton, and I won't enlighten her on the other company you've been keeping."

"Huh!" Morton smirked as if he wasn't unduly bothered.

"But I shall naturally expect no less than marital fidelity from this time forth. Otherwise, as you can see 'Morton', I have plenty of cards in my pack.

Morton gave Robartes an ironic salute. "I think you will find me everything you expect in a son-in-law."

And certainly neither Gwendoline nor her mother noticed any change in his behaviour towards them.

Their return to London was scheduled for the day after next, and Gwendoline had set her heart on showing him round the castle and the headland. They would see it at its best before the site opened to tourists.

They set off at dawn, and Gwen gave him a knowledgeable and individual tour of the medieval castle on both sides of the landslip. He'd lagged behind on the steps to the island, relying heavily on the handrail while she darted ahead. Outside the castle, she swung right along the headland towards her childhood lookout. She was determined he'd see everything through her eyes.

Gwen dragged him to a point where the land sloped steeply down and then fell away in sheer, black cliffs. Driven by an onshore wind, the waves beat furiously upon the rocks that tumbled round their base.

Morton dropped onto a large boulder, still holding her hand. Her pace had left him breathless, but he made the best of it. "Not an inch further. You know what your mother said about being careful."

"What does she know?" The girl's voice was exultant and laughing. She slid her hand out of his and advanced further towards the edge. She stopped less than two feet before the drop and stood facing it, her arms spread wide, letting the wind tug at her clothes while she braced herself against it. A dark figure against a glittering stream of dancing water.

"Be careful, Gwen. If the wind drops for a moment you could go over."

"It won't drop. The wind is my friend. I know it like the pulsing of my own blood."

Morton did not reply. An idea formed in his head and he did nothing to stop it. What if the wind did drop, just for a second? That would leave Gwendoline falling through space and smashing onto the rocks – or falling into the surge and being dashed against the cliff. Either way she would be dead, and he would be free of what had turned out to be a poor investment.

In a way it was a shame. She was young and fresh, and he could have enjoyed her for a few months yet. But he was growing tired of her immaturity, her interminable enthusiasms about things which left him cold, her bright eyes on his, so expectant, so trusting. Well she wouldn't expect this. It would all be over before she knew what had happened. She wouldn't even have time to suffer. He didn't particularly want that. But he did want to be rid of this silly little girl. And he did want to get back to the experienced arms of his lover ... he smiled ... his several lovers. And Robartes wouldn't be able to do a thing about it!

He rose quietly to his feet.

In front of him Gwendoline's attention was focused on the horizon, and her face was lit with wonder. A red sail had cut the slow curve of the ocean at the midpoint. A dark vessel was being carried towards her on the speed of the wind. It grew rapidly larger. Now she could see the oars heaving in and out of the waves, propelling the craft forward in great lurches. It seemed to be borne on the crest of the water towards the Iron Gate.

Behind her stood Morton, intent on silence. She would not hear him coming.

Behind him a flood of men poured over the line of the hill. They pounded towards him, their faces dark and angry. At his first step towards her, a tall figure broke ahead of the rest, and his arm flung back. As it hurled forward, a javelin glittered in the air. It rushed towards the guilty man with deadly aim. It would not miss its target.

For a second, Morton was aware of something – some other presence. Was he observed?

As he turned, and turned, and turned, the javelin spun, and spun, and spun. He received the full force of it in his chest. He dropped to his knees, clutching the shaft. Blood gargled from his throat, and he fell forward across the boulder. He didn't know what hit him.

Gwendoline heard the crowd surging up below her. Then the first figures appeared on the slope. At their forefront was Arthur, fist raised in triumph. At his shoulder, his picked men, the sweat of battle still gleaming on their faces. All around rose up the cries of victory.

When he neared the point where she stood, Arthur stopped and turned to the pursuing crowd. He raised the great sword with one hand.

"The traitor is dead. So die all traitors!"

The risen sun glanced off the gleaming blade. He turned to face the group of men behind her. His towering figure surrounded by a blaze of gold which burned in the water. The crowd fell silent. Gwen took a step towards him, her eyes dazzled by his brilliance.

And then he was past her, and so were his cohort, a babble of noise sweeping on towards the homestead.

Suddenly the sound stopped. She became aware of the bell heather tapping lightly against her ankle. Its rough touch made her realize how close to the edge she had come; the slope that the warriors had ascended now fallen into the sea. How long had she been standing here?

Then she remembered Morton, and thought how he must be chafing behind her. She couldn't expect him to be as wrapped up in the place as she was.

At first the hillside looked deserted. Surely he hadn't gone off without her. His idea of a joke perhaps.

Then she noticed his body, crumpled behind the rock he'd been sitting on. She rushed across with a great cry. She rolled him over, but his grey eyes stared up at her with no recognition. She realized he was dead. She dropped at his side and cradled his head in her arms.

And that was where they found her, hours later, stiff with cold, eyes glazed in shock. They had to prise her off him. Her father wrapped her in a rug, and Rob carried her to the car. Others lifted the body of Morton and took it back to Trevena Manor, where it lay in state until the burial in Tintagel churchyard.

Heart attack, the doctor said, probably precipitated by the steep climb to the headland, though there was clearly an underlying heart problem.

Gwendoline's parents refrained from comment, but they gave their daughter the space she needed and plenty of time to recover from her loss. Her father thoughtfully extracted the Trust document from Morton's luggage.

In time Gwen married a local man, one she had known since childhood and whose quiet attentiveness eventually broke through her numbed defences. Her young heart warmed to a better tune.

Her new partner shared her passion for Tintagel and the old legends. He appreciated the traditions that shaped their lives. Her parents were delighted with her choice. And it wasn't long before they saw the future clambering on the Sheraton sofa and knocking a ball about the gracious lawns.

Most weekends there were trips around the wilds and beauty spots of Cornwall. And the children grew to the tales their mother told them, sitting among the vanished walls of the garden at Tintagel.

THE MACHINES STRIKE BACK

Fred lay quietly in the corner of his shed. Moonlight filtered through the dust of the windows and picked out the assortment of clutter that shared his space. Toppling stacks of plant pots were occupied only by spiders and centipedes. Garden implements in varying stages of rust and disrepair were ranged along one wall. Against the other were some sacks of sprouting seeds, several empty packets of weedkiller and the specky remains of containers for the transport of biological control agents.

The beetles imported for the purpose of dealing with Japanese knotweed had proved more of a problem than a help. The Japanese knotweed still flourished, but a recent crop of gigantic cabbages had foundered beneath the weight of chewing and champing insects. Once fleshy leaves were twisted and curled into pouches to house the next generation of pests in a sooty mesh. The few unaffected areas were scarred, blotched and tattered into holes.

The wife had refused to spend hours sorting the eatable from the uneatable. Besides, she was exhausted with having to help her husband keep the garden at bay on top of all her other duties. Quite apart from the insects, there was the ever encroaching grass. It choked the vegetable patch and strangled the once resplendent perennial beds. The woman had been a keen flower arranger. Her masterpieces of floral ingenuity had won cups at the local Produce Fair; her altar displays had lifted the congregation's spirits above the vicar's platitudes; and her house, with its living colour and fragrance, had drawn the admiration of visitors. Now she was obliged to substitute delphiniums and roses with hogweed, stitchwort and red campion. It was a tribute to her versatility that she still drew compliments from friends and parishioners, but of course there were no more Annual Shows. Everybody was too busy hacking their way through the rampant vegetation. The priority was keeping open a path to the door, or an area where you could still sit under the necessary shade of a garden umbrella, and enjoy a much deserved cup of tea and a quiet moment.

It was such a quiet moment that Fred was attempting now. Like the vegetables, he too had started to develop spots and rough patches on his formerly gleaming coat. He was feeling old and stiff. Every day when the husband returned from the laboratory, he dragged Fred callously from the shed and set him to work. He ignored all his protests, his reluctance to start, and the creaking and rattling that came

156

from his gears.

To give him his due, Fred's owner was a dab hand with the oil can, and he always used the best fuel refined from lupins. Luckily they still managed to grow in the close and damp conditions of the Baltic states. True, they had to be bought in at inflated prices that had almost ruined the national economy, but fortunately his owner had a fairly lucrative job. As a scientist he was paid well over the minimum wage. His laboratory was investigating a new way to shield the atmosphere from the radiation of a blistering sun that had reduced great tracts of the Earth into deserts. So far they had been conspicuously unsuccessful.

Fortress Britain had at this point managed to keep out the hordes of desperate refugees with her disciplined army and squads of affluent and ruthless immigration officials. Besides, the clouds that brought torrential downpours and tempests every other day kept the country comparatively tolerable.

Meantime there was the grass problem. And that was Fred's problem too. No amount of oil would stop his spindles from wearing. The constant sharpening of his blades was reducing them to whiskers. His owner was none too gentle with the coarse rasp either. Fred flinched every time he saw it coming at him. It was more than a traditional lawnmower could bear. Had he not been such a sturdy model and built to last, he would never have survived this long. His owner could replace most of his parts at present, but Fred knew that the older his model the more unlikely it was that the parts would continue to be available. One day soon he would probably be made redundant. After a lifetime of ceaseless drudgery, he would be thrown on the scrapheap.

It wasn't as if it was his fault. His motor had done better than anyone had been entitled to expect, but all this long grass was taking a heavy toll on him. Every time he was returned to the shed it took him hours to cool down, and his operation these days was accompanied by an alarming smell of burning as his motor overheated. His engine had begun to smoke, and he feared for the future. Lying out on a dump somewhere in the rain and the heat, he would soon grow rusty, despite all the oil he'd soaked up over the years. Even his parts would be rejected by other owners trying to service their failing machines. In times past he would have continued to work for several generations and ended up in respectable retirement in some Museum of Garden Implements.

It was all so unfair. What had he done to deserve this? Nothing. It was those humans with their feckless ways. How long had they known about global warming? Decades! And what had they done about it? Nothing! At least not in time. Didn't they have some expression about not putting off till tomorrow what you could do today? They didn't even listen to themselves. Too complacent, selfish and greedy to change their ways and protect the environment. Shortsighted too. Complained it would cost them the earth and their competitive edge. Well, now it was costing the earth. Even he could have told them you can't mess with Nature. And they had done worse. They had neglected it. All the signs were there: the hurricanes, melting icecaps, rising sea levels. But they'd buried their intelligent heads in the sand and failed to notice how the clock was ticking. Well, they'd plenty of sand now, and nowhere to bury their heads. And they'd lost all the time they used to spend enjoying themselves, enjoying the fruits of their prodigality, thinking that rainy day would never come. Well come it had. And serve them right.

But it didn't serve him right, and he wasn't going to put up with it.

So that night, after another hot day scalding round the enemy that was the lawn, he devised a plan. He would go on strike. His owner of course would take him to bits to see what was wrong. He'd reassemble him and know that he should work. But he wouldn't. His owner was not the kind to accept defeat easily, so he wouldn't just junk him at the first hurdle. He'd have a period of grace to get on with his master strategy.

The next day went exactly how he'd envisaged. He soon lay in pieces on the patio, where the weedkillers still allowed a clear area between the house and the garden. The scientist poked and peered at him and cleaned all his cogs and wheels. He changed all his oil and even polished his casing, with characteristic thoroughness. Fred had to admit that, once he was reassembled, he felt better than he had done for years. He almost felt a spasm of gratitude. But he hardened the metal of his heart. This was no moment to give way to weakness. Otherwise nothing would change.

His owner had no time to tackle the lawn that day, since it was dark, and people were no longer allowed the use of lights for inessential purposes.

By the next afternoon the lawn had grown another six inches. If Fred gave in now his mechanism would probably get so choked up he'd break down anyway. So he took the more obvious course of refusing to start. Hadn't some wise-guy said that a decision not to act was an action in itself? That was very true, and in this case it was an aggressive lack of action. He felt not a qualm of conscience when his owner resorted to kicking him. If anything it stiffened his resolve. And he never knew his owner could come out with such a string of blue language. This aroused the wrath of his wife, as she was even more bothered by what the neighbours would say than the fact she would soon have to wade waist-deep to the washing line.

The mention of neighbours sent the scientist scuttling round next door. They had a maxi version of Fred, and it was still working. Not for much longer though, if Fred had anything to do with it. It gave him real satisfaction to hear his master grovelling at their door, when normally he was complaining about their kids and their dogs. Cats were now sanctioned as a necessary way of reducing rodents, but dogs were still persona non grata. And as for kids! Nowadays, what with the height of the undergrowth, you couldn't even see if they were in your garden.

Next door's machine cut a reasonable swathe round the lawn, but Fred could hear him grumbling away to himself, though the man took no notice, of course. It wasn't his lawnmower after all. But Fred took the opportunity to have a quiet word with Edgar - Ergonomically Designed Grasscutter and Advanced Reaper! With the mood he was in, it didn't take much to persuade him.

The following day when his owner went next-door with a packet of his wife's best biscuits for the kiddies, he heard the grim news that Edgar had broken down too.

Gradually the wave of industrial discontent spread across the country. And this time the Government had no tools in their armoury: no unions to threaten, no Local Governments to starve of funds. There were angry voices calling for action. Radio phone lines were jammed with anguished callers for heads to roll. Then the miners went on strike. For some weeks, there had been demarcation disputes over who should clear the foliage which daily fouled the winding gear. The miners were in any case fed up with being regarded as environmental pariahs. Besides, they had no time to work for keeping their gardens in check with secateurs, shears, scythes and scissors.

Fearing the lawnmowers would lose their leverage, other machines came out in sympathy. The strike spread to trains, planes and automobiles. Somewhat irrelevantly, a new political party was formed for the abolition of all machinery and a return to a simpler lifestyle. Society was rapidly breaking down. The Government fell. The generals squabbled as to who should take over. Anarchy roved the streets.

Those living outside the cities were not immediately affected by all this political upheaval. Besides they seemed to have lost contact with all radio and television coverage. Not that they'd have had time to listen to news anyway. They were all far too busy fighting the jungle to get hot and bothered about anything else. Those with huge estates for once were worse off than those without. Nobody had time to deal with their abandoned grasscutters.

Those who believed in conspiracy theories suspected some kind of plot. Perhaps a resurgence of Communism. Some blamed international terrorism. Others muttered about the thinning of the ozone layer and malign influences being allowed to reach the Earth in preparation for alien invasion. Yet more thought this was the long promised Armageddon and wished they had read their bibles while they could still find them - the advancing greenery having reached their spare rooms and their attics. A formerly scorned religious sect was jubilantly heralding the end of the world.

Eventually society collapsed, not only in Britain but across the whole globe. People resorted to eating grass, but suffered appalling digestive consequences and accusations from some quarters that they were adding to global warming with all the methane. There were quarrels among neighbours, and stabbings and shootings. Wars started between nations considered to be encouraging their vegetation to encroach across State borders. America, China and the former Soviet Union launched nuclear attacks on anyone who functioned on different ideologies or had more verdant soils than anyone else. Not surprisingly, this spelled the end of Mankind as we know it, along with a great many species of animal and plant life.

The dust cloud that enveloped the Earth for a few months after the holocaust gave it a chance to cool down. Gradually the Earth returned to some kind of balance. Anything that lived on grass and greenery had on the whole done rather well. Various small tribes, ignored on remote islands in the southern hemisphere, had also somehow survived the radiation. There was no trace of the master race. The survivors were mostly short, squat and low browed, though in some parts of the planet there were a handful of humans who appeared to be taller and thinner and given to sitting for hours on end, cross-legged, doing something they called thinking. Fortunately for them, most of the big predators had not made it this far.

The world was once more green. Fish swam in the seas, birds flew through the oxygenated skies and animals ranged through the burgeoning forests and over the silky prairies. The deserts started to

160

bloom. And the meek inherited the earth.

Fred never knew about the long-term consequences of his actions, of course, but he wouldn't have cared anyway. After all, it had all been their fault. They had brought it on themselves.

He settled down to a life of inactivity in the corner of his shed, until the shed was crushed by the advancing walls of creepers and brambles, and he and his kind disappeared beneath the soils and were fossilised into thick seams of coal.

THE RECKONING

A twig slashed back across his eye. Flashes of pain erupted in his brain, and he yelled a resentful curse. His face was almost numb with cold, and he had given up trying to keep dry. Water droplets showered from every branch he touched; he no longer felt the trickling down his collar. He was getting fed up with this wood. It seemed to be going on for ever.

A sudden bolt of lightning snaked down among the trees. He felt the impact under his feet. Then came the detonation of thunder and the increased onslaught of rain. What the hell was he doing here anyway? He should just give up and go back.

Another flash of lightning revealed the dark mass of a building beyond the trees. Of course! That's where he was heading. Its outline echoed in his memory. It looked no nearer than before. Yet here he was, stumbling and staggering about from one boggy puddle to the next trying to reach it. The rotting leaves seemed designed to conceal the stinking ooze. He'd sunk up to the ankles in one place and slipped down a bank in another. He'd ended up in black mire, his hands scratched, his city suit torn and covered in mud.

Was it worth it? What kind of ridiculous stubbornness was it to press on? It was like some form of compulsion. What possessed him to leave his nice warm car and tackle this nightmare of a wood in these conditions?

Then he remembered. Of course, the car had broken down! He'd been travelling along this country road on his journey north. Like an idiot, he'd turned off the main road to cut off a triangle. It had already started to rain, and he'd been glad of the car's efficient heating. His fingers tapped on the steering wheel to the beat of his favourite CD. He'd checked the clock - eleven forty. He should be at the hotel by half past twelve. Quick drink in the bar, hot shower and a comfortable hotel bed. In the morning, he'd have a leisurely breakfast and arrive fresh and ready for the killing at his promotion meeting.

Then the wind had got up. Sodden leaves dragged and skittered across the road in his headlights. The rain grew heavier and guttered down his windscreen, defeating the struggling wipers. As he rounded a bend, he felt the pull of water under his wheels and he veered off to the side. A tree loomed towards him - he stamped on the brakes. Thank God for ABS. The car juddered to a halt and the engine cut out. He tried the ignition - nothing. He tried again, giving it some accelerator - nothing. Perhaps the water had got into the engine. That's all he needed.

He climbed angrily out of the car. There'd been no flood warning, no ford sign; it hadn't even been raining that long - unless it was very local. The wheels were firmly embedded in a drainage ditch - that's a laugh .... obviously on strike! He kicked the tyre in frustration. Damned thing!

Send for help, that's what. He reached into the car for his mobile. No signal. It was fully charged, so that wasn't the problem. Probably all these trees. He walked up the road to the top of a small rise - still nothing. The trees stretched on in both directions as far as he could see. A dead zone obviously. What should he do? It was miles since he'd passed anywhere. Should he walk on? Or should he just wait in the dismal hope that someone else would drive past? Fat chance! It was the middle of the night and the middle of nowhere.

He got out the AA book, but it was too small a scale to be helpful.

He was preparing to spend the night in the car, when he'd noticed a light shining through the trees that skirted the road. A house! What a bit of luck! He'd be able to make a phone call and wait there for the breakdown truck.

He couldn't see a gate so had clambered over the fence and set off through the strip of trees. It should have taken a few minutes, yet here he was still battling weather and undergrowth, getting more and more vexed. His torch had failed half an hour ago, leaving him benighted. Creepers hampered his feet, and brambles clutched at his legs. It was as though this damned wood didn't want him to get there!

Just as he'd lost the will to live, he stumbled into a clearing alongside a high stone wall. He felt its roughness under his fingers as he groped his way along it till he came to some iron gates. Snarling gryphons topping the gateposts flared to life in another flash of lightning - unwelcoming sentinels. Rough grass grew beneath the gates, sure sign they were no longer used. He supposed he'd have to carry on along the wall to another entrance, but to his relief the rusty chain that kept the gates closed had no padlock. They creaked open on ancient hinges, and he found himself in the garden of the house.

It was intensely quiet, not even the rustle of a mouse. And it was flooded with moonlight, which deepened the shadows and threw everything else into relief. It carved out the leaves of ivy which trailed

163

up the concealed forms of statues humped silently before him. He peered under a veil of creepers at lips gnawed away by time and frost, and the balls of sightless eyes. He felt a wave of revulsion. You'd never think he'd spent his boyhood watching horror movies. But the atmosphere of this garden was at once haunting and disturbing.

And what had happened to the rain? The tangled mat of weeds and tussocks that should have been the lawn was bone dry. No breath of air disturbed the stillness of this place. It was as if it was cut off from time.

But this wasn't getting him anywhere. He picked his way towards the house among half buried chunks of carved masonry. The obscured shape of what must be a sundial stood incongruously in the middle of the area. Its gnomon cast a black shadow across the corrosion - twelve o'clock. That should've been about right except for that cursed wood. But moonlight always was deceiving. He could believe it would always say twelve o'clock, whether midnight or midday. The shadow was probably eaten into the metal. And night seemed like a permanent condition here.

Certainly any light that had streamed from the house was extinguished now. The range of windows looked blankly back at him, impervious to his lost hope. But there had been a light! Or maybe it was just the moonlight after all. The place certainly looked deserted. Wait a minute - that couldn't be right. It had been pouring with rain. Dirty great clouds. It had to be a light from the house.

Enlivened by fresh hope, he started forwards. They could only just have gone to bed. They wouldn't refuse to help someone in such obvious trouble. He hoped his dishevelled appearance would not alarm them. But he had always been good at persuading doubters of his best intentions.

He mounted past more gryphons up the cracked steps. The heavy door was studded with the usual ironware. He searched for the bell but couldn't find one. No knocker either. What did visitors do here - yell for admission? Then he noticed a frayed rope to the right of the door. He gave it a sharp tug, expecting the eruption of a strident clanging. Nothing happened, but a partridge rose tocking out of the vegetation, making him jump.

Oh well, here goes. He rapped on the wood and barked his knuckles for this trouble. "Hello there ... hello?" Again nothing. Emboldened by rising temper, he thumped forcefully on the door with the edge of his fist. The door swung slightly open.

"Oh, I'm sorry, but I couldn't get anyone to hear." He needn't have bothered. There was no-one there. He put his head round the door and peered into the darkness, which was just as black as the garden was moonlit. He hesitated about going in. People got shot in places like this without so much as a by-your-leave.

But he'd got to do something. The door now seemed to be stuck. He squeezed past it and into the hall. A smell of mildew and decay met his nostrils. They could do with a damp course apparently. He had a feeling of space, though he could still see nothing. Sliding his hand around the wall, he could find no light switch, but he could make out the shape of panelling under his fingers - cold and damp. Unlived in. But what about that light?

Light! Of course! He felt in his pocket for a book of matches. Striking one, he managed to make out a broad flight of stairs going up from the middle of the hall. The steps widened at the bottom, graced by curving banisters. The floor consisted of wide, heavy boards. It looked dull, as if coated with grime. The match was down to his fingers. He struck another. Dark figures looked down at him from ornate frames. The windows were draped stiffly in dank-smelling cloth that might once have been velvet. My God the place must surely be empty, forsaken some years back by the looks of it. Any phone would probably be disconnected. No contact with the outside world then!

The hall guttered into darkness as he dropped the wizened match, swearing. He struck another. Its sudden bright flame lifted his spirits. At one end of the hall was an imposing clock; both hands pointed upwards. Wouldn't you just guess it! On a small table next to it stood the stub of a candle in an enamelled holder. He put the flame to the wick and obligingly it flickered into life. The flame stretched upwards, revealing more detail of the hall.

Suddenly the place didn't look so bad. It didn't even smell so bad. Perhaps he was getting used to it. The curve of the banisters almost gleamed along the edges, and even the floor had a subtle sheen. Curtains started into a warm, rich brocade, and the eyes of doubtless venerable ancestors gazed down dispassionately from the golden patina of aged paint.

And then a door opened. A girl with apron and cap appeared carrying a covered dish. She scudded down the passage to the right of the stairs. A murmur of conversation followed her out.

"Excuse me, miss!" She didn't even turn. He watched her black skirts retreat and disappear through another door. In too much of a hurry I suppose. And then he turned towards the door she'd come from. A rim of light now blazed round the edges. Thank goodness. Help at last.

He pushed open the door to a stunning sight. Elegant women, necks decked in pearls and other jewellery, were seated alternately round a mahogany table. Their long skirts draped artfully to the floor, they sat as straight in the chairs as their right bodices dictated. The men who separated them wore tailed coats, closely fitted and double-breasted, sporting gold or ivory buttons and high collars. Either this was a fancy dress party or he'd strayed into the past - or perhaps into one of those gilt-framed pictures! The table was awash with dishes of carved meats and guinea fowl - nothing so common as chicken drumsticks. Glowing decanters and ruby-filled glasses clinked and passed from hand to hand. The whole scene glittered under pewter candelabra and what seemed to be thousands of candles. The women's cheeks were flushed and their eyes bright. In the kinder light of candles even the older women looked attractive.

He paused for one timeless moment before tackling the nearest flunkie. "I'm sorry to intrude, but I need to use your phone. I've broken ..."

The man swept past as if he wasn't there. He probably took him for one of the local peasants and below his notice. He tried again with someone sporting less gold braid. The result was the same.

He was just about to create a scene at the dinner table, when he became aware that he was being watched. Turning to the end of the table, he found himself looking straight into the eyes of the lady of the house. Her gaze did not falter but stayed levelly on him. Her stare was at once assured and disconcerting, almost imperious. He felt as if he was being stripped down to his very soul. He stood mesmerised, incapable of moving or speaking.

She rose slowly from her seat and walked with silent dignity behind the line of guests. She no longer looked at him but crossed by him to the door. He understood that he was to follow. The other guests still studiously ignored him. They might look well bred, but they certainly had no manners. They could at least have offered him a drink.

To hell with them. At least the hostess was aware of her responsibilities. He saw her leave the room and turn right into the passage. He hurried into the hall, but she had vanished. He heard a door close somewhere in the distance, but was too late to see where she had gone.

He set off down the corridor, which seemed to grow longer and longer with every step. Doors opened off to right and left, but he could hear no sound behind them. The further away from the hall he got, the darker it became. Something soft touched his face, and he leapt a mile.

This was ridiculous. Where the devil had she gone?

He opened a door to his left. That same smell of mildew and decay met him. He almost retched with the stench of it. The room seemed to be a nursery, but no child would flourish here. The little cot was covered in mouldy blankets, the hangings torn and discoloured. The floor was littered with droppings from an infestation of rats. The rocking horse had lost its painted eyes and its coat was peeling and patchy. A tin soldier lay on the floor, legs mangled and twisted. Had some tragedy happened here that the place was so neglected? Something ran over his foot. He banged the door to, his handkerchief to his mouth.

The next door was no more promising. He pushed it open and saw a room shrouded in sheets. They had been white but were now yellowed and stained. The same mouldy smell hung over everything. Perhaps they only used one part of the house. It was certainly very big.

Discouraged, he came to the last door, which faced him at the end of the corridor. He had run out of options. As he pushed his way towards it, his legs felt heavy, unwilling to go on. He struggled forward, cursing himself. Whatever was wrong with him? It was only a few yards, but it was like wading through treacle. He dragged his feet step by step, the distance remaining stubbornly the same. He could hear himself snivelling with vexation. Fingers of floating cobwebs curled about his face and body. His flesh winced. He tore at them desperately but became more and more entangled in their meshes.

Then the handle was within reach. His hand stretched towards it. He watched as it grasped the knob. Everything in him rebelled at the idea of turning it. He tried to wrench his hand away, but it wouldn't budge. The more he tried the more clenched on it became. The knob began to turn. His hand began to turn with it. A cold sweat covered his body and he began to scream. The scream whirled round in his skull but stayed silent on the air.

As the door opened inwards he felt himself falling, sucked down as into a vortex. Laughter and screams reverberated into his brain. The sound swelled and faded, bruising and sliding in and out of his consciousness. A bell clanged and jangled closer and closer, insistent, lacerating. The confused cacophony jarred his distorted senses. It was like the descent into hell. And somewhere in the middle of it all the sound of sobbing, a woman sobbing - heart wrenching, beating at his mind.

He jerked awake to the sound of the phone ringing and ringing in his ear. He snatched the receiver off to stop the noise. His heart thudded violently and his body still shook. The bedclothes were wet with sweat and in a tangled heap all round him.

He tried to steady his voice. "Hello?"

"Oh Mike. Were you asleep? Sorry old man."

Mike grabbed onto his shattered senses. "Doesn't matter. I was having a bloody awful nightmare anyway."

"Yeah I bet. Old girlfriend eh! Listen Mike, I was just phoning to say we'll pick you up at eight. Better not be late, or the old boy might throw a wobbly. You know what a stickler he is for "decorum". Must lick up to the new boss, eh? - at least for a bit!"

"Oh, right. Yes. Best bib and tucker. See you later then. Thanks for the reminder."

He put the phone down and staggered to the dressing table. He picked up his watch. Five past six. Plenty of time.

In the bathroom the mirror showed him a face drawn and haggard. "My God I look terrible."

As the steam from the handbasin obscured the spectre, another rose up before him. Why on earth would he think of her now? He pushed the memory aside and wiped the mirror clean.

He tried to concentrate on his shave, but fragments of the past kept invading his consciousness. Angrily he dismissed them. "What did she have to do that for anyway? Who'd have thought she'd do that?" He lathered his beard furiously. "Stupid bloody cow."

He clattered the brush down and took up the razor. "Why didn't she just get rid of it!"

He stretched the skin slightly and began to comb down with the bladehead. "Plenty of other women do. Why not her?"

He wiped the foam off on his towel and continued the downward strokes. Better than electric if you'd got time.

"I gave her the money didn't I? She didn't have to keep it." He carefully shaved up his neck. "Her decision!"

Towelling off the rest of the foam, he splashed his face with cold water. "Anyway, I did my best."

He tried the effect of a smile in the mirror and was pleased with the result. Yet as he turned from the basin, he flung the wet towel onto the tiles as if he hated it.

"God rot her! Why did she have to do that?" He stamped on the towel in angry mortification.

Nevertheless, the hot downpour from the shower soon soothed his ruffled feelings, and he began to recover his poise.

By the time he had pulled on his dress suit and tied an expert bow tie - no clip-on for him - he felt ready for anything. He snapped on his Rolex, patted on a touch more aftershave and admired his reflection in the mirror. Irresistible!

In the car with Max and Geoff, all the talk was of the company takeover and Mr. Big, the tycoon who had swept through their ranks making cuts and changes on all sides - mainly to staff.

Still, the three of them had done all right out of it, and here they were spinning along the roads to the glittering celebration of the new business venture. Old Stokes was loaded, so it should be a swanky affair. And they were staying the night, so they could down as much booze as consistent with their newly exalted status. "The taller they are, the longer their legs," said Geoff, winking.

"The taller they are, the harder they fall!" countered Max.

They all laughed and changed the topic to talent. There ought to be plenty about. There were going to be masses of guests. All packing fortunes, shouldn't wonder. Good pickings.

The journey passed in such amiable speculations, and they found themselves on the approach roads to the manor hall. There was something familiar about them, but then one country road looks just like another. Not many landmarks. Odd pub. Odd farm. But mostly trees, fields, hedges, fields, trees - oh yes, and more trees.

They pulled in through high gates into a sweeping courtyard. Plenty of parking space. The old man knew what he was about. Light poured from every window. It cut across the pebbles of the forecourt and picked out lines of gleaming cars, sleek and prosperous under its fingers. A hard-eyed moon, which frosted the fields about, paled into moody insignificance in the blaze from the house.

Up the steps to a heavy oak door with a bell rope to the side. "How delightfully old fashioned," said Max.

Mike gave a hefty pull on the rope and the bell jangled loudly inside. "Nothing as common as a push-bell for him then."

The door was opened promptly by a butler, no less. All three sniggered involuntarily. The butler seemed entirely unperturbed. If young men didn't know how to behave themselves, it was all the same to him. A sidekick took their coats and scarves and another their overnight bags. The butler led them into the reception room across a vast hall. Mike noticed the black and white tiles in modern imitation of some Dutch Old Master, and the cavernous height of the ceiling. Very palatial. Acres of richly polished wood, and portraits which clearly had no connection with the current owner. Job lot to impress the hoi polloi no doubt.

As they entered the room, mine host came to greet them, all affability. It was as if they were the only guests that mattered. Neat trick that. Although, thought Mike, when you considered it, all this affluence was ultimately down to the skills and experience of people like him. To give him his due, old Stokes introduced them to various other guests with suitably flattering comments on how they were his right-hand men and how he could see them going far. Mike began to feel distinctly at home. He could get used to this.

Then Stokes said something which seemed to promise more than the simple statement. "You must come and meet my daughter." Mike found himself propelled across the room to where a young woman stood surrounded by attentive acolytes. Max and Geoff trailed along too.

"Connie, my dear. Let me introduce you to three of my brightest young protegés."

She turned to meet them. Her dress was the deepest emerald, shot through with the colour of flame. The subtle sheen enhanced the whiteness of her skin. Mike's eyes ran lightly over the curving softness above the scooped neckline. He didn't allow them to linger. Briefly he took her in. Her neck glittered with diamonds. The setting looked vaguely antique, but the stones alone would be worth a mint. Odd how these city magnates couldn't resist the temptation to flaunt their wealth. Expensive taste allied with a streak of vulgarity.

The three young men gathered round her, Max and Geoff vying for notice, chattering and laughing in their most engaging vein. They littered their offerings with compliments about her father, the décor, the company and her own accomplishments. She smiled sleekly back at them, nothing if not well groomed. But a glimmer of ennui flitted through her eyes.

Mike knew better how to impress. He stood opposite her, framed by his colleagues, his stillness contrasting with their animation. If anything he looked slightly aloof. When he saw her attention beginning to flicker, he stepped forward with a cool inclination of the head.

"Can I fetch you another drink, Miss Stokes?"

"Thank you. I'd love one."

He returned to find his friends had succumbed to the coolness in her manner and had wandered off in search of easier prey. She stood alone in a constant movement of guests passing and re-passing, a silent point at the centre of noise.

He held out her glass. "For those who dare to be different, Miss Stokes." She clearly understood that he included himself in the description.

"Oh, Connie," she offered. He gained a glimpse of sharp, white teeth.

"Connie," he acceded, caressing her with his voice. He raised his glass in a slightly mocking salute, and allowed his gaze to fall directly into hers.

The eyes that met his were taunting and knowing. This was no virgin. Her air of diffidence was all a feint. She might deceive her old man, but she didn't deceive him. Underneath the illusion of chastity she was a slut.

A spasm of lust seized him. This was going to be easy. But he knew a good lay might cost him the main prize. He'd keep her dangling until she was gagging for it. Stir her up and then deny her. Starve her until she was ready to take the bait. He knew exactly what he was doing. She'd even pursue it as far as the marriage bed. With the daughter in hand, the father and the power of money would be his also.

A muted gong brought an end to the bustle and prattle around them. It gave way to a hum of expectation as the guests began to move towards the dining room.

"You must excuse me," Connie murmured, reverting to formality. She indicated her father, who would conduct her to dinner.

"Of course." With a slight nod, he turned instantly away and proffered his arm to a young woman standing conveniently, and understandably, by herself. He congratulated himself on his own charity and self-possession. Connie could not fail to note his considerate manner and regret that her role as hostess deprived her of his company.

Connie was seated a few places up from his and on the opposite side of the table. The blaze and brilliance of chandeliers struck fire from her diamonds. The feast, as expected, was sumptuous, carried by endless streams of waiters, doubtless from some exclusive caterers. This was more his style. He could have been born to it.

He devoted all his attentions to the young woman he'd escorted to dinner. She must be congratulating herself on her good fortune. He was certainly on top form, and soon had her simpering and giggling at his flattering banter. The merriment rose from the table and danced around them, held by his personal magnetism. As to Connie, he constantly felt her eyes upon him, stroking his cheek and loitering over his mouth. Yet whenever he glanced her way he found her focused intently on the fellow opposite. She was almost as good at this game as he was!

At the end of the meal, he half expected "the ladies" to retire and "the gentlemen" to settle down to port and cigars. Odd how the place suggested something archaic, almost timeless. Instead he found himself flanked by a mixed group which included his colleagues and still included the young woman, who was showing signs of becoming clingy. Soon he would have to shake her off, but for the moment he allowed her to capture some of his notice, while beginning to foster a more presentable piece, who would at least pose some competition to Connie.

So absorbed was he in his own machinations that he didn't immediately register the presence beside him. As she passed, he felt her skirts flow round his legs, and her hand brushed against his. It was quite deliberate. He felt the challenge.

He didn't immediately react. He carried on talking as if nothing had happened. When he judged the time was right, he turned to see her, as expected, hovering near the door. Her eyes fell fully upon him, dark, almost sullen. Then she left the room. It was a clear invitation.

He followed her out. In the hall he saw the hem of her dress flick into the broad entrance of a corridor to his right. By the time he reached the opening, however, he could no longer see her. He recognised the ploy.

Setting off down the passage, he pushed open one or two of the nearer doors. Nothing but darkness met him. No sense of someone in that darkness. He cursed under his breath. So she was going to lead him a dance, was she? Well, let her. That wouldn't last long.

He whispered her name into the blank air, quietly, not wanting to alert anyone else. He gave a low, flirty call. "Oh, Connie ....where are you?" Still nothing. He was beginning to be annoyed. Still, her millions were worth it, if she wasn't.

Then laughter, light and tantalising, shivered the spaces round him. Well, let her have her fun. Soon he'd be having his.

As he went further, it began to grow darker. He hadn't noticed how he'd left the lights behind. He began to feel uneasy. Now when he pushed a door, he didn't really expect to see her. Yet he felt compelled to go on. She had to be somewhere. The air was becoming thick, and the walls seemed to close in about him. He felt caught in a web of his own making. And he would see it through.

Groping past the recess to one doorway, he thought he heard a strange, rhythmic, grinding sound. Something rocking invisibly on bare boards. A shadow of recognition floated through his brain. Weakness washed over him.

Then he heard the voice, low and sultry, coming from ahead. "Come along now ….. How much longer are you going to keep me waiting?"

His heart began to thud, dangerous, urgent. Desire raged through him. He felt an impulse to violence, unaccountably tinged with fear.

His mouth grew dry and his throat contracted. His tongue felt swollen and throbbing. He ran the tip round his teeth, but to no effect. His legs grew heavy with the heat surging through them.

His mind began to reel, his vision swimming. He blundered against a wall. It felt sticky and clammy. A sickly smell engulfed him, permeated with the stench of mould. What in fuck's name was happening? Was he ill? Had they spiked his drink?

He began to feel no longer in control. What had they done to him? He found himself snivelling with rage and futility.

A flicker of light played under the door that ended the passage. Shadows passed and re-passed beneath it. Laughter batted on his ears, mocking, tempting. The bloody bitch! She was playing him for a fool.

Lust and fury battled inside him. Whatever they were up to, he'd give them a run for their money.

A desperate sense of loathing overwhelmed him, whether of himself or them he didn't know. His brain slipped and slithered around these unnerving emotions. But he'd show them. He'd teach them to mess with him.

A steely anger gave strength to his legs. He staggered the last few yards to the door and thrust out his hand. The knob was ice beneath his fingers. Panic pulsed through him, his mind tilted, but he wouldn't submit. He couldn't submit.

His fingers locked round the searing brass. The knob began to turn.

Epilogue:

THE LESSON

Miss Nancy Greer
Was taken queer
In the middle of Sunday service.
She was seen to expire
By the whole of the choir
And the vicar, whose name was Purvis.

They took her outside
To make sure she had died
In the light of the grey churchyard.
She was set on the hump
Of a grass-covered lump,
Since a tombstone would be too hard.

Her pulse was just fleeting,
But then it stopped beating;
The doctor declared she was dead.
The people all muttered;
The verdict was uttered:
"It was boredom that killed her," he said.

Once they'd heard this grave word,
The crowd heaved and stirred;
The vicar was mortified:
He had fought for each soul,
To make spirits whole,
With a sermon he thought cut and dried.

The fixed intent stare
Became more a glare,
As the minute hand whirred on the clock.
These starved, mortal sinners
Just thought of their dinners,
The vicar concluded in shock.

While he stood in a daze,
The rest turned to gaze
At Miss Nancy's unfortunate body.

To leave her like that,
With one shoe and no hat,
Seemed just a bit callous and shoddy.

Her friend, Mabel Birch,
Went back to the church
To recover the missing regalia:
The heeled shoe from the pew,
The flowered straw from the floor,
A lace glove and such paraphernalia.

In her neat Sunday best,
Her prayer book on her chest,
And the halo of flowers on her forehead,
She looked like a bride.
With a quiet touch of pride,
They agreed she looked slightly less horrid.

What to do with her next
Was the question that vexed.
Should they take her back home to her bed?
But in just a short space
She'd be back in this place;
It seemed such a waste, it was said.

The cry then began
That it seemed a good plan,
Though many had set up a grumble.
Some took the suggestion
To ease their digestion,
Since stomachs had started to rumble.

The vicar just stood there,
Hands folded in prayer,
And appeared unaware of the clamour.
The undertaker made tracks
To change into his blacks,
Fetch his measure, some nails and a hammer.

Since that was decided,
The others subsided
And hurried away to be lunched.

With a terrible sigh,
And to eat humble pie,
The vicar went off pale and hunched.

Since the evening was fine,
In a trickling line,
They returned to the scene after teatime.
But, through hops much fermented
To toast the lamented,
No work had begun in the meantime.

The next day the sexton
Was outraged to find
That a funeral had gone on without him.
He flung down his spade
And would not dig his grave,
As he thought it was done just to flout him.

The rage of the verger
Was next to emerger
From a notice he stuck at the sidey,
Polite, but quite bitter,
At finding such litter -
"Will you PLEASE keep the churchyard tidy!"

To mollify these two,
The vicar was pleased to
Challenge the funeral directors:
Said his duty was spurred,
If she wasn't interred,
To call in the Health Inspectors.

So the full congregation
Soon stood at their station
To pay last respects to the lady.
They'd selected a spot
Which would not be too hot,
As the yew trees were massive and shady.

But the place that they chose
And marked with a rose
Could be seen from the pulpit quite clearly.

The reverend burned
Whenever he turned,
And it troubled his conscience most dearly.

With his thoughts fixed on heaven,
If, at half-past eleven,
His sermon had not reached a close,
All heads turned that way
And the vicar turned grey,
So well versed he concluded his prose.

So that's why on the green
A worn bench can be seen
With a plaque in the best of traditions:
"Oh rest and be thankful
In memory of her
Who rescued the suffering parishioners."